FOR THE
LOVE
OF THE
LAND

FOR THE
LOVE
OF THE
LAND

A NOVEL

BONNIE LEON

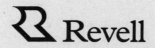

© 2005 by Bonnie Leon

Published by Fleming H. Revell
a division of Baker Publishing Group
P.O. Box 6287, Grand Rapids, MI 49516-6287

Printed in the United States of America

Library of Congress Cataloging-in-Publication Data
Leon, Bonnie.
   For the love of the land : a novel / Bonnie Leon.
      p.   cm. — (The Queensland chronicles ; bk. 2)
   ISBN 0-8007-5897-8
    1. Pioneers—Fiction. 2. Queensland—Fiction. 3. Americans—Australia—Fiction. I. Title. II. Series.
   PS3562.E533F67 2005
   813'.54—dc22   2004029368

Scripture is taken from the King James Version of the Bible.

Acknowledgments

Thanks to Mike Martin, my friend and equine practitioner. You lent me your expertise, and because you were willing to help, the horse savvy characters in this story became real people. If there are any errors, they are on my head.

Kudos to my editor, Lonnie Hull DuPont. You made me work hard. Sometimes I growled at you, but you stuck to your guns and required more from me. Tenacity is a valuable asset, and yours made for a better book.

Also, to Kelley Meyne, my copyeditor. You went above and beyond the call of duty to ensure that the scenes in this book fell together just as they should, and your eye for detail kept my characters true to themselves. Your commitment to quality gave me confidence that this story would shine. Thank you.

1

December 15, 1872

The Thornton kitchen smelled of stew and rising bread. Rebecca pressed the heel of her hand into a lump of dough, then folded the resilient mass and pressed again. "What time is it?"

Willa's blue eyes sparkled with mischief. "I'd say about ten minutes later than the last time you asked." She crossed the kitchen, placed an arm around Rebecca's waist, and gave her a squeeze. "I thought baking might take your mind off your aunt's arrival. I should have known better."

"The minutes are passing too slowly." Rebecca rolled the dough into a ball and set it in a ceramic bowl.

"She'll be here soon enough, I dare say." Willa smiled.

"I can't stand this waiting." Looking into her mother-in-law's kind eyes, Rebecca said, "It's been three months since I received word that she would be visiting. I've been anxious ever since." She glanced out the kitchen window. "I can't imagine Aunt Mildred traveling all that way by herself. If only I could have gone along to meet the stage."

"It appears boldness runs in your family." Willa steered Rebecca to the table and sat her down. "Now, you know what the doctor said. And if I don't keep you close to home, he'll have my hide."

Rebecca leaned an elbow on the table. "I know . . . no trips into town, keep my feet up . . . rest." She laid a hand on her rounded abdomen. "The baby isn't due for another few weeks." As a familiar pain pulled at her lower back, she said, "Maybe the doctor's right. I haven't been feeling quite myself today."

"Are you unwell?" Willa eyed her.

"I'm fine, but I think the baby is preparing for its arrival." She stared at her stomach. "It will be nice to have my body back to myself." The pain subsided and she let out a slow breath.

"Are you laboring?"

"No. I don't believe so."

"You're sure you're all right?"

Rebecca nodded. "You worry too much."

Lily, the cook, picked up the bowl with the dough Rebecca had prepared and placed it on the warming shelf of the oven. "Looks just roight. Ya done a good job." She grinned, revealing a gap in front where teeth belonged. Lily's smiling dark eyes were spaced far apart in her square black face, giving her a friendly appearance.

"I thought myself a fair cook when I arrived, but you've taught me so much more. Aunt Mildred will be pleased, I'm sure."

"Ya've learned roight well. Daniel 'as every roight ta be pleased with ya."

"Only because you took the time to teach me." Rebecca gazed out the window at the dusty yard. Her eyes rested on the place where the drive disappeared over a small rise. "Woodman must be driving especially slow today. The stage was supposed to be in two hours ago."

8

"I expect he's being exceedingly careful with your aunt," Willa said, walking to the stove.

"Auntie must be exhausted," Rebecca said, remembering her own arrival more than a year ago. The ache in her back returned, and she rubbed at it.

Willa placed a cup of tea on the table in front of Rebecca. "Maybe this will help some." She settled a gentle hand on Rebecca's shoulder. "Your aunt will be here in no time, you'll see."

Rebecca covered her mother-in-law's hand. "You're so good to me."

"You're a love, so it's easy." Willa returned the teakettle to the stove, then removed a lid from a hefty pot. Steam puffed into the air. She stirred the contents, then peered inside. "This looks wonderful, Lily. And smells heavenly."

"Just a stew, mum. Hope it's ta yer likin'." She looked at Rebecca. "And I hope yer aunt will like it. It's one of me specialties."

"I'm sure she will," Rebecca said. "In fact, it seems to me that when I lived in Boston, Auntie made a rather good stew." Rebecca stirred a half teaspoon of sugar into her tea. "They must be nearly here, don't you think?" She looked at Willa.

"Perhaps."

Rebecca set the spoon on the saucer and sipped her tea. Stretching out her legs, she cradled the cup in her hands and closed her eyes. "That's better. I practically feel calm. How is it tea nearly always seems to help?"

"Can't say, dear, but it's what my mother always gave me. Whether it was a stomach ailment or nerves, it would be just the thing."

Rebecca took another drink. "I wish my father were alive," she said sadly. "I miss him terribly." She rested a hand on her abdomen. "He would have made a wonderful grandfather."

In the distance a swirl of dust rose into the air. Setting her cup in its saucer, Rebecca stood. "That must be her!" She pushed out of her chair, and as quickly as her added girth allowed, she walked to the front door. Pushing open the screen, Rebecca stepped onto the veranda.

Callie, the housemaid, hurried down the broad staircase leading from the second story. "They're comin', mum! I saw them from the upstairs window!" She joined Rebecca on the porch. "They're not far."

Keeping her eyes fixed on the drive, Rebecca moved toward the steps.

The front door opened and closed again, and Willa stood with Rebecca and Callie. "I wish Bertram were here."

"We all do," Rebecca said, remembering her powerful father-in-law, Bertram Thornton. Their first meeting had been painful, but in the end they'd learned to love one another.

"I dare say, I feel badly for your aunt—I know how miserable the trip from Brisbane can be."

Rebecca's mind reeled back to the days she'd spent traveling from Brisbane. The journey had been nearly unbearable—dust, heat, and several days in an uncomfortable coach. "I arrived in November last year. Remember?"

"Indeed I do," Willa said, her eyes soft with the memory.

Dust churning, the top of the surrey appeared just above the rise. Then a set of stallions and Woodman sitting in the driver's seat came into view. Rebecca strained to catch a glimpse of her aunt. She sat beside Daniel.

"There they are, mum," Callie said, sounding nearly as excited as Rebecca felt.

Gripping the handrail, Rebecca walked down the front steps and waited at the bottom. Her heart drummed. Smiling broadly, she waved and called, "Auntie!" She hurried toward the surrey.

Daniel stepped out and offered Rebecca's aunt a hand. She looked a bit undone and worked to straighten her bonnet before taking the proffered hand. Then she stepped out with as much dignity as she could muster.

When her eyes found Rebecca, the weariness evaporated. "Oh, Rebecca! How wonderful you look!" She folded her niece in thin arms and held her tightly. A few moments later she stepped back, holding Rebecca away from her. Blue eyes brimming with tears, she said, "Let me get a look at you. In spite of everything you are as beautiful as always and seem in quite good health."

"And you look just as you did. I declare, you haven't changed a bit. I've missed you so."

"Oh, you'll never know just how much I've missed you."

"And life at your sister's?"

"It's not been so bad." Mildred smiled. "I rather enjoy the children."

Rebecca hugged her again. "Sometimes I've wondered if I'd ever see you again. I can't believe you're here."

Mildred chuckled. "I must say, I'm a bit surprised myself." A shadow touched her eyes, and she quickly went on. "It was quite an adventure. And I've had few adventures in my life, so I suppose it was time."

Her gaze moved to Rebecca's abdomen, then back to her face. "You're feeling well?"

"Yes. Very."

"It's hard to believe so much time has passed. When I saw you last, it was the day of your wedding. And now here you are having your own child." Using a handkerchief, she dabbed at tears.

Daniel stepped up. "I'd like to introduce you to my mother, Willa Thornton. Mum, this is Mildred Williams, Rebecca's aunt."

"A delight to meet you," Willa said. "Welcome to Douloo."

11

"It's a pleasure to be here." Using the handkerchief, Mildred patted her moist neck and squinted at the bright afternoon sky. "It's quite warm. There was snow on the ground when I left Boston."

"You'll adjust," Rebecca said. "Somewhat."

"I'm sure I will." She smiled brightly. "I've had quite an exciting journey."

Daniel took Rebecca's hand. "Seems she had a time of it crossing from Hawaii. There was a gale much of the way."

"Oh no. Was it awful?"

"Dreadful. Most of the passengers were ill. Like them, I spent much of my time in my room." She dabbed at her forehead with her handkerchief. "I pray the seas will be kinder when I travel home." Her eyes took in the dry, flat world surrounding Douloo, and Rebecca understood she would be happy to face the trip home if it meant leaving this place.

"Please, come in out of the sun," Willa said. "Let me show you to your room."

After getting Mildred settled, Rebecca joined Daniel and his mother on the veranda. "She'll be down shortly."

"I like her," Daniel said. Removing his hat, he combed back his blond hair. "She did quite well on the way out of town—she's a real trooper."

"She has a bit of brass to her, even for a Bostonian," Rebecca said.

"Well, I should say so; you're a Bostonian and full of brass." Daniel chuckled.

"She seems like a fine person," Willa said, glancing at the front door. "I hope her room is comfortable enough."

"Oh, I have no doubts. I'm sure she's impressed." Rebecca

crossed her swollen ankles. "She loved the flowers you put on her desk. Presently in Boston nothing is blooming."

"Of course. It's winter there now."

Looking somewhat refreshed, Mildred appeared at the door.

"Are you faring well, then, Miss Williams?" Daniel asked.

"Better, I think. I just needed to get in out of the sun. And my room is lovely," she added, turning to Willa.

"I'm glad you like it."

Looking at Rebecca, Mildred asked softly, "Can you tell me where the necessary is?"

"We don't have indoor facilities, Auntie, but there is a dunny. It's alongside the house."

Mildred paled slightly but started down the steps. "And which way is it?"

"I'll show you," Rebecca said, following her aunt. "It's just as well I go along. I'd hate it if you had an encounter like I did on my first day here."

"And what encounter was that?"

Realizing the last thing her aunt needed to hear was a story about local snakes, Rebecca hesitated. "Well . . . when I got inside the outhouse, I discovered I had a visitor."

"A visitor?" Mildred's skin tightened over the bones on her face.

"Yes . . . a snake had sought shelter indoors."

Mildred blanched. "A snake? You never mentioned snakes in your letters." She glanced about the grounds. "Are there many?"

"Some," Rebecca hedged.

"Poisonous?"

"Most of them aren't," Rebecca answered, sorry she'd mentioned her first day's excitement. "I'll make sure to check inside for you." Another pain tightened Rebecca's abdomen. It was nearly enough to make her stop, but she managed to maintain a normal façade. She didn't want to cause a stir without reason.

With a smile, Rebecca said, "It's quite all right, Auntie. Woodman sees to it that the snakes and spiders near the house are destroyed."

"Spiders?"

"Yes . . . I'll tell you all about that later."

When they reached the dunny, Rebecca glanced inside, then threw open the door. "See, no snakes," she said brightly.

Mildred leveled a serious look on Rebecca. "What is this place you've come to? I've been so worried about you, and now to discover my fears were valid, well . . . I don't know what to say."

"It's not so bad as it seems. I have a fine life here, and this is home to me now." Rebecca knew she wasn't being completely truthful. Although she'd adjusted to living at Douloo, it wasn't exactly home. She still missed Boston.

With a stiff nod, Mildred disappeared inside the dunny.

Rebecca strolled to the garden along the edge of the house and with some effort kneeled and plucked emerging weeds from their beds. She pressed her nose to a batch of lavender, breathing in its sweet fragrance.

The outhouse door creaked. "I can't imagine living so primitively. How do you do it?"

"We manage. Truly, you become accustomed. And it's really not primitive. Of course, we haven't the conveniences you enjoy in Boston, but it's satisfactory." She walked beside Mildred as they made their way back to the porch.

"I should think you might be a bit anxious about having a baby in such a primitive setting."

"Not really. I feel quite at home here."

Stepping out of the front door, Lily said, "Supper's ready, mum."

14

"Wonderful." Willa stood. "Shall we go inside? Lily's a marvelous cook."

"She's been teaching me, and I'm not doing too badly," Rebecca said.

"When you lived in Boston, you were quite accomplished in the kitchen, as I recall," Mildred said.

"Yes, but I should have spent more time under your instruction." Rebecca linked arms with her aunt.

"I do remember some adventurous cooking lessons," Mildred said with a smile.

Willa sat next to Bertram's place at the head of the table. Since his death, it had remained empty at every meal.

After everyone had seated themselves, Willa looked at Daniel. "Could you say the blessing? And please, remember your father. This is an especially joyous occasion."

Daniel glanced at his father's place. "Of course."

Mildred settled concerned eyes on Willa. "I was terribly sorry to hear about your husband's passing."

"It was a shock to us all, but we've managed quite well." Glancing at Daniel, she added, "Of course, I never would have gotten by without my son. He's been a great help to me."

Rebecca caught Daniel's pained expression. So much responsibility had been placed on his shoulders since his father's death. His mother depended upon him a good deal of the time.

"We miss my father terribly," Daniel said solemnly, then bowed his head. The others at the table did likewise. "Thank you, Lord, for bringing Mildred here safely. It is truly a blessing, especially as the day of our child's birth approaches. Thank you, Father, for this food, and may you bless those who prepared it. And I ask that you would bring much-needed rain to the district. There are some who have already lost their water supply. Also, Lord, this is an important occasion . . . and we think of the man who for so many years watched over this family. He is greatly missed—let him know how much we love him. And may you bless us all. Amen."

Willa dabbed at tears. "I apologize. It hasn't been long since his passing, and I'm still struggling a bit."

"That's to be expected," Mildred said. "I remember how my brother Charles grieved when his dear wife died. It will take time."

Willa offered what looked like a forced smile.

While Callie circled the table filling water glasses, Rebecca helped herself to some carrots and then passed them on. "I was stunned when I heard about the fire. Was it as bad as the Chicago Fire?"

"Not that bad, but it was horrible. I believe it took three days to get it under control."

"How is the reconstruction coming along?" Daniel asked.

"It hasn't even begun. The fire ate up a lot of the city. We've barely managed to do the cleanup." Mildred took a sip of water. "It was frightening. We could actually see an orange glow in the sky from home."

"It must have been terrifying," Willa said.

"Very. I was beginning to believe the entire city might go up in flames." She settled her napkin in her lap. "It burned right down Franklin Street and Congress and included much of Federal Street."

"It's hard to believe. One never thinks such misfortune will strike." Rebecca tried to imagine what the business district must look like. She'd always felt at home there.

After serving herself some carrots, Mildred passed them along. "I was beginning to wonder if I'd have to postpone my trip. Downtown is quite a mess."

"Do they have any idea how long it will take to rebuild?" Daniel asked.

"From what I've heard, the city commissioners just don't

know. It's impossible to estimate." Mildred took a bite of a dinner roll. "Mmm. Delicious."

"Rebecca made those," Willa said proudly.

Mildred raised an eyebrow. "So you have been learning."

"Yes, Lily's a wonderful cook and teacher."

"Lily?"

"She's one of the servants. She keeps to the kitchen most of the time."

"Oh. Yes, of course." Mildred took another bite of roll. "I must admit to being a bit surprised at how big everything is here. It's wide open and seems to go on forever. And you're quite a long way from town."

"That we are," Daniel said, "but we've got the finest station in the district."

"Really? I'd like to see this place you call Douloo."

"I'd like to show it to you. We could take the surrey. I couldn't show all of it, but you could get an idea."

"That would be lovely. And what does Douloo mean? It's an unusual name."

"It means to be bonded to the land," Rebecca said.

Using her index finger, Mildred bumped her glasses up a smidge. "Intriguing."

"I'm thrilled you'll be here for Christmas. We've scheduled a special program at church, and of course, there will be a family celebration here at home."

Mildred's eyes met Daniel's. For a moment Rebecca thought some sort of mischievous exchange transpired between them. "Do you two have a secret?" she asked Daniel.

"Us? No. Of course not. What would give you that idea?" He glanced at Mildred.

"Well, I could swear you . . . never mind. It must have been my imagination."

"Rebecca, you were telling us about Christmas," Mildred said.

17

"Oh yes. Well, it will be nice, certainly."

"This will be our first Christmas without Bertram," Willa said softly.

The room turned silent. No one seemed to know what to say.

Finally Willa smiled. "I dare say, Bertram would want it to be especially fine this year. He always loved Christmas." Her voice sounded cheery, a contrast to the sorrow in her eyes.

"We'll have a first-rate celebration," Rebecca said.

"Yes. There's a lot to celebrate. Daniel's doing a grand job of running the station and watching over us all." Willa smiled at her son.

Yes, Rebecca thought. *But Daniel isn't Bertram, and he shouldn't be expected to behave as if he were.* She took her husband's hand and squeezed. So much had been required of him. And his father's shoes were difficult to fill.

"I do the best I can," Daniel said. "But I'll never measure up to my dad."

2

Daniel swung up into the saddle and rode to the surrey. "You ready to go, then?"

Woodman glanced back at his female passengers. "Roight, we are."

"This is quite exhilarating," Mildred said. "I've never had a tour of a station before."

"We won't be able to see it all," Daniel explained. "The surrey can't go everywhere, and there's more than can be seen in a day, but you ought to have a better idea of its size and purpose by the time we're done." He smiled, his blue eyes crinkling at the corners.

"I wish I could ride," Rebecca said with a pout.

"No riding." Daniel lifted his eyebrows. "You know what the doctor said. We're disobeying as it is."

"Perhaps we shouldn't go," Mildred said. "I'm not certain it's wise for you to venture far from home at all."

"I'll be fine."

"How could you even consider riding in your condition?"

Rebecca offered her aunt a sideways grin. "I was teasing. In this condition I doubt I could get on a horse."

"I'd probably have a better chance of accomplishing such a feat." Mildred sat back and folded her hands in her lap. "Well now, I thought we were going to take a look at this grand station."

"Right." Daniel turned his horse and trotted toward the road.

Woodman flicked the reins, and with a click of the tongue the horses set out.

"It's such a shame Willa was unable to join us," Mildred told Rebecca. "I would have enjoyed her company. I'm sorry she's feeling poorly."

"I think she just wanted to give us time to ourselves."

Mildred took Rebecca's hand. "Very wise. It is wonderful to see you." Her eyes bright, she added, "I'm still having difficulty believing I'm here."

"Well, I'm glad you are." Rebecca squeezed her aunt's hand. "What made you decide to come? It's a long journey."

A flicker of secrecy touched Mildred's eyes. "I missed you and wasn't about to neglect the birth of my greatnephew."

Rebecca had never known her aunt to lie, but she was fairly certain she was holding something back. "I must say, I was a bit unsettled when I received your letter telling me of your visit. I don't know that it's safe for a woman to travel so far alone."

"Oh, I was fine. A spinster like me has little to fear. And besides, I told myself I was coming, and I wasn't about to let anxieties keep me away."

Daniel rode ahead and turned his horse onto a narrow road that cut across a field. Woodman followed. "It's goin' ta get a bit bumpy, lydies," he called over his shoulder.

"It certainly can't be worse than the sea voyage I just had. Or that trip overland from Brisbane."

Woodman offered her a friendly grin, and she smiled in return.

"He's quite nice," she whispered to Rebecca.

"Yes. He is."

"I've never been around blacks much." Mildred scanned the partially cloudy sky. "Thankfully, it's cooler than yesterday. How do you tolerate such heat?"

"One does adjust, and the veranda is usually cooler than most places. I must admit to still yearning for the cool breezes of Boston. However, during the winter it's much cooler than now. Actually chilly at times. Strangely, we generally have more rain during the summer months than during the winter. We usually get a fair number of storms during the hot season."

Daniel pulled up alongside the surrey. "Thought you might like to see some of the cattle right off," he said, nodding toward a nearby herd. "This is a small mob. We've a fair number of them about the place."

Mildred fixed her eyes on the grazing cattle. "My, there seem to be a lot of them. And you say you have many more?"

"Right."

She gazed at the open spaces about them. "I can't remember ever seeing anything quite like this. Everything seems so . . . unrestrained."

Daniel grinned. "We Aussies *are* a bit unrestrained, eh, Woodman?"

"Yais, a bit wild ta be sure."

"You seem quite civilized," Mildred said, then pointed at a grove. "And what kind of trees are those? We've nothing like them back home."

21

"Gum trees and acacia." Daniel peered across the baking plains.

Mildred's eyes automatically followed his. "It's very flat, isn't it."

"We've some knolls, and there's a river or two, even a gibber now and again."

"Gibber? I've never heard such a word."

"Means large rocks or boulders."

"Hmm. How interesting."

The sound of the wind was all that accompanied the creaking of the wagon and jangling of harnesses. It cut across the open land, buffeting the sea of grass. Daniel rode quietly alongside the surrey.

Mildred rested her head against the back of the seat. "This is quite peaceful."

"That it is," said Rebecca.

"It is very different from what I'm used to, but I rather like it."

"Really, Auntie?"

"There's a certain tranquillity to it."

Daniel grinned. "Too right. Ya might be a true Aussie, eh?"

"You think so?" Mildred asked, clearly pleased at the label. "I do believe I've a distant cousin who lives in Australia." She smoothed back wisps of loose hair.

"There you go, then. You do belong," Daniel said. "We've one of our barns right up 'ere." He nodded at a large structure, open on two sides. "Every now and again we'll come across a storage barn like this," he explained. "We've got them scattered about. They're good for laying up hay and sheltering other odds and ends."

"Do you cut your own hay?" Mildred asked.

"Right, we do, except for bad years."

"Does that happen often?"

"We usually have enough rain for growing hay. Bit dry this season though."

When they reached the huge barn, Daniel dismounted and then walked around to help the women out of the surrey.

Mildred was the first to step down. "Oh, that feels much better. I needed to take a stretch."

Daniel gave Rebecca a hand. "You feeling all right?"

"Fine, just a bit uncomfortable."

⁊

Daniel led his horse inside the barn. "A bit cooler in 'ere."

Mildred's eyes roamed through the interior of the large structure and to a mountain of hay piled beneath a lofty ceiling. "Unbelievable. I've never seen anything quite like it."

Daniel grinned, pleased with Mildred's admiration. "Figure it's easier to keep feed in several places on the station. That way we can get it to the cattle easier." He plucked a piece of hay from the stack, stuck one end in his mouth, and chewed on it.

"That makes sense."

"In spite of the lack of rain, we managed to get a fair amount cut this year. We'd be hard done by if not for the moderate rainfall last season." With a sense of apprehension, he gazed outside into the burning sunlight. "Seems we might be in for it this year though."

"In for what?" Mildred asked.

"Drought. We get enough clouds but no rain. They move along without giving us even a small drink."

"What will you do if you don't get rain?" Mildred furrowed her brow.

Daniel shrugged. "Not much we can do, except pray. If it gets real bad, we'll sell off some of the bullocks." Daniel didn't want to talk about drought; he already spent too many hours thinking about it. He walked toward a small doorway. "We keep medicines and such in here—lot easier when the stock needs doctoring."

"That seems prudent." Mildred gazed out at the land stretching away from the barn. "Just how big did you say Douloo is?"

Daniel leaned on the wall. "According to your American measurements—I'd say about five hundred thousand acres. A fair bit to look after, eh?" He lifted a canteen off the saddle horn.

"It's a bit daunting. Seems a lot for a man to manage."

"I've plenty of help, and my father taught me well." He took a drink. "We better be off, then." After taking another drink, he replaced the lid on his canteen and led his horse outside. Helping Rebecca and Mildred into the surrey, he said, "You might want to have a go at some of that water of yours." He looked at Woodman. "Could you get the ladies a drink?"

"Yais, sir."

"This heat will get the better of you if you don't take care to drink."

"No fear of that," Rebecca said, swallowing a mouthful. "I think I've had more than my share already."

"Do you need to go back, Rebecca?" Daniel asked.

"No. I'm enjoying myself. I've been cooped up inside far too long." She glanced at Mildred. "Would you like to return to the house?"

"Absolutely not. I find this far too interesting."

Daniel remounted. "Right. Well, if you get too hot or uncomfortable, tell me."

He led the way, moving toward what looked like a cloud of dust. He stopped at the top of a low rise. A sea of mooing, tail-swishing cattle moved across the dry ground, their noses close to the earth, biting off precious clumps of grass. Dirt sifted about the sightseers.

"Oh my, I don't think I've ever seen so many cows at one time," Mildred said.

"We've a fair number of calves this year—ought to do well at the market," Daniel explained. "We'll be moving them south to the train in a few months."

Keeping her eyes on the herd, Mildred said with obvious admiration, "You seem to be handling things quite well without your father. I'm certain he would be proud of you."

"I'm giving it a fair go." He pressed his feet down against the stirrups, straightened his legs, and pushed himself up off the saddle. "Sometimes it feels like my father's 'ere watching me." He settled back into the saddle and rested his hands on the saddle horn.

"That must be comforting," Mildred said.

Daniel nodded, but rather than feeling peace at the idea of his father's presence, he felt exposed and deficient. No matter how hard he worked or prayed, he knew he'd never be good enough to replace the man who'd overseen Douloo for so many years.

Flies swarmed the spectators. Mildred sputtered and swatted at the niggling pests. "I don't mean to whine, but could we move on?"

"Sorry about the flies," Daniel said. "I'm used to the little beasts." He turned his chestnut stallion away from the herd and prodded him forward. Woodman followed, and they moved along yet another dirt road, leaving most of the flies behind. They started across a shallow river, stopping midstream to allow the horses to drink.

Rebecca and Mildred also took the opportunity to sip from their canteens. "Rebecca dear, is the water in the river always this low?" Mildred asked.

"No. As Daniel said, it's been a bad summer—not enough rain. I'm sure it will come though. It always does."

Daniel plucked a burr from his mount's mane, then glanced at the blue sky. "It will. I'm sure of it."

"I did some reading about Australia before setting out on this journey. One of the books said you sometimes have droughts."

"We get 'em, all right. No worries though."

"You seem very nonchalant about the whole thing. Seems to me without water your station could be ruined."

"Could be. But it does me little good to worry." Daniel smiled. "My grandfather started this place more than forty years ago. I figure it'll take more than a drought to run us out of 'ere. In fact, I've plans for improvements."

"Improvements? Really?" Mildred looked at Rebecca. "Seems you've married an ambitious man."

"I'm building up the herd—got my eye on a fine bull. He'll add life to the mob."

Daniel's gaze moved across the open land. "Figure on putting in some wells too."

"Why, that makes wonderful good sense. But will there still be water if there's a drought?"

"We may be hard done by, but we'll manage." Daniel pulled up on the reins and nudged his stallion forward, splashing through the stream and climbing up the bank.

Woodman expertly steered the horses up the rutted incline and followed Daniel, who silently led the way along the eastern boundary of the station, then followed a path cutting diagonally across the grasslands. The wind sighed, and it sounded as if the flats were breathing.

"There's a place close to home that I'd like to show you," Daniel said, studying the three in the surrey. "From the looks of you, it'll do you some good."

"What's wrong with our looks?" Rebecca teased.

"You seem a bit done in." He looked at Woodman. "A bit overheated, wouldn't you say?"

Woodman glanced back at the women in the surrey. "Too roight." He grinned.

"I must admit to feeling slightly overheated. And my feet are swelling." Rebecca lifted her right leg and examined her puffy ankle and foot.

A mob of kangaroos bounded across the field in front of them. Daniel pulled back on the reins, and his horse danced. "Well, have a look at that, will you," he said, wearing a grin.

"Kangaroos!" Mildred exclaimed. "I saw a picture in one of the books I read."

"Roight," Woodman said. "Roos. Big reds."

"How wonderful. I never actually believed I'd see one close-up. They're somewhat peculiar looking though, don't you think?"

"Peculiar? How?" Woodman asked.

"They look strange. Up on their back legs like that, I mean."

"They're good eatin'."

Mildred blanched.

Daniel pointed at one. "That one there's got a joey." A tiny head protruded from a pouch in the front. The small roo peered over the edge of its mother's pocket, seemingly content to ride.

"The babies stay put til they're big enough to keep up on their own. That one looks like he might be adventurous."

Mildred laughed. "Amazing. I never thought I'd see the day." She shook her head side to side. "This place is full of surprises."

"That it is," Daniel said with a smile, feeling proud of his home and pleased that Mildred was impressed. "Come on, then."

He spurred his horse forward. About a kilometer farther on, they stopped to watch a group of aborigines in the distance. They'd been quietly moving across the grasslands until they caught sight of Daniel and the surrey. Now they crouched and stared at the travelers.

"Ought to give them their space," Daniel said.

Mildred had gone slightly pale. "Why is that? Are they dangerous?"

"No."

"Daniel, they look as if they're afraid, don't you think?" Rebecca asked.

"Too right. And they're smart to stay out of sight, I'd say."

"Why is that?" Mildred asked, partially standing in the surrey to get a better look.

"Some blokes 'round these parts just as soon shoot 'em as look at 'em," Woodman said, his tone surly.

Daniel rested his hands on his saddle horn. "Shame too. They're no trouble, really."

The color had drained from Mildred's face. "Doesn't the law have something to say about that?"

"Out 'ere the people are the law. We pretty much take care of ourselves."

"And who takes care of them?" Mildred nodded toward the aborigines, who were now cautiously moving away.

Daniel didn't have an answer. It's not something he'd ever given much thought to. "I guess they take care of themselves pretty much."

The blacks continued moving until they disappeared into the shimmering heat rising from the flats.

Mildred sighed heavily and sat down. "I must say, Rebecca, I have some qualms about you . . . and the baby living here."

"There's no reason, really, Auntie."

28

"I'm concerned about your safety."

"You've no worries," Daniel said, riding alongside the surrey. "Rebecca and the baby will be well looked after."

"I admit this is a tremendous place, but it's quite wild. What about medical facilities? Are there any?" Without waiting for an answer, Mildred continued, "When a woman's having a baby, you're never certain what emergency might arise."

"We've a doctor. He's been looking out for my family a good number of years. When her time comes, he'll be sent for. He's a fine doctor."

"I mean no disrespect. I'm sure he's a fine doctor, but you must admit, the facilities in Boston are . . . superior. What if something goes wrong? Or what if the baby's not quite right?"

Daniel squeezed the reins and forced down defensiveness. "Women have been having babies out 'ere for generations, and quite successfully, I might add." His eyes went to Rebecca.

"Auntie, I'll be fine. I'm not afraid."

"Well, you might want to rethink that." Mildred set her jaw. After a moment she conceded, "I suppose we must trust in the Lord."

"Rebecca's a strong one," Daniel said. "She'll be fine."

"I pray you're right." Mildred sounded solemn.

"I know it must be hard for you to understand our ways. I suppose it seems isolated, but this is home to Rebecca and me. We feel secure 'ere. There are dangers, but then there's troubles everyplace. I'd say it's better for a bloke to live out in the open among God's creation than it is to be crushed in the middle of a city. More than likely, mankind began in a place like this rather than a place like Boston." He grinned.

Mildred pursed her lips. "I'm sure you're right, but that doesn't mean we were meant to remain in such surroundings." Her eyes took in the barren spaces. "Adam and Eve started out in the Garden of Eden. And as much as I admire this station . . . to be perfectly honest, this looks more like the place Adam and Eve were banished to."

Daniel chuckled. "You may be right. But Rebecca and I aren't afraid. Living 'ere makes a person stronger."

"I don't know that Rebecca needs to be any stronger," Mildred quipped, a half smile on her face.

Wagon and rider continued moving through the grasslands until a green smudge appeared in the distance. Daniel reined in his horse, and Woodman stopped the team. "This place is grand. You'll like it," Daniel said before moving on.

Following a river, a strip of lush grasses sliced through yellow fields. The waterway widened and seemed to rest in a patch of green before continuing. The sightseers moved closer. There amidst dry ground and gnarled trees lay an oasis. The trees looked stronger and healthier. There were gum trees and acacia, shrubbery, and green grasses. It was shaded and cooler. The small river drifted into the lushness, then curled back on itself, creating a pool before flowing on again.

"Why, I never," Mildred said. "What is this place?"

"It's a billabong," Rebecca said, standing. "Isn't it lovely?"

"Yes. Absolutely."

Daniel climbed off his horse. "For us, it's kind of a secret garden. Except it's no secret, really. This is a place we come to rest and cool off. The pool is good for swimming."

"Absolutely lovely," Mildred said, allowing Woodman to help her out of the surrey. "If I had a blanket I think I could just lie down right here and take a nap."

"Brought one," Daniel said, grabbing a blanket out of the back of the carriage.

"Oh, how wonderful, Daniel," Rebecca said, taking Wood-man's hand and clumsily stepping out of the surrey.

Daniel spread out the blanket beneath a tree. "Have a seat, Mildred."

"I think I shall."

"Oh, I'd love to put my feet in the water," Rebecca said. "Will you join me, Auntie?"

"No. I think not. I'll be just as happy to remain right here." Mildred leaned back on her arms and closed her eyes. "Daniel?"

"Can't wait," he said, taking Rebecca's arm and guiding her toward the water.

☙

Leaning back, Mildred stretched out her legs in front of her. She watched as Rebecca and Daniel disappeared down an embankment. Breathing deeply, she closed her eyes. "This is quite marvelous. Do you come here often?" she asked Woodman, who sat at the base of the tree with his back pressed against the smooth bark.

"Now and then."

"Does Rebecca?"

"Yais, mum. As often as she can." He smiled and his dark, round face crinkled into deep lines. "She feels closer ta Boston 'ere, I think."

"I suppose she would. Back home she and that horse of hers, Chavive, traipsed through the grounds at every opportunity. She loved that animal. It nearly broke her heart when she was forced to sell her." She gazed at the water, a small smile playing at her lips. "Why does it pool up that way?"

"Can't say exactly. Guess it's what the river wants ta do, eh?" Woodman rested his arms on bent knees and studied cattle farther downstream that stood on the bank slurping up water from the river. Their soft mooing sounded like a lazy song.

31

All of a sudden a raucous cry splintered the air.

Mildred startled. "For heaven's sake, what was that?"

"A kookaburra."

"A what?"

Woodman laughed. "It's a bird. Kind of sounds like they're laughing, eh?"

"I suppose it does." Mildred looked up into a nearby tree. A stocky white and gray bird sat in its upper branches. Once more it let out its discordant cry. "It doesn't look particularly distinctive, but its voice certainly is."

"Too roight," Woodman said and then returned to staring at the river. His eyes drooped.

Mildred said, "This is a fine station. Daniel must be proud of it."

"Yais, mum. That he is."

She plucked a piece of grass and twirled it between her fingers. "Can't say I'm completely comfortable with Rebecca living way out here, but . . . she seems happy."

"I'd say she is. She and Daniel 'ave a fine life."

Mildred gazed at the surrounding countryside, which was nearly hidden by the greenery. "I must admit, Douloo is quite spectacular, even beautiful in some ways. I might actually miss this place after I return to Boston."

"What's there that ya 'ave ta return to?"

"Why, I have a life there. Of course I must return," she said, but inside Mildred considered the secret thought she'd been afraid to look at squarely. She had hoped this would be a suitable place where she might stay. She'd missed Rebecca terribly, and although her brother-in-law had offered her a comfortable place to live, she felt smothered by his constant attention. And then there was Thomas. She didn't know what to do about him.

"Woodman!" Daniel's voice sounded sharp. He ran toward the shaded area where Woodman and Mildred sat.

Woodman stood.

"Smoke! There!" Daniel pointed at a billowing white cloud rising up from the ground several kilometers south.

Mildred pushed to her feet and leaned against the tree. "Oh, dear Lord!" she said, gazing at the apparition.

"I'm going to take a look."

"Ya best not go on yer own."

"And whose 'ere to go with me?" Daniel asked. "You get the women back to the house." Daniel untied his horse and climbed into the saddle.

"Daniel?" Rebecca called, clambering up the bank as quickly as she could. Breathing hard, she lay a hand on the horse's neck. "Please be careful." She grasped Daniel's hand.

"I'll be fine. No need to worry."

"I'll be there straightaway," Woodman said.

"Right. And bring any roustabouts or drovers about the place, eh? Might need them." Daniel kicked the stallion in the sides and galloped off.

3

Riding hard, Daniel moved toward the billowing smoke. Anxiety and his worst imaginings fed his racing pulse.

Purposely he turned his thoughts elsewhere, to the early days with Rebecca in Boston. At her father's estate they'd ridden with abandon, racing across open fields and tramping through forests of oak and fir. It had been an enthralling time. He'd been mesmerized by Rebecca. She was the most beautiful woman he'd ever met. He'd fallen in love with her playfulness as well as her stubbornness. Now a fire threatened Rebecca and the child she carried.

He approached the blaze. It was sizable, spitting and hissing as it ate up dry grass. The fire moved toward a mob of cattle a kilometer away.

The muscles in Daniel's stomach tightened. This was one of the most formidable adversaries he'd ever face. He watched while it gained momentum and threw flames several meters in front of its path.

He searched for some means to stop it. There were no streams or ponds, and all that stretched out in front of the flames were dry grasses. If he wanted to put down this monster, he'd need help.

Daniel glanced in the direction of the house. If the fire couldn't be stopped, it would destroy his home. *Lord, no*, he thought, watching for riders. He needed help.

He moved toward the grazing livestock. The fire moved closer. The animals mooed anxiously, switching their tails and eyeing the approaching flames. If he didn't get them moved, they would likely stampede, injuring themselves and at the very least scattering away from his land and onto his neighbors'. In the maelstrom that could ensue, some might even flee directly into the flames.

Without help, there was little Daniel could do, but he couldn't afford to wait to move them. He approached slowly, and as he got closer he talked to the mob, careful to keep his voice calm. He glanced at the fire. It was moving fast and getting close. Smoke drifted toward the mob, and the cattle were becoming agitated.

Once more he searched the grasslands toward home, hoping to see Woodman and a mob of other riders. The plains were empty. *Come on, Woodman. I need you.*

With a quick look at the encroaching fire, he continued to move in on the cattle. Lifting his rope and swinging it over his head, he rode up to a young bullock. "Come on, now, move along. Hep, hep, hep." He kept his voice calm, although his insides felt tight as a string on a crossbow.

The bullock sauntered forward; others joined him. Daniel moved back and forth around the animals, trying to keep them close together. All the while, he kept an eye on the menacing fire. He'd have to move faster if he wanted to save the cattle.

Again he looked across the flats, hoping to see help approaching. In the distance dust swirled up. Daniel kept working but watched the brown cloud. Soon he could make out a rider. It was Woodman. A group of other riders rode along-side him.

"Good to see you!" Daniel said as Woodman rode up with Jim at his side.

Jim glanced at the fire. "Figured you could use some help."

"That I can." His tone turning serious, he said, "We'll need men fighting the fire and men moving the mob. You drovers look after the cattle. The rest of you need to go to work on a fire line." He glanced around at the group of riders. "Glad you came prepared. Use your shovels to dig up the grass and turn the sod. If luck goes our way, we'll stop this right 'ere."

Woodman dismounted and tied his horse to a thatch of brush. Several men did the same. Jim and a group of drovers set off toward the herd.

"Steer them toward the north," Daniel called as he untied a shovel strapped to the back of a saddle. "Woodman, glad to see you were thinking ahead," he said, holding the shovel slightly aloft.

"Brought all I could find. Figured ya'd need somethin' ta fight with. It's not much."

Daniel trudged closer to the blaze but made sure to stay a good distance ahead of it. "Let's dig a line along 'ere," he said, pointing at the place he wanted the men to work. "Make the patch as wide as you can. Less chance of flames jumping the line that way." He pushed his shovel into the earth. "We got to work fast," he said, turning over his first clump of sod.

Too soon the fire was so close that choking smoke whirled around the men. Daniel tied his handkerchief over his mouth and nose, but it did little to keep out the pungent smoke. His eyes burned and teared, and his throat felt raw. Coughing, he kept working. The flames were moving fast.

With the fire nearly overtaking them, Daniel called, "All

right. Get out of 'ere. Let's go!" Carrying his shovel, he sprinted toward his horse, climbed on its back, and rode to a safe distance. He watched and waited to see if the line held.

Grasses crackled and sizzled as flames gobbled up the prairie. Smoke grew thicker; the world seemed to turn dark. Daniel could barely see. Smoke scorched his throat and burned his lungs. Choking and coughing, he waited. Would the barrier stop the flames?

Jim joined Daniel. "Doesn't look good."

"What about the herd?"

"Got 'em moved. They ought to be all right. There's a couple of drovers still with them. Figured you could use help here."

More ferocious than ever, the blaze moved toward the barrier. Then, with little more than a pause, it leaped the fire line and caught hold of the grasses on the opposite side, where it moved on.

Daniel stared at the blaze. It seemed fiercer than before.

"What are we gonna do?" Jim asked.

Fighting panic, Daniel didn't answer right away. Then with ferocity he said, "We dig another line!"

For a moment longer he watched the flames. Hungry, they continued to consume prairie grass and reached for more, moving toward the house. *Lord, how do we stop this?* Daniel grabbed his shovel and moved farther out ahead of the flames.

"All right," he called to the men. "I'll need all of you on this line, digging as if your lives depended on it. They do. We've got to stop this thing! Now!"

Immediately the roustabouts and drovers went to work, digging and turning sod. Sweat mixed with soot and dirt trailed down their faces and necks. There would be no surrender.

Flames grew taller and more insistent, pressing closer to

the band of warriors. Sparks fell on shirts, hair, and skin, burning through material and flesh. Yet the men continued to battle.

The fire was too close. Daniel realized that to stay and fight could mean someone would die. "All right! We got to find another place to fight. Everyone back!" Some continued to work; he shouted, "Now! It's moving too fast!"

The men grabbed their horses, swung up onto their backs, and moved away. Holding his shovel aloft like a saber, Daniel shouted, "Get the mob moved." Using his handkerchief to wipe sweat and dirt from his face, he gazed at the ravenous fire and prayed, *God, help us.*

Rebecca fanned the hot air and watched the open plains, searching for Daniel. Where was he? It had been hours since Woodman and the other men had charged out of the yard.

"What time is it?" she asked.

"Nearly four," Willa said. "Try not to worry, dear. I'm sure the men are fine. It's not the first fire they've had to fight."

"It's the first time something like this has happened since I've been here."

"Yes. But recently we've been blessed with its absence. Fire is something we always watch for. The tall grasses and the eucalyptus are like sweet treats to a fire—they energize a blaze."

"Really?" Mildred asked, keeping her eyes on the plains. "Could the fire come here?"

"Yes. I suppose so. The house has been in jeopardy before. But I'm sure we've nothing to fear. The men are strong, and Daniel knows just what to do." She turned a reassuring smile on Mildred, who clutched the front seam of her dress.

"It'll be dark soon," Rebecca said. She wanted to believe

Daniel would be all right, but inside she couldn't quell her fear. *Lord, please protect him, and the others.*

"What would we do if the fire came here?" Mildred asked.

"The men would fight it off, and we'd help them."

"What if they don't come back?" Mildred's voice trembled.

"Well, of course they'll be back," Willa said. "We've nothing to fret about." She picked up her embroidery. "Perhaps it would be a good idea if we busied ourselves with something other than our worries."

"They've been gone a long time, Willa," Rebecca said.

"It's not been so awfully long. And there's been no sign of fire from here, not even the smallest wisp of smoke. I dare say that if there were a large fire, we'd see smoke." She concentrated on her sewing. "We're fine and so are the men. God is looking out for them, I'm certain of it."

"I pray you're right," Mildred said. She walked across the porch and sat in a wicker chair. She sucked in a deep breath and returned to watching the flats.

"You look a bit pale, Rebecca. Are you all right?" Willa asked.

"Yes. I'm fine."

"Perhaps a drink of water would be good?"

"I am thirsty."

"Callie, could you get Rebecca some water?"

"I can get it." Rebecca started to rise.

"Oh, no you don't. You stay off your feet. The doctor was very explicit about that."

"No trouble, mum. I'll get it." Callie walked into the house.

Her insides quaking, Rebecca gazed out past the cottages and the barns and studied the plains. "If it was a small fire, wouldn't the men have returned by now?"

"We'll learn all the details when they get here," Willa said calmly.

"I wish I could feel as calm as you," Rebecca said. "You always remain tranquil, even in the worst situations."

"Oh, I get myself in a dither from time to time, but over the years I've learned it does little good except to give someone a stomach upset. Worry drains one's vitality, and I have too little vitality left." She smiled.

Callie carried out a tray with three glasses and a pitcher. "The water's cool, mum," she said, pouring a glass and handing it to Rebecca.

"Thank you, Callie." She sipped. "It tastes wonderful."

"Would ya like some, Miss Williams?"

"Yes. That would be lovely." Mildred stood and stepped toward Callie, accepting a glass of water. She walked to the balustrade. "I do hope they return soon."

✿

Another hour passed before a puff of dust appearing from below the rise told of approaching riders. The women stood expectantly.

"It's them," Rebecca said, seeing the top of Daniel's hat as he crested the rise. "Daniel!" Gripping the handrail, she made her way clumsily down the stairway. Daniel loped into the yard, then walked to the porch. Grabbing the horse's reins, Rebecca waited for him to dismount. "Thank the Lord you're all right."

Daniel removed his hat and circled an arm protectively about Rebecca's waist.

He was dirty and reeked of smoke, but Rebecca didn't mind.

"Right good to be back," Daniel said with a smile. His teeth looked very white against his blackened skin.

40

"Is everything all right?"

"Yeah. It was like a miracle." Ignoring his filthy condition, Daniel hugged Rebecca.

"What happened?"

"You look hot and thirsty," Willa said. "Callie, could you fetch more water, please?"

"Roight, mum." Callie hustled into the house.

"What happened?" Rebecca asked again.

"Well, it looked bad, right bad. The flames were huge and the fire was growing stronger. We built two fire lines, but neither one stopped it."

"It was a fight for sure," Woodman said.

Rebecca had been so intent on Daniel she hadn't even noticed Woodman. "I'm so glad you're all right." She turned her attention back to Daniel. "You said something about a miracle?"

"Right. The fire was really cooking. And I have to admit to being a bit scared. We couldn't stop it. And it was moving fast."

Callie handed Daniel and Woodman glasses of water.

Daniel chugged down a few gulps, then continued. "The wind came up—strong. At first I thought we were in real trouble. The fire seemed to burst with life, but then all of a sudden the direction of the wind changed and chased the fire back on itself. I figure God stepped in, eh?" He grinned.

"Praise the Lord," Willa said.

"And what would have happened if the wind hadn't changed?" Mildred asked, her face looking pinched.

Daniel finished off his water. "Well, to be honest, it was heading this way. We could have been fighting it right 'ere."

Mildred blanched. "Are you sure it's out?"

"Yes. No worries."

"You could have lost everything."

41

"Right, but it didn't happen, and it's not likely to."

Mildred still wasn't appeased. "What would you have done if it had come here? How do you fight a fire?"

"We'd have beat it back," Daniel said, his voice reassuring. "You've no worries. This house has been 'ere a good many years, and it'll be 'ere a good many more."

Rebecca pressed closer to Daniel. "You're safe and so is Douloo. That's all that matters."

4

A searing evening sun settled on the horizon as Rebecca followed Willa into church. Although instructed by the doctor to stay close to home, she'd managed to convince her family it would be safe to attend Christmas Eve services. Feeling tremendously swollen and uncomfortable, she walked down the aisle. Neighbors offered nods and smiles. Daniel kept a hand protectively on her arm and, following his mother, guided Rebecca into a pew.

Rebecca lowered herself onto the wooden seat and looked about the sanctuary. Sunlight slanted through windows, casting a shimmering glow over the room. Parishioners whispered among themselves, their enthusiasm and anticipation radiating throughout the church.

Daniel sat beside Rebecca. Smiling at her, he clasped her hand and held it. Mildred took the spot just to Rebecca's right and patted her arm sympathetically.

Cambria sat a few rows in front of Daniel and Rebecca. She turned in her seat and smiled at them. Her cheeks had more color, and the blue in her eyes seemed brighter than usual.

Rebecca waved to her, then whispered to Daniel. "She

looks nervous. I can't imagine how it must be to sing in front of all these people."

Daniel nodded. "Right. Not to mention, it'll be the first solo ever sung in this church."

Rebecca remembered the tongue-lashing she'd taken from her father-in-law months before when she'd suggested Cambria sing a solo. She was certain that now he would be pleased with the special music. *Elvina Walker must be fit to be tied*, she thought with pleasure. Elvina had been one of the most ferocious opponents of solo music.

Rev. Cobb took his place at the front of the church. The room quieted. *He looks healthier and happier these days*, Rebecca thought. Rather than dreading the sermons as she once had, she looked forward to hearing what he had to say. Although still a bit long-winded, his messages were now inspired, each carrying her into the Father's presence or bringing personal conviction.

Free of Bertram's tight controls, Rev. Cobb had blossomed. She wished her father-in-law could be here to see the changes. At the end, he had grieved the negative result his strong hand had placed on the church. He would be happy to see how it was now moving forward.

"G'day to you." Rev. Cobb gazed out at the parishioners. "Bless you all for being here. This is truly a night to rejoice." He smiled. "Let's begin by worshipping together in song. Please stand and open your hymnals to page ninety-three."

Organ music resonated throughout the small church, and harmonious voices sang "Angels We Have Heard on High" and then "Away in a Manger." The songs were familiar to Rebecca, and she sang out as much as her swollen tummy would allow. Although the baby now sat low in her abdomen, she still had difficulty catching her breath.

Daniel held her hand against his chest. Glancing at her handsome husband, Rebecca wondered why it had taken her so long to fall in love with him, then surmised that really it hadn't. *I did love him, even in the beginning. I was just afraid to completely offer my life to anyone.*

The baby kicked, and she rested her free hand on her stomach. Rebecca's heart galloped. Was she up to motherhood? She'd never even held a baby.

The song ended, and there was a hushed rustling as parishioners took their seats. Rev. Cobb returned to the lectern. "It's time our church moved forward in what some might consider a daring step but I believe is an example of our growing trust." He smiled as his eyes found Cambria. "One of our own will bless us in song."

A hushed murmur moved through the congregation.

"As it turns out, Cambria Taylor has quite a lovely voice, and she's going to lift us to new spiritual heights as she shares 'O Holy Night' and 'It Came upon a Midnight Clear.'"

Cambria walked to the front of the church, and the reverend stepped aside and sat in a chair alongside the wall.

Silence pervaded the sanctuary. Cambria stood at the front, hands clasped at her waist and the heels of her shoes pressed tightly together. She trembled slightly. For a brief moment she closed her eyes. Rebecca knew she was praying. A prelude was played on the organ, and then Cambria sang the first chords. Her soprano voice filled the silence with the words of "O Holy Night."

Rebecca felt gooseflesh on her arms. No longer overly hot, weary, or achy, all she knew was the sweetness of God's presence. Closing her eyes, she allowed the reverent voice and words to carry her into a heavenly place. With only a brief pause, Cambria moved on to the next hymn—as lovely as the first. When the final note faded, a hushed reverence lingered over the congregation.

Rebecca glanced at Elvina, who sat one pew ahead of her.

Her eyes glimmered, and her cheeks were moist with tears. Rebecca smiled. *Thank you, Lord.*

Cambria quietly took her seat, and Rev. Cobb returned to the lectern. "Thank you, Cambria. That was lovely. Once again music has carried us into the presence of God—what a gift he has given us." He smiled at the congregation and glanced down at the outline in front of him.

"Christmas is a time to reflect on the greatest gift ever given to mankind—a Savior for a lost world, a Savior given for each one of us. He knew you even then . . ."

Dusk settled over the church. The glow of candles and lanterns replaced sunlight. Rebecca felt secure. A sharp kick from her unborn child reminded her of the miracle that would soon take place, and she felt the mingling emotions of fear and anticipation. Would she be up to the task? Would the baby be healthy?

⚅

The service ended with a resounding rendition of "O Come, All Ye Faithful," which seemed fitting to Rebecca. She walked out of church feeling ready for a mission of service—exactly what her calling was she didn't quite know, but she felt certain the Lord would lead.

As she stepped toward the door, Meghan Linnell brushed past her. She started to excuse herself and then realized whom she'd bumped into. She stopped midsentence.

"Merry Christmas to you," Rebecca managed to say.

Meghan glared at her, and then her eyes dropped momentarily to Rebecca's rounded stomach. "Merry Christmas? I think not. Rather, I pray for your misfortune." With that, she turned and walked away.

Rebecca pressed a hand to her stomach, stunned at the

sharp words, so like a curse. *I don't believe in curses*, she told herself. *And what else should I expect from Meghan?*

"Dear heavens," Mildred said. "Who was that?"

"Meghan Linnell."

"Why is she so angry with you?"

"She was in love with Daniel and wanted to marry him. I guess I can't really blame her for being upset."

"Yes, well there's a limit to what is brokenheartedness and what is simply too much." Mildred placed an arm about Rebecca's shoulders. "I believe Daniel ended up with the woman of God's choosing."

Rebecca rested a hand over her aunt's. "Me too." Sadly she watched Meghan and prayed, *Lord, replace her bitterness with your love*. There had been a time when simply seeing Meghan had stirred up anger and resentment, but that had changed. Now more than anything else, she felt sorry for Meghan.

Daniel circled the back of her waist with his arm. "She's made her bed; she'll have to lie in it."

Cambria approached. "You were wonderful!" Rebecca said, reaching out to hug her friend. "I was carried away to heaven."

"Ya were? I was right scared. Nearly decided not ta do it, but knew I'd never hear the end of it from ya." Cambria smiled, then hugged Rebecca again. "Ya have a grand Christmas, now."

"You too."

$\mathcal{D}$

The moon was large and round in the night sky. Its glow over the flats made the countryside appear as if it were covered in snow. "This is nearly how it looks in Boston in December," Rebecca said. "Of course, you must imagine it's cold."

Mildred gazed at the moon. "I'd rather not. I prefer this

to shivering beneath a blanket with our breath hanging in the air."

"I remember," Willa said. "December in England was usually quite cold. I agree. I rather like this."

Rebecca leaned against Daniel and closed her eyes. "It was a beautiful service, don't you think?"

"Right nice," he said.

"Lovely, quite lovely," Mildred added. "I must admit, I was a bit surprised. Being so far away from everything, I didn't expect something so nice. Your friend Cambria has a delightful voice."

"I could never do something like that," Rebecca said. "I'd be too frightened. Of course, I don't have a voice like hers, so I've nothing to worry about."

"Well, that's true enough," Daniel quipped.

Rebecca pinched him.

"But you have so many other fine qualities," he added, pulling Rebecca closer.

She snuggled against him.

"I'm just thankful we managed to get through the evening without having to send for the doctor." Willa smiled at Rebecca.

"Dr. Walker was there," Rebecca said. "And he gave me a piece of his mind. Then he told me he understood and wished us all a merry Christmas."

⟡

Unable to sleep, Rebecca listened to Daniel's even breathing. Hoping to find a more comfortable position, she rolled onto her other side and pressed her back against his. Staring into the darkness, she wondered how long it would be before her child would be born. She felt a prickle of fear.

She knew having a baby wouldn't be easy. So many things could go wrong.

She took a deep breath and tried to relax. In spite of open windows, the air was still and hot. She dropped her feet over the side of the bed and pushed herself upright. Pressing a hand against the small of her aching back, she crossed to the window and stared out at the yard. A light was on in Callie's house.

She pushed her feet into slippers, grabbed a robe, and quietly walked out of the bedroom and down the stairs. A kerosene lamp at the end of the hallway and along the staircase gave off muted light. She stopped at the sitting room door and studied a rather fragile-looking Christmas tree with a small mound of gifts beneath it. The morning would bring a celebration, one that was made sweeter this year by her aunt's presence. If only it also included her father. With a sigh, she looked at her abdomen and rested a hand on it. *You would have loved him.*

She opened the front door and stepped onto the porch. The moon was still bright, although lower in the sky. She stood at the rail and gazed at the grounds. Someone stood on Callie's porch, then walked down the steps and moved across the yard toward the main house. It was Callie.

"Ya all roight, mum?"

"Fine. But I can't sleep."

"Me either. Was just sittin' and thinkin' 'bout things." She studied Rebecca. "Ya ought ta get yer rest, with the little one comin' soon."

"I would if I could," Rebecca said dryly. With a sigh she added, "I feel as if I'm about to pop."

"The baby knows the roight time." Callie smiled lovingly. "I'm anxious ta see 'im."

"You think it's a boy?"

"I do. And I'm mostly roight."

49

"How can you tell?"

"Don't know for sure. Just do."

"Hmm. Well, I hope you're right, for Daniel's sake. I don't really care one way or the other as long as it's healthy." Rebecca turned toward the door. "I have something for you. I was going to wait until tomorrow, but . . . well, just a moment."

She trudged inside the house and headed for the Christmas tree. Callie followed. "Oh dear, where is it?" Rebecca asked, studying the pile of gifts. Clumsily she knelt and shuffled through packages. "Ah, here it is."

"Let me help ya." Callie offered her a hand and assisted Rebecca to her feet.

Rebecca held out the package. "For you."

"But why? Ya shouldn't 'ave."

"I consider you a friend." Rebecca shrugged. "And it's Christmas."

Callie untied a red ribbon. "Looks like a book." She grinned and carefully tore away the wrapping, revealing a black leather volume. "A Bible? For me?"

"I know you don't believe, but I wanted you to have one . . . just in case."

"It's a fine gift." Callie ran a hand over the cover, then looked at Rebecca. "But I will use it only to practice my reading. I will not believe."

Rebecca nodded. "I understand." She grasped Callie by the shoulders and kissed her cheek. "Merry Christmas."

"Merry Christmas ta ya." Callie grinned and picked up something from behind the tree. "I 'ave something for ya too." She handed Rebecca a handwoven bag. "It's a dilly bag ta keep yer things in."

"It's lovely. What beautiful handwork. How did you make it?"

"It's nothin' really. I just used strips of bark, and after softening 'em I wove 'em together."

50

"There are so many bright colors."

"Wal, that was simple enough. I used roots and bulbs ta make dye."

"Thank you." Rebecca opened the bag and looked inside. "I never expected . . ."

"I don't believe in yer holiday, but I wanted ta give ya something anyway." She smiled, glanced at her Bible, then said, "Good night, mum." Like a mist moving silently away, Callie left the room without making a sound.

Rebecca crossed to the settee, enjoying the quiet of the house. A creaking came from the stairs, and a few moments later Daniel walked into the room.

"I woke up and you weren't beside me. Is everything all right?"

"Yes. I'm fine, just uncomfortable. Seems each day that goes by it becomes more difficult to sleep."

Daniel sat beside her, and she leaned against him. "So much has changed in such a short time." Rebecca brushed dark hair off her shoulder. "When I think about what our life was like at this time last year . . . well, it's just nearly unbelievable."

"Hmm, let me see. Seems we were living in a marriage of convenience and quite unhappy."

Rebecca smiled softly. "Thank the Lord for his mercy."

Daniel squeezed her shoulders. "I have something for you. I was going to give it to you tomorrow, but we're both up now and I just can't wait any longer."

Rebecca straightened. "What is it?"

Daniel stood. "Come on, then." Wearing a half smile, he grasped her hands and pulled her to her feet. Keeping a hold of one hand, he led her toward the front door.

"Where are we going?"

"You'll see." He opened the door and stepped outside.

"You have something for me outside?"

Daniel grinned, and his dimple creased his cheek. He led her down the front steps and to the barn.

"Daniel, what's going on?"

He didn't answer. Instead, he grabbed a lantern from just inside the barn door and lit it. "Ah, that's better. Come on, then."

He moved toward the back of the barn and stopped just before the last stall, where he hung the lantern from a post. "I've been thinking and thinking about what to get you for Christmas. There didn't seem to be anything that was just right. And then I realized there was only one thing you would really love."

Rebecca's excitement and confusion grew. "What is it?"

Daniel grinned and then picked up the lantern and moved to the last stall. "Merry Christmas," he said, holding the lantern high and then clicking his tongue.

A horse emerged from the shadows. A roan mare nickered. Rebecca stepped closer and studied the horse. "Chavive?"

A familiar whinny answered her.

"Oh, my Lord! Chavive!" Rebecca wrapped her arms around the animal's neck and hugged her. Tears wet her cheeks. She rubbed the animal's face with the palm of her hand. "Oh, Chavive! I never thought I'd see you again." Rebecca looked at Daniel. "How?"

Daniel smiled broadly. "I inquired about who bought her and made them an offer. At first they didn't want to part with her, but when I told them how you two belonged together, they relented."

"But how did you get her here all the way from Boston?"

"It was a bit complicated, but I had Mildred's help. It was perfect timing, with her coming over. If she hadn't been traveling on the same ship, I don't know that I'd have trusted anyone to oversee the voyage. But Mildred made sure she had a first-rate stall onboard ship, and a good handler was hired to see to her all the way to Brisbane."

"It must have cost a fortune."

"Not exactly, but close. It was worth it though." He smiled broadly. "Jim went to Brisbane to fetch her. We've had a real time of it, trying to keep her presence from you. And I was afraid Mildred would let the cat out of the bag. She was so excited about the whole matter that she's had a terrible time of it."

"So that's what Jim was doing in Brisbane."

"Right."

Rebecca crossed to her husband. "Oh, Daniel! I love you!" She held his face in her hands. "You're the most wonderful man on the earth!" She kissed him. "Thank you! Thank you!"

"Don't know that I'm exactly the most wonderful, but close to it, eh?" Daniel grinned broadly.

Chavive whinnied. Rebecca turned and patted the mare. "She's thin."

"The trip over was a bit rough on her. No worries though. She'll fill out."

"She's dressed for a Boston winter." Rebecca ran her hand down the horse's neck, imagining the sheen that would soon appear as the horse shed her winter coat.

Rebecca longed to ride her, right now under the light of the moon. She glanced at her swollen abdomen, then caressed Chavive's face. "You're a fine lady. We'll ride soon."

5

Rebecca picked a sprig of lavender, held it to her nose, and breathed deeply. "Mmm, I love this smell."

Mildred pulled a weed, then sat back on bent legs. "It's one of my favorites. It has a distinctive fragrance. We ought to include it in a bouquet." She gazed up at an overcast sky. "I'm thankful for the cool weather; working in the garden is a delight."

Willa dropped a rather large weed into a bucket. "I've always found gardening to be soothing. No matter what my trouble might be, I feel more at peace when my hands are busy tidying up my garden."

"Yes. Absolutely," Mildred said.

Rebecca wondered about the sadness she saw in her aunt's eyes. "Is everything all right, Auntie? You don't seem yourself. Is something troubling you?"

Mildred hesitated before answering, as if trying to decide whether to share the truth or not. Finally she said, "No. I'm fine." She looked over the garden and changed the subject. "But I do wish I'd done more gardening over the years." She dusted the palms of her gloved hands. "When I lived with you and your father, we had someone to do such things, and my brother-in-law, Sterling, doesn't think it's ladylike." A resolute expression settled on her face. "However, I've decided that when I return I'm going to tell him I don't much care what he thinks—I'm going to do as much gardening as I like." She smiled triumphantly.

Such boldness was out of character for Mildred, but Rebecca liked it. "Bravo," she said.

With a harness draped over one shoulder, Woodman joined the three women. He smiled. "Roight fine day. Good for workin'. Fresh air and hard work's good for a body. A soul needs ta get close ta the earth." He shuffled the harness, then with a "G'day," he walked on.

"Woodman seems a fine person," Mildred said.

"He is that." Willa pushed to her feet. "I dare say, I don't know what we'd do without him."

"Is he leaving?"

"Oh no. Well, I can't say for certain. He's been known to go on walkabout without a moment's notice."

"Walkabout—I've heard of that. Just what does it mean?"

"I don't understand it completely." Willa tucked a stray strand of hair into place. "The aborigines feel some sort of call from the earth. They walk for days and days, listening to . . . the earth. They continue on until they've finished. I'm not quite sure just what they're doing, but I heard something about their listening to and following songs. Sometimes they're gone for months."

"Really? How peculiar."

"I'd like to go with Woodman sometime," Rebecca said. "I think it would be fascinating."

Willa grinned. "You won't be going anywhere. Soon you'll have a child to look after. And most likely Woodman wouldn't take anyone along with him. It's usually a solitary experience.

55

And I don't think without hardship." Willa retied her straw bonnet, cinching it tightly under her chin.

"Daniel said that when he was a boy he went on walkabout with Woodman."

"Yes, now that you mention it, he did. He was still a lad. Woodman thought it would be a good experience for him, and Bertram agreed. They weren't gone too awfully long, only a few weeks as I recall."

Adding a sprig of lavender to the beginnings of a bouquet, Mildred said, "How curious to just walk off and wander about. I'd be afraid of getting lost."

"They never get lost," Willa said. "Aborigines seem to know the earth and its ways very well. At times they're rather surprising people."

"Woodman is kind. He was a great help to me when I first arrived," Rebecca said, rubbing an aching back. Feeling weary and sore, she let out a slow breath. "I'm rather tired. I think I'll sit on the veranda for a while."

"You look flushed," Mildred said. "Are you sure you're all right?"

"Yes. Just a bit hot and achy." Chavive whinnied and trotted along the edge of the corral. Rebecca's eyes went to her. "I can hardly wait to ride again."

"It will bless me to watch you," Mildred said.

"Auntie, I'm amazed that you said nothing about her. You were so good at keeping the secret."

"It wasn't easy. I wanted to tell you so badly. But I'd promised Daniel."

Rebecca dropped a kiss on Mildred's cheek. "Thank you for taking such good care of her while you traveled. I've heard terrible stories about animals who have been mishandled while being transported."

"I checked on her every day. It was rather nice, really, becoming reacquainted with her. And the stable hand who watched over her was a fine young man. He worked for the previous owners. I think he was sad that she'd been sold."

Rebecca studied the horse. "She doesn't look as robust as she did when she lived with us. But I'm sure she'll be herself again soon."

"You best get out of the sun," Willa said, taking Rebecca's arm and guiding her out of the garden and up the porch steps. She steered her toward a chair, seated her, and then pulled another chair up close. She lifted Rebecca's feet and set them on the additional seat. "There, now, that ought to help." She glanced at Mildred, who'd dropped onto a settee. "I'd say we've worked long enough for one day. I'll have Callie get us some tea and biscuits." Taking the small bouquet from Mildred, she said, "I'll put these in water."

Willa disappeared indoors. A few minutes later she reappeared with a bowl of water and a washcloth. "Here, now, this should be cooling," she said, wringing water from the cloth and gently patting Rebecca's face. Her sky-blue eyes full of concern, she placed the cloth on Rebecca's forehead.

"That feels nice. Thank you." Rebecca closed her eyes.

"It's not hot, but you're looking overheated," Mildred said.

"I'm better now, Auntie. Don't worry." Rebecca's eyes went to the corral. Chavive trotted restlessly around the enclosure, ready for a ride. "It will be so lovely to ride her again. It's still hard to believe she's actually here."

Mildred smiled. "Oh, I remember the hours you spent on horseback exploring the pastures and forests near our home." She cast a glance at the dry flatlands. "I don't suppose it's quite the same here."

"No. But it's still very nice," Rebecca said. "There's a feeling of freedom here that I didn't have in Boston. I'm certain once Chavive becomes accustomed to the openness, she and I will have a grand time together."

"I'm sure you're right," Mildred said. "I must admit, however, that this is not what I had expected . . . or hoped for."

"What do you mean, Auntie? Hoped for?"

Callie appeared carrying a tray with a teapot, cups and saucers, and delicate-looking jam-filled biscuits. She set it on the table between the women. "Anything else, mum?"

"No. That's all for now."

"I'll pour," Mildred said, lifting the teapot. Daintily balancing a cup and saucer, she filled the cup with the honey-colored brew. After handing a cup to Willa, she poured tea into the two remaining cups, adding sugar to one and giving it to Rebecca. "If I recall, you like just a bit of sugar."

Rebecca sipped. "It's just right."

Willa offered the plate of biscuits to Rebecca. "Would you like a sweet?"

"No. I'm not hungry."

Willa extended them to Mildred.

Mildred took one, tasted it, and chewed thoughtfully. "Mmm. Delicious. I believe I detect a hint of almond?"

"You'll have to ask Lily. She made them." Willa took a biscuit and set the plate down. "She's a wonder in the kitchen."

Rebecca dipped the cloth in the water, wrung it out, and patted her face and neck. She wasn't feeling quite right. An ache had settled around her abdomen and lower back, and she felt restless. She closed her eyes and tried to relax. The muscles in her abdomen tightened, sending sharp pains into her pelvis. She tried to breathe normally.

"You're not looking well," Mildred said.

"Actually, I'm not feeling well."

"What is it, dear?" Willa asked.

The pain subsided. "It might be time for the baby."

Mildred's face blanched. "Why do you think that?" she asked, her voice tight.

"I'm not feeling like myself, and I had a rather unusual pain just now. However, it's gone."

Rebecca took a sip of tea and gazed out over the yard and beyond to the grasslands. Where was Daniel? The last several days, he'd been working on the outer ranges, and Rebecca had worried her time would come and he'd not be close enough to be sent for. *Please, come home soon*, she thought.

Quiet settled over the three women. A breeze rustled the greenery about the veranda, carrying with it the sharp fragrance of lavender. Rebecca drank her tea while making an effort to release her tension. Then again the muscles in her abdomen tightened and a throbbing settled into her lower back. The ache wrapped itself around her, gradually increasing in intensity. She let out a soft moan.

"Rebecca, what is it?" Willa asked.

"I'm having another pain."

Willa and Mildred both stood. "We best send for the doctor," Willa said. "Callie! Callie!"

Almost immediately the housemaid appeared at the door. "Yais, mum?"

"We need Woodman to go for the doctor. And someone needs to find Daniel. Please ask Jim if he'll go. It's time for the baby."

"Yais, mum," Callie said, bustling across the porch and then taking the steps two at a time before running across the dirt yard toward the carriage house.

"We should get you to bed," Mildred suggested.

"If it's all right with you, I'd rather stay here. The pain isn't so bad that I belong in bed, and it's much nicer here than indoors."

"I suppose you're right." Mildred clasped her hands together and held them close to her chest. "I don't really know much about these things. I've never had a child, and I've never been present at a birth." She walked to the balustrade. "What does one do?" She looked at Willa.

"For now, we wait." She patted Mildred's arm. "Everything will be fine. Rebecca's young and strong, and Dr. Walker is a fine physician."

"I'm sure you're right," Mildred said, her nostrils flaring as she breathed in.

It wasn't long before Rebecca's contractions became strong and close together. Gratefully she moved to her bed. Her labor seemed to be progressing quickly, and Daniel still hadn't returned.

"Willa, do you know where Daniel is working?"

"No. I suggested he stay close to home. But you know how men can be. They see a job that needs doing and they do it." She leaned over Rebecca and said gently, "Jim's gone to look for him, and I'm sure he'll be here in no time." She straightened and walked across the room to Mildred. "Things seem to be moving along rather rapidly," she whispered.

Rebecca overheard. "Does that mean something's wrong?" she asked.

"Oh my, no. Don't you worry. Every woman's labor is different. No doubt everything's fine. We just want the baby to wait for the doctor."

Rebecca felt a pulse of apprehension. "What do we do if he doesn't get here in time?"

"We have Lily. She's brought many babies into the world. Perhaps she ought to have a look at you. I'll get her." Willa opened the door and found Lily waiting just outside. "Ah, there you are."

"Yais, mum." The cook grinned, the gap in front taking

over her smile. She walked toward Rebecca. "So it's time for the bybie, eh?"

Mildred paced. "Willa, I don't know about this. I expected there to be a doctor here."

"And I'm sure there will be," Willa said, the usual serenity missing from her voice.

"How much longer do you think he'll be?"

"I'm certain Woodman's doing his best to get him here. There's no reason to be alarmed."

Lily placed a hand on Rebecca's abdomen and left it there through a contraction. "Yer pains are strong. That's good."

"It is?" Another contraction hit, and Rebecca gritted her teeth.

Lily placed both hands on Rebecca's stomach and felt for the baby. "It's still kind of high up, mum. Do ya feel like pushin'?"

Rebecca shook her head no.

"Roight, then. No worries." She stood and turned to Willa. "Do ya want me ta stay?"

"No. I just wanted you to check her. She's fine?"

"Yais, mum. But the pains are strong. Maybe very soon that bybie will be 'ere."

"Oh dear. Where is the doctor?" Mildred asked, her voice trembling.

Willa sat on the edge of the bed and placed a damp cloth on Rebecca's forehead. "Mildred, perhaps you should have a cup of tea. I'll make sure to let you know if there is any change."

"I couldn't leave just yet."

The muscles in Rebecca's abdomen tightened again. Feeling as if she were being torn in two, she clutched her mother-in-law's hand. Although she made no sound, when the contraction passed she looked at Willa and said, "It hurts more than I imagined."

"I know, dear. The first baby is always the most difficult. The pain's not something a woman can truly explain, and it usually takes a bit of time for the little one to arrive." She smiled. "But you're doing splendidly."

Mildred hovered in the background, hands clasped. Her lips moved in silent prayer.

"Auntie," Rebecca said. "Come here." She patted the bed beside her.

Mildred approached and sat carefully.

Rebecca smiled at her aunt. "Everything will be fine. Please don't worry. I've been told that Lily's an excellent midwife. She's helped with nearly all the babies born here at Douloo."

Mildred nodded but looked unconvinced.

Another pain crashed over Rebecca. She closed her eyes and clenched her teeth. Like a terrible, ripping wave, it moved through her—she knew nothing but pain. Still, she refused to cry out. When it finally passed, she took a deep breath and blew it out. "That was the worst one yet. Do you think I'm getting close?"

"Maybe we should call Lily in again?" Mildred asked.

"I don't believe that much has changed since she was here. It's only been a few minutes."

Mildred nodded and sat in the straight-backed chair. She pulled a handkerchief from her skirt pocket and folded it, then unfolded it and refolded it again.

Time passed, and the contractions came harder and lasted longer. Willa kept a cool cloth on Rebecca's forehead and periodically bathed her face with the damp cloth.

"Oh," Rebecca groaned and gripped the bedsheets as another contraction moved through her. When it finally let go, she asked, "Did I hear the doctor? Please look."

"Right, dear," Willa said, "I'll check." She stepped to the

window and looked down on the yard. "No. There's no one."

"I think you ought to get Lily," Rebecca said.

Willa walked to the door and opened it. "Lily," she called, "please come right away."

A few moments later Lily stepped into the room. She moved to the bed. "Ya feelin' worse, mum?"

"Yes."

"And ya feel like pushin'?"

"No, but the pain is very bad."

"How often they comin' now?"

"Every couple of minutes," Mildred said.

"That's good." Lily rested her hand on Rebecca's abdomen. "Feels like a big bybie," she said with a grin. Another contraction hit Rebecca. "That's a good one for sure, eh?" She winked at Rebecca. "Ya'll 'ave this bybie soon, I think." She pulled the sheets down. "I 'ave ta check ya, mum."

Rebecca nodded and closed her eyes, humiliated at the examination.

Lily probed. "This one's goin' ta need a bit of help."

"Is something wrong?" Mildred asked.

"The bybie's not comin' down. He's faceup. I'll 'ave ta turn 'im." Lily grasped Rebecca's hand. "It's goin' ta be all roight, but it's gonna hurt, mum." Her dark eyes were filled with compassion.

"Must you do it right away?" Mildred asked.

"No. We can wait a bit. See if it turns on its own."

"I think that's best," Mildred said.

"Someone's comin' up the drive," Callie said from the doorway.

Willa went to the window. "Go down and get the door. It must be the doctor."

A few moments later footsteps were heard in the corridor

and Cambria peeked into the room. "I had no idea," Cambria said. "Are ya all right, Rebecca?"

Rebecca couldn't answer. She was in the midst of a contraction. And she wasn't at all certain that everything was all right. *Lord, please keep my baby safe. Help me.*

"She's just fine," Lily said. "But she's got business ta take care of and there's no time for visitin'. This bybie needs help gettin' 'ere."

"I'll be praying," Cambria said before moving away.

A few minutes later Rebecca heard the rattle of harnesses and the bang of the front door swinging closed. Footsteps clumped down the hall.

"Sorry I took so long getting here," Dr. Walker said, striding into the room. "Woodman had a bit of trouble with the locals. Seems a couple of blokes got tanked up at the pub and decided they didn't want him in my office."

"Well, why in heaven's name couldn't he go into your office?" Mildred asked, her voice high-pitched.

"Blackfellas aren't always welcome in town. Some folks 'round here give them a hard time of it." Dr. Walker grinned. "Woodman gave no quarter though. He laid 'em low."

A new wave of pain rolled through Rebecca. She closed her eyes and gripped the bedsheets. "Oh," she groaned, feeling an uncontrollable urge to push. "I have to push, Doctor."

"The bybie's turned faceup, Doctor," Lily said.

Dr. Walker checked Rebecca. "True, all right. I can turn him. I'll need you ladies to help."

Rebecca took Willa's and Lily's hands and braced for more pain.

"Once I've got him turned, it shouldn't take long, Rebecca. Hold on, then."

Rebecca could feel his hands move inside her. At the same time a powerful contraction tore through her, and the pressure in her back and pelvis seemed unbearable. She screamed.

Mildred stood back, clutching her hands tightly together. She was pale and trembling.

"Mildred dear," Willa said calmly, "perhaps you should join Cambria downstairs?"

"Yes. I do believe that would be wise." She caught Rebecca's eyes. "I'll be praying."

"Almost there," the doctor said "All right. I've got him. Now push, Rebecca. Push."

Moving her grip to the headboard, Rebecca bore down. Desperate, she cried out, "Doctor, help me! Help me!"

"You're almost there," Dr. Walker said, guiding the child as it came down the birth canal. "Couple more pushes ought to do it."

Rebecca pushed with three more contractions.

"All right, then. One more and I think we'll have him."

Pushing through burning pain, Rebecca grasped Willa's hand. She couldn't hold back a shriek. The agony seemed unending. All of a sudden the pain let go.

"Here he is!" Dr. Walker lifted the infant and cleared its mouth.

He wasn't crying, and Rebecca felt a moment of panic. Then a tiny, gurgling wail emerged, then another, and finally a lusty cry burst from the infant's lips. His face was blotchy red, and his eyes looked nearly swollen shut, but Rebecca had never seen anything more beautiful. Tears spilled from her eyes.

Dr. Walker cut the umbilical cord and handed the baby to Lily. She wrapped the newborn in a blanket. "He's outraged, and roightly so, I'd say. Nothin' like bein' born." She settled the infant in his mother's arms.

Rebecca gazed at her son's pudgy red face. Wonderment and joy filled her. An intense love like none she'd ever known engulfed her. She ran her hand over the little one's nearly bald head and kissed him. "He's beautiful, isn't he?"

"That he is," Willa said, leaning in close. "He looks just like Daniel did when he was born." Tears pooled in her eyes. "And even a bit like Elton. Bertram would have been so proud."

❦

After Dr. Walker had declared Rebecca fit and had gone on his way, the new mother rested between fresh, clean linens. Propped up on pillows, she gazed at her infant son, who suckled contentedly. She felt a fierce, deep love. It was a bit frightening. She understood that for the remainder of her life she would be tied to this child, that this tremendous love could never be severed. Even so, she was afraid, wondering if she would be a good mother. She had no experience.

She looked about the darkened room. Mildred slept in a chair, and Willa arranged diapers into a stack. "Has anyone heard from Daniel?"

"No, luv, he's not here yet," Willa said gently.

"He should be here." Rebecca felt like crying. "I wanted him here."

"And what would he have done? Daniel would have been downstairs pacing and no help at all." Willa sat on the edge of the bed and peeked at the infant. "I'm sure he would have been here if he could. But this is a very large station. It's not easy to find someone in a hurry."

"Daniel knew my time was near. He shouldn't have traveled so far." Rebecca blinked back tears. She knew she was being unreasonable. Daniel couldn't choose where he worked. The station told him where he was needed.

6

I have a son! Daniel thought, running down the upstairs hallway. He stopped at the bedroom door, and rather than immediately going in, he stared at the doorknob. Thinking of his son, he smiled. *Me, a dad. Imagine that.* His delight lasted only a moment as the weight of responsibility registered. Would he be a good father? He wasn't even certain what that meant.

His mind traveled back to his own childhood. When Daniel was quite young, Bertram had been affectionate with his boys and even fun. Memories of riding together, fishing, and working side by side filtered through his thoughts. But those days hadn't lasted. Why?

I'll do it right, he told himself, opening the door and stepping into the room.

Willa sat in a chair near an open window. Her eyes glowed with delight as she stood and went to him. "Did you hear? You have a son," she whispered.

He nodded.

Taking Daniel's hand, she led him to a cradle beside the bed, then stood with him, gazing at the newborn.

Daniel knelt beside the cradle and studied the infant. He slept, his lips in a soft pucker. Blond tufts of hair stood out from his head, and he held tiny fisted hands against his chest. Joy and pride coursed through Daniel.

"He looks like you did when you were first born," Willa whispered.

"You think so?"

"Uh-huh." She smiled. "Would you like to hold him?"

"Hold him?" Daniel straightened, feeling insecure. He'd never held an infant before.

Willa picked up the baby and gently placed him in Daniel's arms. "Make sure to support his head," she said, moving his hand so it cupped the child's head. She dropped a kiss on her grandson's cheek, then looked at Daniel, her eyes brimming with tears. "I remember when you were brand-new. It was a lovely time."

Daniel held him stiffly. The baby stretched his arms over his head and opened his eyes. He struggled to hold his father's gaze. "He's got blue eyes," he said with a grin.

"Just like yours."

"Daniel?" Rebecca asked, pushing up on one elbow.

"Yes, luv, it's me."

Balancing the baby awkwardly in his arms, he moved closer to the bed. "I'm so sorry I wasn't 'ere. I wanted to be, but there were some cattle that wandered too far afield and they had to be rounded up." He tried to smile. "Jim had a time finding me."

Rebecca gazed at the baby in Daniel's arms, then looked at her husband. "I understand. We did miss you though."

He looked down at the infant. "He's a real beaut."

Rebecca's eyes returned to her son. "He is, isn't he," she said tenderly.

Daniel smoothed the child's downy hair. "Can't believe how soft he is."

68

"All newborns are like that," Willa interjected. "Nothing in the world has tarnished them yet." Quietly she left the room.

Daniel sat on the edge of the bed. "Are you feeling all right?"

"Yes. Just tired."

"I wanted to be 'ere, but I couldn't let the mob stray. If the rain doesn't come, we'll be hard done by. Can't afford to lose any animals."

"Do you think we're going to have a drought?"

"Looks that way."

The baby yawned and blinked, then stared hard at his father. Finally he closed his eyes and a fleeting smile touched his lips. "Did I see right? He smiled?" Daniel was beginning to feel more comfortable with his son.

"Yes, but according to your mother all babies do that. He doesn't know it was a smile."

Rebecca's eyes turned serious. "I thought droughts were fairly common here."

"Right. But that doesn't mean they're not trouble. We never know how bad one's gonna be."

Rebecca's brow creased with worry. "If it happens will it be dangerous? Will we manage?"

"Not to worry, luv. I'll take care of any trouble." He gazed at his sleeping son. "I've got a family to look after."

"The rains will come. I'm sure of it."

Daniel knew there was no certainty there would be adequate rain, and if not, they'd be hard-pressed to find enough water to see them through a bad season. He forced a smile. "No worries, then." He caressed his son's hand. "Everything will be grand, eh?"

"Of course it will." Rebecca leaned against Daniel and tenderly ran a finger down the front of her son's gown. "How could it be otherwise?"

Feeling a pang of panic, Daniel forced it aside and kissed Rebecca's forehead. "Too right." He looked at the baby in his arms. "Thank you for our son."

"I'm still so overwhelmed by him. It's a miracle."

The baby stretched out an arm and opened his hand. Daniel touched his palm, and the newborn closed his fingers. "Look there, he's holding my hand."

"He knows his daddy."

The baby whimpered and searched for a meal. Daniel chuckled. "I'm of no help to you, lad." He handed the baby to Rebecca. "It's you he needs." He grinned. His grin softened, and so did his eyes. "Lily told me you were quite brave."

"I had no choice. He was going to be born no matter what I did." She put the infant to her breast, where he suckled contentedly. Rebecca caressed the baby's cheek. "It's so hard to believe he's ours."

"What should we name him?"

"I still like Joseph. We talked about it, remember?"

Daniel nodded.

"In the Bible Joseph was a man of great faith. I want him to be like that."

Daniel smiled. "Joseph it is, then."

"And I was thinking that we might give him your brother's name as a middle name."

"Mum would like that. So do I." Daniel touched the infant's clenched fist. "Joseph Elton Thornton."

⟡

Joseph's whimpers woke Rebecca. She opened her eyes and gazed at the ceiling. She didn't feel right. Her body ached, especially her lower abdomen. The baby's whimpers grew louder until he was crying full out.

Feeling groggy and unsteady, Rebecca started to rise. Pain

cut into her abdomen, and she felt a surge of moisture flow between her thighs.

Fear spiked through her, and she lay back down. *Oh, Lord. Something's wrong.* Joseph's wails intensified. She tried to rise again, but the room whirled. *Please, somebody come and help me.*

The door opened. "I could hear him all the way down the hall," Willa said brightly, stepping into the room and striding toward the cradle. She scooped up the two-day-old infant and held him close, rocking him. "There you are. Everything's all right now." Willa looked at Rebecca, and her smile faded. "Rebecca? What's wrong?"

"I don't know. Something. I'm not feeling well. Could you get Lily? I think it has to do with having the baby."

"You look feverish." Willa lay the back of her hand on Rebecca's forehead. "You're hot. I'm sure it's nothing to worry about, but I'll get Lily and send for the doctor." With Joseph still cradled in her arms, she hurried out of the room.

A few moments later Willa, Lily, and Mildred stepped into Rebecca's bedroom. Lily asked, "Ya not feelin' good, mum?"

Rebecca shook her head. "My body aches, especially here." She lay her hand on her lower abdomen. "And . . . I think I'm bleeding more heavily."

Lily gently placed a hand on Rebecca's face. "Ya've got a fever, all roight." She lifted the bedding and checked Rebecca's dressings. "Yer bleedin' more than ya ought. But it's not so bad." She replaced the blankets. "We'll fix it. Don't worry, mum." She smiled, but behind her eyes Rebecca could see apprehension.

Lily glanced at Willa and Mildred. "We'll need some clean cloths, linens, and a clean gown."

"I'll get them," Willa said, quickly leaving the room.

"Miss Williams, can ya stay with 'er? I'll get some warm water for washin'." Lily started for the door.

"Yes. I'll stay right here." Mildred sat on the chair beside the bed and took Rebecca's hand. She smiled at Rebecca. "Everything will be all right."

"Where's Joseph? He was crying."

"He's with Callie. She said she'd see to it that he was fed. Annie's baby is just two months old. Callie said she's got more than enough milk for two."

Rebecca closed her eyes. She'd heard of women who had gotten sick after having babies. Some died. Would she? Tears escaped and seeped from the corners of her eyes. *Lord, I have a son. He needs me. And I have a life that I love. Please don't take me now.*

✦

After Rebecca's nightgown and undergarments had been changed and the bedding replaced, Rebecca settled down in her pillows. She was drained and needed to sleep.

"Ah, now ya look roight comfy."

Rebecca strained to open her eyes.

Lily smiled. "I made some tea, mum. It ought ta help ya some. 'Ere 'ave a sip, eh?" Willa and Mildred helped Rebecca sit up while Lily offered the tea.

Rebecca caught a whiff of it. "Oh." She turned her face away. "It smells awful. What is it?"

"Just eucalyptus, mum. It's good to fight sickness. I seen people so sick they ought ta die, but they got well instead. Drink some." She pushed the cup to Rebecca's lips.

Rebecca allowed the warm brew past her lips and fought to keep the bitter tasting liquid in her mouth long enough to swallow it. Lily offered her more, and she took it. Finally, unable to tolerate even one additional drop, she pushed away the cup.

"That ought ta help," Lily said, straightening. "Ya can 'ave more later, eh?"

"Where is Daniel?" Rebecca asked weakly.

"One of the roustabouts is looking for him," Willa said. "They ought to be here straightaway."

Rebecca closed her eyes. Sleep drew her down into its comfortable depths. If only the pain in her abdomen would go away.

The sound of a buggy approaching carried up from the yard and through the window. Mildred looked out. "Thank goodness. It's the doctor. He'll know what to do."

A few moments later Callie ushered in Dr. Walker.

"Now, what is this I hear about your being sick?" He leaned over Rebecca and felt her forehead, then took a thermometer out of his bag, glanced at it and shook it hard before placing it in her mouth.

Rebecca was so weak she could barely hold it in place. *Lord, what's wrong with me?*

Dr. Walker rested a stethoscope on her chest. "Can you take a breath for me?"

Rebecca breathed in. The doctor listened. "Once more." Rebecca obeyed. Dr. Walker moved the stethoscope to her abdomen and listened. Allowing the stethoscope to hang freely from his neck, he placed his hands on Rebecca's abdomen. "This might hurt a bit." He pressed down, palpating her stomach.

Rebecca winced and moaned. The pain was severe.

Dr. Walker removed the thermometer, studied it, and then returned it to his bag. "You're good and sick, all right. But you ought to be fine." He smiled.

"What is it, Doctor?" Mildred asked.

"My best guess is childbed fever."

"And just what is that?" Mildred asked, her tone suspicious.

"It's a condition women sometimes get after having a baby. We don't know what causes it. It's fairly common."

"Will she be all right?" Willa asked.

The doctor lowered his eyes slightly. "I think we ought to let Rebecca rest." Before anything more could be said, he walked out of the room.

$\mathcal{D}$

Willa and Mildred followed the doctor into the hallway. Daniel strode down the corridor toward them.

Dr. Walker cleared his throat, glancing at Daniel. "I'll be honest. It's not good."

"What do you mean . . . not good?" Mildred demanded. "I thought you said this was common."

"It is common, but sometimes . . . women die."

"Die? No. Not Rebecca," Daniel said.

Her eyes filling with tears, Willa pressed a hand to her mouth. "No. I won't believe that. Rebecca's strong and healthy. She had a bit of difficulty with the birth, but she did well."

"What can we do?" Mildred asked, her voice weak and trembling.

Dr. Walker reached in his bag and pulled out a bottle. "Give her this for the pain. Allow her to rest. She may recover."

"Give her something for pain? That's all you're offering?" Daniel gazed at the bottle of medicine. "There must be something else we can do."

"Lily gave her some tea made from eucalyptus leaves. Do you think that will help?" Willa asked.

"Some of the aborigine potions work. I've seen them be effective. It won't hurt to try." Dr. Walker rested a hand on Daniel's shoulder and looked him straight in the eye. "I wish I could do more."

"She's not going to die," Daniel said vehemently. "You can do something."

"I wish I could. But it's not up to me. I'm sorry."

"No! I don't believe you."

"Daniel, hush. She'll hear you," Willa whispered.

Daniel balled his hands into fists.

"I'll be back tomorrow," the doctor said and walked away.

Daniel glared at his back, then taking a shuddering breath, he turned and walked into Rebecca's room.

The shades were drawn, making the room look dark. Rebecca slept, her breaths slow and shallow. Daniel sat on the chair beside the bed, took her hand, and pressed it to his cheek.

Opening her eyes, Rebecca looked at him and managed to smile. "Daniel," she whispered.

"Hello, luv. What's this? You're getting sick when you have a son to look after, eh? I'd say it's just a shrewd way to get out of work." He forced himself to smile.

"I'm sorry, Daniel. I don't know how it happened. I just woke up feeling terrible. I'm sure it will pass."

"Right." Daniel kissed her hand.

"I'll be all right. I'm certain of it."

Daniel sucked in a breath. "Yeah. That's what the doc said. Things will be right as rain in a few days."

"I'm so tired. I'm going to sleep for a while. All right?"

"I'll be 'ere."

The sound of a didgeridoo echoed from somewhere outside. Its deep-throated hum resonated in Daniel's heart. Tears pressed against the back of his eyes.

"Is that Woodman?" Rebecca asked.

"Maybe. He's a good one with the didgeridoo."

Rebecca managed to nod slightly and then closed her eyes.

Daniel gazed at her. *Lord, please don't take her from me. I*

can't live without her. And Joseph needs his mum. Daniel choked
down a sob.

⌓

Hours passed, and then a night and another day. Rebecca
grew weaker. She slept mostly, rousing only for sips of Lily's
special tea and water. Daniel remained at her side. Callie,
Willa, and Mildred came often to sit with him and to help
nurse Rebecca.

The second day, Cambria and Jim came to visit. When
Cambria started to step into Rebecca's room, Jim released
her hand and remained outside the door.

"Jim?"

"I better stay out here," he said.

Daniel moved to the door.

Jim rested his hand on his friend's shoulder. "How you
holding up, mate?"

"Not so good."

"I'll be here if you need me," Jim said. "Anything I can
do, let me know."

"Thank you," Daniel said and returned to Rebecca's
bedside.

Cambria stood over the bed, staring at Rebecca. Her eyes
were red rimmed, and her face looked splotchy. She fought
tears. "Is she any better?"

Daniel shook his head no.

Cambria leaned close to Rebecca and spoke to her. "Ya can't
die. Fight, Rebecca. Stay with us. Please. I couldn't bear it . . ."
She couldn't finish what she wanted to say. Instead, she kissed
Rebecca's cheek and then straightened. Tears brimming, she
looked at Daniel. "I'll be back tomorrow." Covering her mouth
with her hand, Cambria walked out of the room.

The next evening Rebecca roused slightly. Daniel caught her staring at him. He'd dozed off in the chair. "Rebecca?" he asked.

"I'm thirsty," she croaked.

Daniel smiled and grabbed a glass of water that had been sitting on the bed stand. "Evening, luv," he said, helping her to sit. "'Ere you go." He held the glass to her lips.

Rebecca managed a few sips, and then Daniel lowered her back to the bed. "You don't feel so hot."

"I think I might be better," she said feebly.

"I'll get Mum." Daniel sprinted to the door. "Mum! Mildred! Lily!" He returned to Rebecca.

The women hurried into the room, Mildred first. "What is it? Is she all right?" Mildred moved to Rebecca's side, staring at her niece.

"Yes. She's better." Daniel smiled.

Rebecca managed to look at her aunt. "I . . ." She swallowed and licked cracked lips. "I want to see my baby. Where is he?"

Callie stood in the doorway. Wearing a broad smile, she said, "I'm roight glad ta hear yer voice, mum. And I'll get Joseph." She walked to the nursery.

"Praise the Lord," Mildred said, hugging Rebecca. "You've been so sick."

"I knew you would prevail," Willa said, laying a hand on Rebecca's arm.

"It's the tea. I seen it work before." Lily grinned. "Good stuff. Ya keep drinkin' it and ya'll get well roight soon."

Callie walked in, carrying Joseph. She handed him to Daniel. "He'll be glad ta see his mum."

Rebecca's eyes went to her son. "Oh, he's so beautiful."

Tears glistened. "I was afraid I'd never be a mum to him again."

Daniel leaned in close and settled the infant next to Rebecca. With Daniel's help, she cuddled her son. "Joseph, this is Mummy." The baby responded by opening his eyes and gazing at Rebecca's face.

"Ah, you see. He knows you," Mildred said.

Smiling, Rebecca kissed his cheek. "Mummy loves you."

7

Rebecca sat on the veranda, the cradle beside her. Taking a deep breath, she breathed in morning air. The day would heat up, but for now the warm breeze worked with the roses, geraniums, lavender, and wisteria to create a sweet-smelling aroma that wafted over the porch.

It felt good to be well and strong. In fact, today she planned on picnicking. Gazing down at her son, she felt the powerful love that had overtaken her. She never tired of looking at him.

She'd found being a mother a challenge. Everything about it was new to her. She hadn't even known how to change a nappy. And she had been petrified to bathe Joseph for the first time. Willa had refused to do it for her, but she'd stood beside Rebecca and offered support and guidance. Now Rebecca felt more proficient at such tasks. With each passing day she and Joseph both grew stronger.

Mildred stepped onto the veranda. "Oh, there you two are," she said, bending over to peer at the baby. "What an angel."

"He is a good baby."

"Why, I've never known a child to be so content." Mildred straightened and brushed a free strand of hair back into place. She gazed at the carriage house, where Woodman worked on the surrey.

Worry lines etched Mildred's forehead.

"What is it, Auntie? Something's troubling you. Does it have anything to do with Woodman?"

"Oh, heaven's no. I've just been wondering what life would have been like for me if I'd had someone to share it with."

"You had me and Father."

"That's not the same." Mildred looked at Rebecca kindly. "It's not that I didn't love you . . ."

"I understand."

Mildred settled in a chair across from Rebecca and folded her hands in her lap.

"There is something wrong. What is it?"

"I'm fine, really." She wet her lips. "It's just that I had more than one reason for coming here . . . to Queensland."

The baby whimpered, and Rebecca rocked the cradle with her foot.

"My brother-in-law has an accountant who comes to the house quite regularly. In truth, he's more a friend to Sterling than a business associate." She pulled a handkerchief from beneath her blouse cuff and twisted it between her hands. "Anyway, over time he and I have become friends . . ."

"Auntie, are you saying you have a suitor?" Rebecca asked with delight.

Mildred didn't answer right away. "I suppose I do," she finally said, uncertainty touching her pale blue eyes. "I just don't know what to do about him."

"Is there something wrong with him?"

"Oh no. He's a fine man, a perfect gentleman."

"Do you love him?"

Mildred rubbed her thumb across an embroidered flower

on the handkerchief. "I don't know. Perhaps. At this late juncture how does one really know such a thing?"

"I don't know, Auntie. But it seems to me that love is love no matter how old a person is."

Mildred tucked the handkerchief back in place beneath her cuff.

"And what does he have to do with your being here?"

Mildred's head bobbed up, and she looked straight at Rebecca. "He asked me to marry him. And I just couldn't face him."

"For heaven's sake, why not?"

"I . . . I don't know what to tell him. So coming to visit you seemed appropriate. And seeing that Chavive had a safe journey gave me a good reason to visit, as well as seeing you of course."

"You ran away . . . to Australia."

"I suppose I did."

"Why?"

Mildred studied perfectly manicured nails. "I can't marry him. I can't marry anyone. I'm far too old for that kind of thing."

"Don't be silly. You're quite youthful . . . for someone your age. And when you were young didn't you plan to marry one day?"

"Yes, but Mother and Father needed me. I couldn't leave them."

"Oh, Auntie. It's your turn now."

Mildred shook her head. "I don't know . . . it's too late for me. I'm very set in my ways. And although his wife died several years ago, I'm certain he still loves her. I don't want to be a substitute for someone else. I'm not up to that."

"That may be, but how do you know he feels that way?"

"I see it all the time, the way he talks about her and how she's still a part of his life."

"I don't see that as being so unusual." Joseph let out a small wail, and Rebecca picked him up. "As much as I love having you here, I think you ought to go back. This may be your only chance for love."

Mildred looked a bit bewildered. "I don't know. I need time to think."

"You can stay as long as you like, but . . . well, your suitor may not wait."

Mildred lifted her eyebrows. "I won't be coerced."

Wearing a mischievous smile, Rebecca said, "All right, then. I won't push."

⅏

With Joseph in her arms, Rebecca walked down the staircase. The house seemed empty and quiet. She peeked into the study.

Willa sat at her writing desk, pen in hand and stationery in front of her. She looked up and smiled. "Good day, Rebecca. And how's my grandson?"

"He's wonderful. His tummy is full and he's content." Rebecca walked into the room. It enveloped her as a sanctuary might. Heavy curtains shut out much of the late morning sunlight. The furnishings were made of deep mahogany, and an Oriental rug covered a large portion of the floor. Heavy bookcases held hundreds of books. "I remember being afraid of this room."

"Afraid of it?"

"Yes. It was the place I'd have to face Bertram when I was in trouble." She rested a hand on Bertram's desk and gazed about the room. "Now it feels peaceful here."

Willa smiled softly. "Yes. I rather like it. I can feel his presence."

Rebecca nodded and then asked, "Are you writing a letter?"

"As a matter of fact, I am. To my aunt Ada. She lives in Melbourne. I thought she'd be thrilled to hear the news about the baby. Last time she wrote she mentioned a desire to come up on holiday, but it's just too much for her. She'll be eighty-six in February."

"Oh. I would have enjoyed meeting her." Rebecca gently patted Joseph's back.

"She's a sweet woman. I miss her." Willa set down her pen. "I was hoping to make a trip down soon. Would you be interested in accompanying me?"

"To Melbourne?"

"Yes. It's a lovely city. We might actually attend a concert or go to the ballet."

"That sounds wonderful! When do you want to go?"

"I was thinking possibly in November. The weather is so hot here at that time of year, and Melbourne is much cooler. It would be a nice change for us."

"Sounds just right. Joseph will nearly be a year old, and I ought to be an expert at mothering by then." She glanced down at her son, who slept on her shoulder.

"Right. We'll plan on it, then. I'll tell her to expect us." Willa smiled and picked up her pen again.

"I was hoping you would like to accompany Mildred, Daniel, and me on a picnic this afternoon at the billabong."

"That sounds lovely. I won't be long. We'll have Lily prepare something."

"All right. I'll speak to Daniel. That is, if he's working nearby. Do you know where he is?"

"I thought he said something about a job that needed to be done in the barn."

"That's lucky. He's been working so hard, I barely see him. I thought it would be nice if we had a family outing."

"It would be delightful."

Keeping Joseph cradled against her shoulder, Rebecca walked into the kitchen where Lily was baking bread. "Lily, could you make a picnic for the family? We're going to the billabong."

"Roight, mum. I can do that."

"Wonderful." Feeling carefree, Rebecca hurried through the kitchen and out the back porch door. Supporting Joseph with one hand, she lifted her skirts with the other as she walked toward the barn. *I hope Daniel's here*. The smell of hay greeted her as she stepped into the shadows of the barn. It reminded her of the stables back home. She glanced about. "Daniel?"

"I'm 'ere," he called from a back stall.

Rebecca moved toward the sound of his voice. When she reached the stall, she stood at the gate. "Here you are. How lucky for me that you're working close to home."

Daniel pounded a nail into the wall and straightened. "Needed to replace a few boards 'ere." He glanced at the walls and roof. "A lot of it needs repair. It's getting a bit old."

"When was it built?"

"Before I was born."

With a grin Rebecca said, "That means it's very old, then." She leaned a hip on the gate. "I was wondering if you'd join Joseph and me for a picnic lunch at the billabong."

Daniel thought a moment. "I'd like that, but I've got a lot to do, luv."

"You have to eat no matter how busy you are."

"Right. But to go down to the billabong and relax and visit with you would take more time than I have. A place like this never really lets go of a man. The work never ends."

"That's my point. The work will never end. It will still

be here tomorrow, so I was hoping you'd make time for us today."

Daniel moved close to Rebecca and rested a hand on one shoulder. Gazing down at his son, he said quietly, "I want to. I do. It's just that right now is a bad time."

Rebecca wanted to get angry, but she knew all stations required a lot from their owners. "It would be lovely to spend time together."

"I wish I could. But how would it look if I went off and had a picnic with my beautiful wife and young son while the men worked?"

"Don't you think they'd understand?"

"Maybe, but it's not right. And if I stopped work every time I wanted to, we wouldn't have a station. I thought you understood."

"I do." Rebecca tried not to pout. She knew he spoke the truth. "It's just that I miss you. We've barely seen you the last couple of weeks."

Daniel planted a kiss on Rebecca's forehead and smiled down at his son. "I'll make time. I promise. Just not today." He took Joseph's hand in his. The baby grasped his finger. "He'll know me well. I'll see to it." He kissed the tiny fist.

"You work too hard. Since your father died your time has been consumed with this station."

"It's a big station. I've no choice. I've never had to oversee the entire operation. I've a lot to learn." He caressed Joseph's nearly bald head. "You go along and have your picnic. A bit of bread and cheese will do me just fine. I'll try to join you next time."

"All right. We'll see you at dinner, then?"

"I'll be there." Daniel lifted his hat slightly and smiled. His cheek dimpled and his blue eyes crinkled, turning down at the corners the way they always did.

Rebecca could feel the tremble of her heart. Then sadly

85

she turned and walked back toward the house. She stopped. She had more to say.

Returning to the stall, she said, "Daniel, I'm worried about you."

"Me? Why?"

"I think you're pushing yourself too hard." Joseph whimpered and Rebecca patted his back. "You think you've got to be like your father."

Daniel didn't say anything. He shifted his weight to his other foot and stared at Rebecca.

"You're not Bertram Thornton. You weren't meant to be him."

Daniel took off his hat and wiped his forehead with his shirtsleeve. "I admire my father and what he did 'ere. He took *his* father's hard work and sweat and made it into something truly grand. He was a great man. And I suppose there's some truth in what you say. I do want to be like him. But I know better than to expect that."

"But you can—"

Daniel cut her off. "I've got to do my best, work hard. And if it's possible, make this place finer than it is now. If I can't do that, at least I've got to keep it going. We're facing hard times."

"I don't think you see what you're doing. You're trying to step into your father's shoes. But you must go about living in a way that's suitable for you, not him." Joseph whimpered more loudly, and Rebecca gently bounced him.

"I'm not trying to *be* him."

Rebecca didn't want to argue, but why couldn't he see the truth? Struggling to keep her voice quiet and calm, she said, "You may not be able to see it, but I can. You want more than to be as good as he was; you want to be better than him." Rebecca hesitated. Did she dare go further? Deciding there was nothing to be lost, she plunged ahead.

Joseph's whimpers were becoming more demanding. "You've even taken to overseeing people in the district like your father did. Do you also intend, one day, to rewrite the reverend's sermons?"

"Of course not. You're not being fair, Rebecca."

"I'm trying to be rational, but I'm afraid. Remember the mistakes your father made? He cared so deeply for his family and the people in this district that he did too much."

Daniel glowered at Rebecca. "I'm a Thornton. And people look up to me. Some need help. I must do what I can. Doesn't the Lord ask us to do for our neighbors?"

"Yes, but—"

"Rebecca, I've said all I'm going to. I won't argue with you." He placed another nail against a board and pounded it in.

"I'm sorry," Rebecca said. "I don't want to fight, but please, can't we talk about this?" She boosted Joseph onto her shoulder.

Daniel blew out a breath. "All right, then." He moved his hammer from one hand to the other. "I guess I do feel a bit as if I'm living in my father's shadow. And it's frustrating to know that no matter how hard I work, I'll never be as good as him." Tormented eyes looked into Rebecca's. "Don't you understand? Douloo is my responsibility now. You and Joseph and Mum, you're *my* responsibility." He walked to the window at the back of the stall and gazed out. "Sometimes I wake in the night in a sweat. I dream I've ruined the station, lost it all. And then I see my father and my grandfather standing side by side staring at me, their faces filled with disappointment and sorrow. And I know it's all my fault."

"Daniel, it's just a dream. We're not going to lose the station. You're doing a fine job."

"Right. I'm not going to lose it. But it takes hard work to hang on to something like this. I've got to make sure everything is being done as it ought to be. Overseeing Douloo is my duty. If I don't watch over it, who will?"

"Daniel, you're not alone. You have me, your family, and God."

He moved to Rebecca and grasped her arms. "I know what you say is true, but it feels as if I'm carrying a great burden. I've always known that one day Douloo would be mine." He straightened and looked at his son. "He depends on me to keep it safe for him."

*

Her heart aching for Daniel, Rebecca walked back to the house. She wished there were something she could do to make his burden lighter. *Lord, show me what I can do to help.*

Willa stood on the bottom step of the porch. "Is everything all right?"

"Yes and no."

"What is it, dear?"

Rebecca sat on the step and Willa sat beside her.

Willa rested a hand on Joseph's back. "He's such a love, so much like his father."

"In what way?"

"His looks and his disposition. He's temperate and good-natured." She raised an eyebrow and glanced back at the barn. "And what is troubling you about Daniel?"

Rebecca smiled slightly. "You know me so well." Taking a deep breath, she continued, "All he thinks about is Douloo and how he *must* watch over it and help it transcend into something finer than it already is. He's working too hard. And he worries too much."

"He takes his responsibilities very seriously . . . as he should." Willa bent and picked up a slender eucalyptus leaf. "Too much though, I must admit." Twirling the leaf between her fingers, she offered Rebecca a smile. "In time he'll find his place. It hasn't been that long since Bertram died. Be patient."

"I'm afraid. Is this how things began to change with Bertram? Was he different in the beginning?"

Willa's eyes teared. "I must say, in the early years we had quite a lot of fun. Oh, Bertram was serious minded, but he also knew how to play. He spent quite a bit of time with the boys." A frown furrowed her brow. "Gradually he moved away from us."

"I'm afraid that's how Daniel and I will end up."

"He's always been quite different from his father. Bertram had a forceful presence. He was driven. Since Daniel was a lad he's always been a follower, never a leader. Although when he found something of real interest, he'd give it his all." She patted Rebecca's arm. "And I dare say, I'm sure that's what he's doing now. Taking care of Douloo isn't just for him but for you and me." Her eyes fell upon Joseph. "And for his children."

"I think he feels a need to live up to his father's memory. He's working to please Bertram."

"He and his father didn't settle things before Bertram died." Willa dropped the leaf. "I wish they had. There was so much that needed to be restored." She rested a hand on Rebecca's arm. "Daniel always wanted to please his father and never felt that he could. Whatever he did never seemed to be enough for Bertram. He may still be working that out. Pray for him and love him. I'm convinced things will get better."

"And if they don't? What am I to do then?"

"He'll come around. His father's only been gone six months." Her eyes glimmered and she brushed away tears.

Rebecca felt a rush of grief. "I can't imagine what it is like to lose your husband."

Willa straightened slightly and smiled. "And you won't have to know for many years, I'm sure." She stood. "Well now, the picnic things are ready; would you still like to go?"

89

"Absolutely."

The sound of an approaching rider echoed from the road. Rebecca shaded her eyes and looked toward the drive. A man riding a short, stout horse galloped over the rise and into the yard.

He stopped a few feet from Willa and Rebecca. Removing a black bowler hat, he said, "Good afternoon. I'm Thomas Murdoc. I was hoping I might find Mildred Williams here."

Rebecca felt a pulse of surprise. Obviously this man was not a local. What could he want with her aunt? She stood. "Yes, she is visiting here. She's my aunt. What can I do for you?"

"Actually, I've come all the way from Boston to see her."

Curiosity replaced Rebecca's suspicion. "Did you say your name is Thomas?"

"Yes. I'm a friend of Mildred's."

"I believe she mentioned you." Rebecca smiled. "Please, won't you come in out of the sun. Let me get you something to drink."

Thomas dismounted. He wasn't a very large man and couldn't have been more than two or three inches taller than Rebecca. He bent forward slightly, obviously stiff from his ride. Pressing a hand against the small of his back, he forced himself erect. "I'm not used to riding much. I came all the way from Thornton Creek." He dusted off his shirt and pants. "That's quite a road you have. Several times I nearly lost my way." He smiled and his lined face looked friendly.

"I'm Rebecca Thornton, and this is my mother-in-law, Willa Thornton." She hefted Joseph slightly. "And this is Joseph, my son."

"Oh yes. It's so good to meet you. Mildred's spoken of you."

"You must be thirsty."

"Yes, very."

They walked toward the house. When Rebecca reached

90

the stairway, she hurried her steps, anxious to surprise her aunt. "Auntie . . . Auntie Mildred," she called as she crossed the veranda and opened the front door.

Willa stepped inside. "She must be upstairs. I'll go and find her. You two sit. I'll have Callie bring you something to drink." She disappeared indoors, leaving Rebecca and Thomas on the veranda.

"This is a fine place," Thomas said, gazing about.

"Thank you. Won't you have a seat?" Rebecca laid Joseph in his cradle and then sat in a wicker chair.

Thomas hobbled across the porch and dropped into a chair across from her. He gazed out over the plains. "A lot of open country here. And I must say, everything looks very much the same—it's easy to get lost."

"That's true. It takes time to learn your way about. I hadn't lived here long when I lost my way. If not for a friend of mine, I might have perished."

"Well, we can thank the Lord you didn't."

Thomas seemed a very nice man and must certainly have some sort of intentions toward Mildred to have followed her halfway around the world. Rebecca studied him from beneath lowered lids. Although his hair was thinning a bit on top, he was quite nice looking, with warm brown eyes. And he looked like someone who smiled easily.

The front screen door creaked open. "Rebecca, did you call me? I thought . . ." Mildred stopped and then slowly stepped onto the veranda, allowing the door to clap shut behind her. She stared at Thomas, who stood to greet her.

"Mildred, you remember Mr. Murdoc, don't you?"

Mildred glanced at Rebecca, then looked back at her guest. A bright flush lit her face. "Why, yes. Thomas, what are you doing here?" Her hand went to her neckline.

"I came to see you. And I haven't done much in the way of traveling, so I thought it was about time I had a look at

91

Australia." He smiled, then added in a tender voice, "I missed you and hoped you'd be kind enough to show me a bit of the countryside."

"Certainly, Thomas." Mildred said his name as if it were honey in her mouth. She moved to a chair and sat. "I wasn't expecting you. You should have written and told me you were coming."

He pulled a crumpled letter from his breast pocket. "I did, but I decided rather suddenly to travel here and thought I'd just hand deliver it." He extended the letter.

Mildred took it. "I'll read it later, if that's all right?"

"Of course—whenever you like."

Callie stepped onto the porch with a tray of filled water glasses. She set it on the table.

"Thank you," Thomas said, taking a glass. "I can't remember being this thirsty." He took a drink, then another and kept on until the glass was empty. He held it out to Callie. "Do you think I could have a little more?"

"Roight away." Callie took the glass and disappeared indoors.

Thomas settled his eyes on Mildred. "You look fine. Seems the Australian sun has been good for you."

"Why, thank you, Thomas." She pursed her lips. "But I still don't understand why you're here."

Thomas glanced at Rebecca, then looked back at Mildred. "Perhaps we could take a walk?" He stood and held out his arm.

Still flushed, Mildred said, "Of course." She stood and rested her hand on his arm. Looking like a much younger woman than she was, she glanced at Rebecca and said, "We won't be long."

8

Thomas stayed close beside Mildred as they walked toward the corral adjoining the barn. Mildred suddenly felt bashful and embarrassed. She removed her hand from his arm and made certain there was enough space between them that they couldn't touch. Thomas didn't speak. Mildred searched for something intelligent to say but couldn't think of a thing. She was still astounded by his surprise appearance.

Thomas stopped at the corral and leaned against the fence. Mildred rested her arms on the top railing and stared at Chavive, who pranced around the edges of the enclosure, as if showing off for her audience. "She's beautiful, don't you think?"

Thomas's affectionate brown eyes rested on Mildred instead of the horse. "Yes, handsome."

Glancing at Thomas, Mildred could feel her face heat up and quickly returned her gaze to Chavive.

The mare trotted toward her visitors and thrust her head over the top of the fence, nuzzling Mildred.

"Oh my. Why, hello there." She patted the mare's neck.

"You seem in high spirits today." She glanced at Thomas. "This is Chavive, Rebecca's horse."

"She's a beauty, all right." Thomas studied the animal. "I seem to recall you mentioning a horse called Chavive. She had been sold from your brother's estate. Is this the same one?"

"You have a good memory. When Rebecca married Daniel and moved here from Boston, she was forced to sell her. To Rebecca it was like losing a friend. And an additional sorrow after losing her father." Mildred felt the sudden sting of tears. "Silly of me. I still miss my brother." She forced a smile and blinked away the tears.

"We never stop missing the ones we love."

Mildred only nodded. What could be said? She knew about Thomas's wife and child. Gwenn had died giving birth; the baby, a little boy, had died along with her. Mildred continued as if nothing had been said about death. "Daniel purchased Chavive for Rebecca this past Christmas. But of course Rebecca was in no condition to go riding then."

"Why not?"

"She was expecting Joseph."

"Oh yes. Of course."

"Rebecca's been anxiously awaiting the day she'll be recovered enough to ride." Mildred glanced back at the house and at Rebecca, who sat on the porch. "That should be any day now. She's doing quite well."

Mildred plucked a handful of grass from alongside a watering trough and offered it to Chavive, who greedily took the tidbit. Mustering her courage, Mildred asked, "Thomas, it's lovely to have you here, but I'm not quite sure why you've come."

Anxiety flashed across Thomas's face. He managed a smile. "Actually, I'm a bit surprised to find myself here as well." He looked at Mildred, unable to disguise his devotion, then rubbed Chavive's nose. "After you left, I imagined what my life would be like without you . . . and . . . well, I decided I couldn't manage." His lips turned up in a crooked smile, and he lifted his eyebrows slightly. "So I decided to come after you and make you understand how important you are to me." He acted as if he might touch her but refrained.

Mildred felt panic close in. "I'm not sure what to say, Thomas. On one hand, it's wonderful to see you, but on the other . . . I wish you hadn't come." Seeing hurt in his eyes, she quickly added, "It's not that I don't care for you; I do."

"Then what is it? Why won't you marry me?"

Mildred didn't know exactly why she didn't want to marry Thomas. He was kind and considerate and attractive for an older man. *It's his wife. He still loves her.* Mildred had never been courted, not since she was young. Now she couldn't help but wonder if Thomas was trying to replace his wife with her. *If I ask him, I'm sure he'll deny it. What would be accomplished by bringing it up? And I haven't known him long enough to speak of such personal things.*

"I'm not certain I can answer your question," she said. "It's difficult to imagine myself married . . . to anybody. I've been on my own for so many years; it just seems absurd that a spinster like myself should suddenly find herself married." She straightened her spine, bringing herself nearly to the same height as Thomas. "And I'm used to being independent, and . . . well, to be honest, I spent so many years caring for my parents that I don't relish the idea of looking after a husband." She gripped the fence so tightly a sliver jabbed her palm. "Ouch!"

"What is it?" Thomas asked, the lines in his face deepening with concern.

"Nothing." Mildred studied her palm. "Just a sliver."

"Here, let me see." Thomas took her hand. "Hmm, this

may require minor repair," he said with a grin. Taking a small knife out of his pocket, he opened the blade and gently probed. "Hold real still. It'll only take a moment, Gwenn." He stopped and stared at her palm.

Mildred sucked in her breath. "What did you call me?"

"Oh." Thomas looked at her. "I . . . I'm sorry. I just had a memory of doing this same thing for Gwenn." He smiled. "She was quite brave just like you."

Mildred wanted to pull her hand away, but Thomas had returned to his ministrations.

"These little pocketknives can come in handy," he said, lifting the splinter from her hand. "That's it, slick as a whistle." He smoothed her skin. "You wouldn't have to look after me."

Mildred took her hand back and examined the spot where the sliver had been lodged. "I can see that you're quite self-sufficient." She nodded at the knife. "You're very good with that thing."

Pressing the back of the blade against his pant leg, he closed the knife and then returned it to his pocket. "I'd be handy to have around."

"You certainly would at that, but . . . Thomas, I don't know that I ever want to marry." She met his brown eyes, knowing that what she had to say would wound. But it was clear that Gwenn was the one he loved.

"When I was young I planned to marry someone very charming and raise a family." She smiled. "I had all the silly dreams that most girls do. But then Father took sick and Mother couldn't cope; I stayed to help. After Father's passing Mother needed me. She never stopped needing me. When she died I was no longer young."

"I'm sorry, Mildred."

She rolled back her shoulders and turned to study Chavive. "Don't feel sorry for me. I've had a full life. After Mother died

I went to live with my brother and his family. When his wife, Audrey, passed, I stayed to watch over Rebecca. It was like having my own family. And I couldn't love Rebecca more if she were my own." She plucked a piece of straw from a crib of hay. "My life has been satisfying."

Thomas rested a hand on Mildred's arm and gently turned her so she faced him. "And how about now? Is it fulfilling?"

"Yes, very. I'm quite happy." Mildred's mind traveled back over the last few years. If she were being truthful, she'd have to admit to not being exactly happy. Since Charles's death and Rebecca's move here, she'd felt as if she'd been tossed aside. She didn't mind too terribly much having to live with her sister, Edith. Her family had accepted her into their home. However, she wasn't really needed. When she'd decided to travel to Queensland, she'd hoped that Australia might be the answer for her. But she wasn't at all sure she could adjust to living here. It was a bit too primitive. She met Thomas's eyes. "I have a fine life."

"That's not what I asked."

"Well, then I don't know how to answer you." Mildred smoothed her collar. "I'm not young anymore, Thomas. I'm nearly fifty."

"And do you think I'm young? I'm beyond fifty, my dear. But I don't intend to stop living because of it."

"That's not what I'm saying . . ."

"Mildred, to me you're still young and beautiful. I want to spend however many days I have left with you."

Suddenly afraid, Mildred stepped away from Thomas. "You must give me time . . . to think. I'm not sure what I feel." She tipped up her chin slightly. "I won't be bullied into marrying anyone. If you care for me you'll wait until I know for certain just what I should do."

"I'm a patient man," Thomas said, his crooked smile reemerging.

With daylight barely touching the sky, Rebecca laid Joseph in his crib and climbed back into bed, snuggling close to Daniel. *If only we could have more leisurely mornings*, she thought, knowing that the moment the sun brightened the room, Daniel would be up and off to take care of responsibilities on the station.

Daniel stretched and yawned. "Everything all right?" He draped an arm over her.

"Yes. Joseph was just fussy."

"Thought I heard the little rascal." Daniel pulled Rebecca close, gently kissing her. "He's a fine lad."

"He is, but his sleeping habits could be improved. I barely get to sleep and then I'm up again."

"Why don't you have Callie get up with him in the night? She could give him a bottle."

"I've been tempted, but it doesn't seem right to have someone else look after my son."

Daniel smoothed soft curls back from Rebecca's face. "Enough sleep or not, you're still beautiful." He kissed her again and then rested his forehead against hers. "Wish I could lie here a bit longer."

"Why don't you? Just for a while?"

"There's work to be done. We can't always do what we like, eh?"

Rebecca rested her hand on his cheek. "I miss you."

Daniel grasped her hand and kissed her fingers. "And I dare say, you barely have time to think of me, with Joseph to look after."

"I love him, but I'll always want to spend time with you," Rebecca said with a smile. She glanced in the direction of the nursery. "I was afraid I'd be a terrible mother, but I've managed to figure out most of this mothering thing. Sometimes

I just stand over his crib and stare at him. I'm still amazed at him and how he came from us."

"Joseph's a lucky little boy." Daniel dropped a kiss on the tip of Rebecca's nose and then rolled out of bed. He walked to the armoire and proceeded to dress.

Pushing up on one arm, Rebecca asked, "Is there any way I can be of help to you . . . so you won't have to work so hard?"

Daniel smiled at her. "Watch over Joseph and take good care of yourself. You've had a hard go of it."

"I do those things already."

"Pray for all of us. That would be a comfort."

Rebecca sat up and dropped her legs over the side of the bed. "I do that as well. I want to do more. There are so many demands on you—not just Douloo and your family but the people in the church and the community. They depend on you too much. They act as if you are your father."

Daniel sat on the edge of the bed. "I don't mind. I want to help, but I'll never be the man my father was."

"You're already a better man."

"Thanks, luv."

Unwilling to let things rest, Rebecca pressed, "I'm quite competent and able to be of assistance. I worked with my father for many years."

"Mum's taken on the paperwork; perhaps you could help her."

"I'll ask her. I wouldn't mind at all."

Leaning close, he said, "Soon you'll be busy chasing after our son and you'll have no time for anything else. Plus, he'll be growing so fast you won't be able to keep up with the sewing. And one day he'll be needing school."

"It will be quite some time before he'll need that."

"Right, but we can't put off thinking about the future, eh?" He grinned and moved to the closet, where he grabbed a pair of work boots and then crossed to the dresser and took a pair of socks out of the top drawer. He sat on the chair and pulled on the socks and boots.

"There's church this morning," Rebecca said.

"Right." He tied the laces. "I'll be there, but I've got to move a mob of cattle before I go."

"It's Sunday. . . ."

"Right. I'll be cleaned up and there on time."

"But Sunday is meant for rest."

"I agree, but I've a couple of drovers down sick. And it's got to be done or the cattle will overgraze. We've little enough grass as it is." He studied Rebecca a moment. "I figure God will understand."

"If Elvina Walker finds out, we won't hear the end of it." Rebecca folded her arms over her chest. "I won't make excuses for you."

"And I don't expect you to." Daniel grinned. "If I'm late you can make up a story . . . say I'm feeling poorly or something."

"But that would be lying."

"You've never told a lie?"

"Of course I have, but only when it was absolutely necessary."

Daniel dropped onto the bed next to Rebecca. "You've got to take life a bit easier—not so serious. It's grim enough as it is."

Rebecca leaned against him, enjoying the smell of his cotton work shirt. "I suppose you're right. I'll do my best to stand up to Elvina."

"Good for you." Daniel stood and buttoned his shirt, then grabbed his hat from the top of the armoire.

"Try not to be late. Church just wouldn't be the same without you."

Joseph started crying.

100

"I'll get him for you." Daniel left the room and returned a moment later with the infant in his arms. "I'd say he's right hungry."

"It's only been a couple of hours since he ate," Rebecca said, taking the little boy.

"I've got to be off. I'll see you at church." He strode out of the room.

With Joseph in her arms, Rebecca followed. "Are you going to work after church?"

"Don't know yet. Depends on how much I get done this morning."

Willa stood at the bottom of the staircase. "Lily has breakfast ready for you."

"Grand. I'm starved." Daniel escorted his mother into the kitchen.

"I told her you'd be leaving early."

Rebecca hurried to keep up.

Daniel grabbed a plate with eggs, bacon, and toast from the warming shelf. "Looks right good, Lily."

The dark-skinned cook nodded but didn't look up from her cooking.

Rebecca stood in the kitchen doorway. Joseph screamed his indignation at not being fed immediately.

"Is he all right?" Willa asked.

"Yes. He just wants to eat . . . again." Rebecca shifted him into her other arm.

"You promise not to be late?"

Daniel bit into a piece of toast. "I can't promise. I'll do my best."

Rebecca bounced Joseph gently, and his crying quieted. "I want to be supportive, Daniel, but church is important."

"I agree. And I'll be there." His voice had lost its pleasant tone.

101

Willa sat across from her son. "Will you be missing church?"

Daniel stopped chewing and stared at his mother. "I said I'll be there." He sounded annoyed.

"I beg your pardon, young man. You may be overseeing this station, but you're still my son. And I don't appreciate your sharp tone."

"Sorry. I didn't mean any disrespect, Mum, but it seems that doing a bit of work on a Sunday morning is a great sin 'round 'ere." He cast an exasperated glance at Rebecca.

"I didn't say it was a sin." Rebecca glanced at Willa. "It's just that if he's late, Elvina and some of the other women will want to know why, and I'll have to explain that Daniel's working. I don't want to face their judgment."

Willa took a slow, easy breath. "You shouldn't worry about what Elvina will think. We're supposed to be living our lives to please God, not people. I don't believe the Lord is going to be angry with Daniel for working when he must." Her gaze settled on her son. "However, I doubt he'd delight in this if it becomes a habit."

Daniel took a drink of coffee. "Mum, even Dad worked on a Sunday now and again."

"Yes. He did. But only when there was no other choice. And I can count on one hand how many Sundays he worked throughout our entire marriage." She folded her hands on the table in front of her. "He certainly had his share of sins, but missing church wasn't one of them. He cared too deeply for the people in this district to disregard his duty to the church."

"Right. I know that. In fact, he sometimes put so much into the church that his own family did without him."

"It was out of love." Willa's eyes filled with tears. "I won't have you speak poorly of him."

"Sorry, Mum. But we've got to tell the truth 'round

102

'ere." He rested a hand over his mother's. "I loved him. And sometimes I feel him . . . watching me. And I can hear his criticism."

"Daniel, you didn't get a chance to say good-bye to your father. If you had, he would have told you how much he loved you and how proud of you he was."

Daniel nodded. "I know, Mum. I know he loved me, but now it's my turn to take care of Douloo. And I've got to show him I can run this place."

"You're doing splendidly. He couldn't ask more."

"I pray you're right." He pushed to his feet. "I've got to go." He gave his mother a kiss on the cheek, then leaned over the table to Rebecca and kissed her. "Don't be angry," he said seriously.

"I'm not angry," Rebecca said, feeling especially tender toward her husband. He was hurting. "I'll see you in a bit, then."

≫

Rebecca started up the church steps, dreading walking in without Daniel. She'd stood out front waiting for him as long as she dared. Willa, Mildred, and Thomas were already inside. She hoped Elvina Walker wouldn't notice her.

Before Rebecca was five steps inside the sanctuary, the gray-haired widow strolled past her mother-in-law and her aunt and walked straight to her.

"G'day, Rebecca." She looked at Joseph. "Isn't he a handsome lad? Looks so much like his father, eh?"

"Yes. He does."

Elvina stared at Rebecca, then glanced behind her and looked about. "And where is that husband of yers?"

"He'll be here. He's just a bit late."

Elvina raised one eyebrow. "Oh? I hope everything is all roight."

Rebecca was tempted to lie but decided that being deceitful wouldn't help. "He had pressing business at the station."

"Seems ta me he's been roight busy these days. Might be workin' too hard, eh?"

"He's working very hard. There's a lot to be done." Rebecca fought to maintain a friendly tone. "And we have a couple of drovers who are ill, which makes us shorthanded. Daniel's needed."

"Well, you might want to remind him that if he makes time for God, God will make time for his work." Looking something like a bristling hen, Elvina continued, "I hope this won't lead to his missing church on a regular basis."

"He hasn't missed church."

Elvina continued as if Rebecca hadn't spoken. "It's bad enough to work on a Sunday. Remember God's commandment to keep the Sabbath day holy."

"G'day, Elvina," Daniel said, stepping up to Rebecca and taking hold of her arm. "Sorry I'm late, luv." He took Joseph. "There you are, lad." He settled him against his shoulder and smiled at Elvina as he escorted Rebecca toward the front of the church.

"Thank goodness," Rebecca whispered. "I was just about to get a lecture on the Ten Commandments from that old biddy. I'm not sure I would have been able to control my temper."

"Now, Rebecca, mind your manners. You're in the house of the Lord." Daniel grinned.

Rev. Cobb moved toward them. "G'day to you." He smiled and rested a hand on Joseph's back. "What a fine lad. He looks quite robust."

"Yes. Dr. Walker says he's the picture of health," Rebecca said.

"Looks like you," the reverend said to Daniel. "Same blue eyes and blond hair."

"I think he's a bit more handsome than his old man though, eh?"

The reverend smiled and moved on to Elvina. "G'day, Elvina. Hope you're in good health."

Rebecca hurried to the pew where Mildred, Thomas, and Willa sat. She slid in beside them, allowing room for Daniel. She leaned close to him and whispered, "Please don't be late again. I don't know if I'll be able to hold my tongue next time."

"I'll do my best," Daniel said.

"I don't mean to be selfish. But I feel very conspicuous walking into the church alone. And I know Elvina will be looking for any little failing on our part."

"Don't you worry about Elvina. God will see to her. I've no doubt."

Rebecca glanced over her shoulder at the elderly woman. "I suppose she must be miserable," she said. "But she'll cause trouble if she can. I think she and Meghan are friends."

"Then they deserve each other, eh?"

9

"Hep, hep, hep," Daniel called and then whistled as he drove a mob of bullocks back onto Thornton land.

In a puff of dust, Jim rode up alongside him. "So we're going to move these closer to the house?"

"Right. They've been nothin' but a nuisance down 'ere. Course, might save us a lot of trouble if we just took them straight to the cattle yards."

Jim grinned. "Might at that. Especially if they keep wandering."

"Looking for good grazing is all they're doing. There's none 'round 'ere."

Jim nodded, then with a whistle mustered the young bulls. Once the cattle were rounded up, Daniel and Jim rode side by side as they drove them toward home.

"Come on," Jim hollered. "Keep moving." He whistled and twirled a rope over his head. "I was worried we might be dealing with poddy dodgers instead of straying cattle."

"Haven't heard of any thievery 'round 'ere lately," Daniel said as his horse cut to the right toward a stray. "Hep, hep, hep," he called, turning the young bull back toward the group.

Joining Jim again, he said, "This mob's only a piece of our trouble. We've got cattle wandering onto our neighbors' land all over the station."

"Thirsty and hungry." Jim eyed the arid plains. "It's dry, the worst I've seen since coming here."

Daniel nodded. "I've not seen it this parched in all my life. But I've heard of worse."

"You think it'll break soon?"

Leaning forward in his saddle, Daniel gazed at a distant ghost gum. Its bare limbs and white bark suited the thirsty landscape. He had prayed and hoped for a change. "Can't say. Dry seasons like this one can be murderous and unwilling to give way." He pulled a handkerchief from his back pocket and wiped sweat and dirt from his face. "We may be hard done by before we're through. Woodman says this'll be a bad spell."

Jim lifted his water flask from the saddle horn where it hung and swilled down a mouthful. "What you gonna do if the rains don't come?"

"Might have to sell off some of the herd, let a few drovers go, and pray—for rain."

"So you figure I'll be looking for work?"

"No. I'll be keeping my best drovers. I'll not be sending you down the road."

The cattle were compliant, and it didn't take long before the bullocks were well onto Thornton land. Daniel pulled up. "I figure we've come far enough. It's Saturday. Take the rest of the day off, eh?"

"You're not going back to the house?"

"I've got something I wanted to look at. I'll be along before supper though. Maybe you could stop by the house and tell Rebecca."

"Glad to." Jim glanced toward the road. "I was thinking about taking a turn by Cambria's."

"You serious about her?" Daniel draped his rope over the saddle horn and looped it a couple of turns.

"Maybe. She's a fine woman, but I'm in no hurry to settle down."

"She's a free-spirited filly, that one. Won't take to the bit well, I can assure you."

Jim grinned. "Sounds a bit like Rebecca, I'd say."

Daniel lifted his hat and resettled it on his head. "You might say that." He grinned.

"Don't know that I'd really want to tame Cambria. I fancy her just the way she is."

"You think her father's going to let her go 'round with the likes of you?" Daniel chuckled.

"I'm working hard to make my way into his good graces. Things seem to be going pretty well."

"Good for you, then."

"You sure you don't need me? I can stay."

"Go on and take some time with your lady."

Jim doffed his hat, turned his horse toward the Taylor place, and rode off.

Daniel watched until all he could see was the dust created by Jim's horse.

Feeling melancholy, he headed toward the place Woodman had once dreamed about his brother Elton galloping his stallion. When Daniel had returned from Boston with Rebecca, Woodman had told him about the dream. He'd said Elton was happy.

That place had always been a favorite of Daniel's and his brother's. The ground was level and mostly smooth. During the wet season, water flowed down the now-dry channel. He and Elton had often raced through the gully, they and their mounts enjoying the tantalizing sensation of splashing water as they charged through the stream. Ghost gums grew along the banks. As a lad, Daniel had imagined the trees were spectators cheering on the two competitors.

Now he moved slowly toward the place where they'd once played. Reining in his horse in the shade of a broad-limbed acacia, Daniel stopped in its filtered sunlight. He drank from his canteen, then replaced the lid and breathed deeply, filling his lungs with overheated air.

His thoughts moved to Rebecca. Again he'd had to leave her while she slept. Every morning he would stand and gaze at her, wishing he didn't have to go. When she'd gotten sick after Joseph was born, he hadn't been able to leave her, and even when it had become clear she would live, he'd lingered a few extra days.

The station demanded his attention, and the stillness of the flats called him to the solitary friendship of the open plains. *If only Rebecca could share this with me*, he thought, studying the dry countryside with its haze of dust and heat. Even as he dreamed of sharing what sustained him, Daniel recognized the futility of the wish. Rebecca might accept her life in Queensland, but she would never cherish the land.

When he reached the dry riverbed, his mind returned to the races between him and his brother. Elton had almost always beaten him. He'd been more driven and more fearless than Daniel had been. "I wish you were here," he said aloud. "I need your help." He watched a small goanna dart across the heated earth and disappear into the roots of a gum tree. Elton had been well suited to managing Douloo. *If only he and Father hadn't quarreled so brutally.*

Daniel had been the one who frequently took the path of least resistance. Now, as inappropriate as it might seem, it was he who carried the weight of responsibility for Douloo.

He'd have to learn to scrap and to defy the odds. He'd never been tough enough for his father, but he now took solace in the fact that he was becoming stronger and more shrewd. Perhaps his father might admire him a bit these days.

His stallion whinnied nervously and danced. "Whoa, there." Daniel looked about to see what was distressing the animal. A snake glided across the ground toward the horse's feet. The stallion's muscles tightened, and he leaped, then sidestepped and reared with a high-pitched neigh.

Daniel pulled on the reins and pressed his knees tightly against the animal's sides but lost his seat and was thrown to the ground. Pain pierced his left ankle as it twisted beneath him. He managed to grab the reins. He wasn't about to let his horse run off. The snake slipped away, and the stallion quieted.

Gripping the reins, Daniel struggled to his feet. Gingerly he put weight on the foot. Shooting pain cut to the bone. He stood, balancing on his undamaged foot. "Must not be all that bad, eh?" He patted the horse. "No worries."

Still not certain that the horse wouldn't bolt, he kept hold of the reins and hobbled to a nearby log and sat. His ankle throbbed. Carefully he removed his boot and studied the limb. Already it was bruised and swollen.

"Could have been worse," he said to the quiet plains. *And if it had been?* Reality hit him with a jolt. His family and Douloo depended on him. He couldn't afford to get hurt—or worse, killed. If something happened to him, there was no one to oversee Douloo—his father's and grandfather's legacy could be lost.

In the distance he spotted a horse and rider moving toward him. He watched as they came closer. It was Rebecca.

Riding astride, Rebecca galloped toward Daniel. She pulled back on the reins and leaped from Chavive's back. "Are you all right? I saw you fall."

"I'm fine. What are you doing out 'ere?"

"Riding." She smiled. "Jim said you might be heading this way. I hoped we could spend some time together." She crossed to her husband and bent to kiss him. Looking at his exposed foot and ankle, she gasped. "That looks horrible. Are you sure you're all right?"

"Just twisted my ankle. There's a bit of bruising, but it's nothing." He pulled on his sock and boot and then cautiously stood but couldn't manage to conceal a grimace. "I thought Jim was off to see Cambria."

Rebecca shrugged. "She must have been gone, because he's at the house." She took a step closer. "Why don't you let me have a look at that ankle."

"No. It's fine."

Chavive nudged Rebecca's shoulder. She turned and smoothed the horse's damp neck with her gloved hand. "It's wonderful to have Chavive here." Her eyes settled on Daniel. "Thank you for buying her for me. I'm still overwhelmed by all you did to get her here."

"You're worth any amount of effort." Daniel studied the animal. "And she's a fine animal."

Rebecca kissed Daniel again. "Thank you. It's wonderful to ride again."

Rebecca's beauty and energy suddenly overwhelmed Daniel. He'd never known anyone like her. He hugged her. "I'm so glad you're mine."

"We belong to each other." Rebecca smiled. "Today is grand. I feel alive, more like myself."

"And where's Joseph? Mum watching him?"

"No. Actually, Callie is. She and Joseph seem to get along quite nicely. Your mother and Aunt Mildred are supervising, of course."

"Right. They're smitten." Daniel grinned. "I believe Mum sees my brother in him."

"Yes. She's told me so."

Daniel let his eyes roam over the dry creek bed. "Elton and I used to ride 'ere. The open ground made for a perfect track. Course, in those days during this time of year there was a stream flowing through the channel."

"I wish I had known Elton."

"You would have liked him. He was a fine mate."

"And if he were here today, he'd probably want to know why you're out here—alone."

"No. He'd understand—I belong 'ere; we both did once." Daniel mounted with only slight difficulty. He settled in the saddle and with a smile said, "Come on, then."

Rainless clouds moved in and shaded Daniel and Rebecca as they rode. Rebecca forgot her worries. Being on Chavive's back again seemed to set her world in order. And today was better than most days—Daniel was beside her.

They rode a long while. Daniel was quieter than usual, barely responding to Rebecca's remarks and questions. Finally she asked, "Is something troubling you?"

"No."

"You're very quiet. Are you in pain?"

"Nah. I'm fine."

Rebecca reined in Chavive and waited until Daniel stopped. He turned around in the saddle and looked at her. "What is it?"

"Something's wrong. And I'm not moving until you tell me what it is."

Daniel turned his horse around and walked back to Rebecca. He didn't say anything for a long while, then finally said, "I'm worried. The fall I took . . ."

"You said it wasn't severe."

"Right. I'm fine, but . . ."

"What is it, then?"

"I've been thinking about what you and Joseph would do if something happened to me."

"But you're fine. No worries. Isn't that what you always say?"

Daniel offered her a crooked smile. "I have said that on occasion, but we have to be sensible—something *could* happen." His horse bounced his head, and the bridle clinked. "Douloo is my responsibility now, and I don't know what would happen if . . ."

"Nothing is going to happen to you. But if it did, Douloo would be fine. There are capable people to oversee the station. Your mother and I are reasonable, intelligent women. I'm sure we could come up with something. And of course, there's Woodman. And Jim is a fine hand. Between the four of us, I'm certain we could hold this place together."

Daniel wore a humorous smile. "Are you finished?"

"No. I'm not. You must trust the Lord, Daniel. He is forever at your side."

"Right. I know. But sometimes it's hard to hang on to faith. When you were sick . . . I was really scared."

"I'm fine now. You can't worry about the past."

"Do you ever doubt that God is in control?"

Rebecca thought a moment. "Yes. But then I think back to all the troubles I've faced and how he's always looked after me."

"Sometimes my faith is right weak. I don't know what I would do without you." He reached across the space between the horses and took Rebecca's hand.

She squeezed his hand and smiled. "I think we ought to have a bit of fun now and then." She smiled mischievously, let go of his hand, and kicked Chavive in the sides. Chavive cantered ahead of Daniel and his stallion. "Are you up for a race?" Rebecca called over her shoulder.

Daniel spurred his stallion and quickly caught up to her, then charged past. Their troubles momentarily forgotten, the two raced across open grassland. At the edge of a dying stream, they reined in the horses and allowed them to drink.

In spite of his injury, Daniel helped Rebecca dismount. "You're very good at riding astride."

Rebecca grinned. "I can just see Elvina Walker's face. She would be appalled."

"Too right." Daniel chuckled.

Rebecca squatted beside the stream and scooped up a handful of water. Her thirst satisfied, she wet a handkerchief and patted her face and neck and then sat in the grass along the bank. She leaned back on her hands. "We ought to return to the house."

Daniel sat beside her, draped an arm over her shoulders, and pulled her close. "We don't have to go back straightaway, do we?"

Recognizing his intentions, Rebecca blushed and said, "I suppose not."

He kissed her ardently.

Rebecca hugged him tightly. "I love you, Daniel. Please try not to leave me so often."

A mewling and yipping sound came from the base of a nearby gum tree.

"What's that?" Rebecca asked. She studied burly roots beneath the eucalyptus. More yips emanated from the tree.

Daniel pushed to his feet and then helped Rebecca up. "Stay put," he said and hobbled toward the sound. When only a few paces from the tree, he stopped and stared down at its exposed roots.

"What is it?"

114

"Dingo pups. By the looks of them, they've been deserted by their mother."

"Oh, Daniel," Rebecca said, joining him. She could see four scrawny, matted balls of fur. Shaking and mewling, the pups crawled over one another. One stopped and gazed at the intruders with wide eyes.

"Why do you think the mother left them?"

"Any number of reasons. She could have been sick or might have been killed. The drought could have driven her away—self-preservation is always the highest order."

"I haven't anything to carry them in. How will we ever get them home?"

Daniel didn't answer right away. When he did, his voice was somber. "We aren't taking them home."

"But we can't just leave the poor little things. They'll die."

Daniel set his jaw. "They may look cute now, but dingoes are a scourge—they kill livestock. The fewer of them, the better."

"Daniel, we can't leave them!" Rebecca moved toward the pups.

"Rebecca, stop."

She continued.

"Stop. I demand you to stop!"

Rebecca turned and looked at Daniel. "You demand?"

"Yes. And you'll listen. Saving those pups makes no sense."

"They're innocent babies."

"No. They're not. They will grow up to be calf killers and sheep killers." He studied Rebecca a moment. "I'm having enough trouble making a place for myself in the district. The men around 'ere expect a lot from me. If I bring home a litter of dingo pups, I'll be a laughingstock. I can't afford to lose the blokes' respect."

Limping back to his horse, he withdrew a rifle from the saddle and walked toward the pups. "I want you to get on your horse and ride away," he said evenly.

Horrified, Rebecca stared at him. "You can't possibly . . ."

"Go. Now." He didn't look at her but stepped closer to the abandoned pups.

"Daniel, please don't."

He turned and stared at her. "We can't save them, and neither will I let them suffer. Go."

Shaking inside, Rebecca climbed onto Chavive's back and turned toward home. At first she cantered and then broke into a run, hoping that the wind and speed could blot out what was coming.

Four shots echoed over the land.

Tears blurring her vision, Rebecca drove Chavive hard. *How could Daniel be so cruel? I never thought of him as merciless.*

Bertram's words came back to her. "Daniel must be strong. And he needs someone at his side who will help him achieve that. A man can't run a station without courage."

Is this the kind of courage he was talking about? What of compassion?

She remembered the helpless pups, and fresh tears filled her eyes. *Would God have saved them?* She sucked in a ragged breath. *Lord, if this is what it means to be strong, then I pray for weakness.*

10

With Joseph resting on one hip, Rebecca stepped out of the house and onto the veranda. "Good morning, Mildred," she said, still feeling some of the previous day's melancholy. She couldn't rid her mind of the slain pups.

"How are you this morning, dear? You look a bit down."

"I'm fine."

Mildred crossed her ankles and leaned back in the chair. "It's rather nice and cool, isn't it?"

"Yes. In fact, I had to throw an extra blanket on my bed last night. I hope we have more days like this." She hitched Joseph up higher on her hip. "Has Thomas gone off with Daniel again?"

"Oh yes. Those two have taken to each other. Thomas really likes working with Daniel. If not for his business in Boston, I'm nearly convinced he'd remain here indefinitely."

"And what about you? It's been nearly four months since you arrived."

Mildred feigned shock. "Are you suggesting I've overstayed my welcome?"

Rebecca chuckled. "Of course not. You can stay as long

as you like. In fact, I'd love it if you would make this your permanent home."

Mildred's expression turned serious. "I have considered it. But this just isn't home to me. I've been thinking of returning to Boston. After all, this has been a rather extended holiday. I've been delaying a decision; I'll miss you terribly."

"Why don't you stay, then?"

"Oh, I couldn't do that. I adore you and Joseph, and I feel as if Daniel's family is mine, but I do have a life in Boston—family and friends, my church." She looked out at the countryside. "Life here is very different. I'm not certain I could ever completely accept its harshness."

Rebecca nodded, her mind returning to the pups. "I understand. I still find some things difficult to tolerate. And although I see beauty here, I still long for the lushness of Boston and sometimes even miss the bustle of the city." She gently patted Joseph's bottom. "Will Thomas be staying long?"

"I really don't know. He mentioned that he has business waiting for him in Boston, but on the other hand, he did say that . . . well, that he is a patient man."

"And what do you think he meant by that?"

Mildred smoothed a strand of hair back up into its chignon. "He wants to marry me. When I told him I couldn't possibly make any promises, he said he was a patient man. What do you think he meant?"

Rebecca smiled. "Oh my. That sounds as if he may stay for some time. That is, of course, if you do."

"I can't tear myself away just yet, and I must admit, I'd hate to see *him* go. I do enjoy his company. He's a fine man."

"He dotes on you. And he spends as much time as he can manage with you. I wish Daniel and I were able to find more time to be together. Some days he's gone before I rise, and all too often I'm asleep before he returns in the evening."

"There's no doubt Daniel wants to be with you, Rebecca.

I can see the love in his eyes every time he looks at you. Overseeing a station this size is a great responsibility and a difficult one for a young man. Do be patient with him."

"I understand, truly. I only wish he didn't have to work so hard." Rebecca shifted Joseph to her right shoulder and covered him with a blanket that she had draped over her other shoulder.

Moving to the railing, she thought of Boston. There had always been some special event taking place, something to stir her interest. And in New England the lushness never completely faded. The seashore had been one of her favorite places. Her mind carried her back to her retreat on her father's estate where she could look out over forested hills and valleys marked with open patches of cultivated land and beyond to the sea that lay like an iridescent gem. *I haven't seen the ocean since first arriving in Brisbane more than a year ago*, she realized.

Rebecca glanced at her aunt. Perhaps she could accompany her when she returned home. A visit might do her some good. However, the idea of leaving Daniel to cope alone seemed heartless.

The ache of homesickness settled in her chest as she realized more clearly that her life was here now. When Daniel inherited Douloo, the station had forever become home. Gazing at the dry surroundings, Rebecca said, "If only the clouds would drop some moisture. We had almost no rain all summer, and now even though the temperatures are cooling and there are clouds, there's still no rain."

Joseph whimpered and snuggled closer. Rebecca looked down at him. "Are you sleepy? Do you want to go to bed?" His bright blue eyes focused on his mother.

"He's such a dear. And he seems big for his age," Mildred said. "What does the doctor say about his progress?"

"That he's strong and healthy," Rebecca said with a smile.

She patted Joseph's back. He pressed a fist into his mouth and closed his eyes. Dark lashes rested against his cheeks. "One difficulty about his being so healthy—he's quite heavy. After holding him for a while, my arms and back ache."

She walked to the cradle that always sat on the porch. After looking through the bedding to make certain there were no poisonous creatures hiding inside, she settled him in it. Straightening, she remained there a moment, looking at him. What did the future hold?

Joseph jerked his hand out of his mouth and let out a small cry, and then replaced the fist and settled down again. *He is beautiful*, Rebecca thought, feeling a swell of love.

Callie stepped out of the house. "Can I put 'im ta bed for ya, mum?"

"No. He's fine." Rebecca felt a twinge of hurt as she watched Callie return indoors. "I sometimes think Joseph prefers Callie over me," she said.

"Oh, nonsense. No one can replace a mother."

"Auntie, that may be true, but he always quiets when Callie holds him, and she's there for him in a moment when he lets out the slightest whimper."

"If it bothers you, perhaps you ought to speak to her."

Rebecca walked to a chair and dropped onto it. "I know I'm being foolish. It would be silly of me to say anything about it. Callie is such a dear, always helping and never complaining. If not for her, I don't know what would have happened while I was ill. She took care of him as if he were her own."

"She was a great help." Joseph squirmed and let out a soft cry. "Is he still getting you up at night?"

"Yes. But only once. Callie's actually taken to sleeping in the room next to his. Sometimes she gets up with him. If he's hungry, she brings him to me. But I must admit, I wish she wouldn't help so much."

"Rebecca, speak to her."

"She's simply trying to make life easier for me, and it is nice to sleep when I can."

Joseph slept, and silence settled over the porch. Rebecca thought back to her childhood. Mildred had stepped into the role of mother when her real mother died. Mildred couldn't have been better to her, but when she explored her memories, she still felt the ache of her mother's absence.

"Although I was only five when Mother died, I still remember. I missed her so much."

"Yes, you did. I tried to help, but you needed her. I always felt I'd shortchanged you."

"No. That's not true. You were a wonderful help to me and always loving. I remember in the beginning when I'd have those bad dreams, you were always there to console me."

"I think your father helped more often than I did. But I was glad to do what I could." Mildred's eyes were suddenly awash with tears. "Since I never had children of my own, you felt like mine."

Rebecca reached over and squeezed her aunt's hand. "And you were like a mother to me. I cherish you."

Mildred smiled softly. "I love you, but no one can fully replace a mother."

Rebecca nodded. "I remember her quite vividly."

"She was a lovely person. And you've always been very much like Audrey, not just your appearance but your personality as well. She was brave and adventurous, just as you are."

"I don't feel very brave or adventurous." She glanced at Joseph and wondered if he would one day feel the bond that should exist between mother and child. She feared she wouldn't be enough—wouldn't love enough or be intelligent enough. "Auntie, I feel so inept at mothering. I love Joseph, but I'm not sure I'm doing a proper job. Much of the time I simply feel tired and overwhelmed."

121

Mildred offered a sympathetic smile. "No one is a perfect mother, Rebecca. Especially in the beginning. It takes time to become proficient and to gain confidence. And what new mother isn't tired?"

"I suppose you're right," Rebecca said, but she wasn't certain she believed her aunt. More than likely, Mildred was just trying to make her feel better. She caught a movement out of her left eye and turned to see what it was. A huge, black spider moved along the top of the railing at the far end of the porch. A funnel-web! She suppressed a gasp.

"Oh my," Mildred said, standing and pressing a hand against her throat. She took a step backward. "I've never seen a spider quite like that. It's big as a man's thumb. Is it dangerous?"

"Yes. Very. I'll have Woodman get it." Rebecca stood. "Auntie, don't worry. He's no danger where he is." She glanced about. "Now, where did Woodman get off to?" The spider moved along the railing.

"He's coming this way!" Mildred squealed and moved backward until she stood against the front railing. The contact startled her and she jumped. "Is that one of those horrid spiders you were telling me about?"

"Yes. A funnel-web," Rebecca said, walking down the front steps and looking about. When she didn't see Woodman, she glanced back at the spider and said, "Well, I suppose I'll just have to take care of it myself."

Trying to get hold of her courage, she returned to the porch. Keeping an eye on the nasty creature, she crossed to a broom leaning against the front door frame. Her heart hammered and her mouth had gone dry. *It's nothing more than a bug*, she told herself. Cautiously she moved toward the spider, broom raised.

"Do be careful," Mildred said, moving to the cradle and lifting out the baby. She held him close as if to protect him. "Oh dear. Didn't you say just one bite could kill a person?"

"Yes . . ."

"Maybe you ought to get Woodman."

"This one won't be biting me or anyone else." Rebecca lifted the broom higher. Seeming to sense danger, the spider darted toward the outside of the rail. Rebecca took a step closer. All of a sudden it moved toward her, lifted its body, and raised its two front legs in an aggressive stance.

She felt a surge of revulsion and alarm, and for a moment reconsidered finding Woodman. *No*, she told herself. *It's an insect. I can certainly kill a bug.* She raised the broom. "You don't scare me. I'm bigger than you." Teeth clenched, she swung the broom down hard, directly on top of the spider. Rebecca pressed firmly to make certain it was dead, then carefully lifted the broom. All that was left of the ghastly thing was a black smear across the broom's fibers. Rebecca knocked the remains loose and they dropped to the ground. With a feeling of confidence, she returned the broom to its place at the door.

"How dreadful." Mildred shuddered.

Wearing a smug expression, Rebecca lifted Joseph out of Mildred's arms and returned to her chair. "It's nothing to worry about, Auntie." Joseph put his feet on his mother's lap and pushed himself upright. He grinned, and his cheek dimpled just like his father's. Rebecca dropped kisses on his face.

"I don't know what I would do if I were to find one of those things in my room."

"No worries, Auntie. I've never seen one in the house. Although, I did hear that Lily came across one in the kitchen once. But that's extremely rare. Woodman's careful to watch for them."

"I'm careful ta watch for what?" Woodman asked, approaching the steps and then leaning on the handrail.

"Funnel-webs. I just killed one. It was there on the railing."

Woodman grinned. "Ya mean ta say ya got up the courage? Ya might be an Aussie after all, eh?"

Rebecca folded her arms over her chest and smiled. "I just might be."

"Proud of ya, mum," Woodman said, tipping his hat before walking away.

Joseph let out a small cry. "You can't be hungry already." Rebecca moved him to her shoulder and patted his back, but whimpers turned into wails. She bounced him gently, but he threw himself away from her and cried more fervently. She tried to cuddle him, but he only became more agitated.

Callie stepped out of the front door. "Let me give 'im a try." She reached for the infant. "'Ere, mum, let me 'ave 'im." She took Joseph and held him against her chest. His cries quieted, and he rested his head against her cotton dress. "There ya are. Yer fine now, eh?" Callie said, rocking gently.

Feeling a pang of jealousy, Rebecca turned to her aunt. "See what I mean. It's always that way. When I can't do a thing with him, she comes along and he quiets right away." Rebecca tried to make her voice light, but she wondered why her son preferred Callie.

"I'm sure it's not you," Willa said, walking up the front steps, carrying a basket of eggs.

"What, then?"

"You can never tell what will soothe a child." Willa knit her brows. "Perhaps you're feeling tense? He might sense it."

"I've heard of that," Mildred said. "And you did just kill that dreadful spider."

"Yes, but all mothers feel anxious now and then. You would think he'd feel how much I love him."

Creases of concern lined Callie's forehead. "Would ya like 'im back, mum?"

"No. He's content now."

"Well, then would ya like me ta take 'im upstairs ta bed?"

124

"Yes, that would be fine," Rebecca said without looking at the servant.

Callie took the baby indoors, and Rebecca rested her head against the back of her chair and wondered what she could do to be a better mother.

Willa sat beside Rebecca. "So you killed a funnel-web, eh?"

"I did. And I was just beginning to feel a bit of confidence, but my own son prefers someone other than me."

"Don't be silly. You're a fine mother. He's always glad to be with you."

Rebecca pushed out of her chair and walked to the railing. "I'm simply not very good at it."

"Rebecca Thornton, you're an excellent mother," Willa said adamantly. She moved to Rebecca's side and rested a hand on her daughter-in-law's arm. "I see how much you love him. And how his eyes light up when he looks at you."

"Oh, that look is the one he uses when he's hungry," Rebecca said with a crooked smile.

"It's more than that and you know it."

Rebecca rested a hand over Willa's. "Sometimes I wonder what would have happened if I'd become a lawyer. I would probably have been better at that than I am at mothering."

"Rebecca Thornton, stop this nonsense!" Mildred's light blue eyes looked angry. "Thank the Lord you've been blessed with a child."

Willa added in a gentler tone, "Being a mother is one of the most important tasks God gives. The man Joseph will become has quite a lot to do with you and what you teach him. I dare say, God never created a more significant job than that of being a mother."

Rebecca could feel the sting of tears. "Yes. I agree, but sometimes I feel like I'm doing a poor job."

"I don't want to hear another word. You're doing just fine."

Not knowing what else to say, Rebecca stared at her mother-in-law. She couldn't possibly understand how inadequate she felt. Willa was the perfect mother. "And I feel I could be doing something more than just helping around the house."

"You underestimate yourself, Rebecca," Willa said. "You've been a great help to me. I'm getting on in years, and with Bertram gone, your assistance is of immense value."

Rebecca took in a deep breath and blinked back her tears. "Thank you for your confidence, but I sometimes think of the days I spent in my father's office and at the courthouse—they were satisfying, filled with anticipation and a sense of achievement. After searching through a case and then deciding an angle of attack, my father would step into the courtroom and bring justice. I was part of something significant."

Sadness touched Willa's eyes. "And now you feel insignificant?"

Rebecca thought for a moment, then said honestly, "Sometimes. Never in my life did I envision that I would one day live in the midst of a great plain and have a son and husband who depended upon me. Life was much different in Boston." She looked beyond the dirt yard. "I love Daniel and Joseph, but there are times when I miss my old life and wish Daniel would take me back to Boston."

Willa's expression turned serious. "God will show you why you're here at Douloo and what you're to do with your life. I'm extremely grateful for your presence."

Rebecca nodded. Her thoughts returned to the funnel-web she'd killed, and the sense of self-assurance crept back. *I can do whatever I set my mind to.*

11

Joseph's crying dragged Rebecca from sleep. She rolled onto her side and stared at the empty space beside her. Daniel was gone. With a heavy sigh, she sat up and ran her hands through tangled hair. *If I just let him cry, Callie will get him*, she thought. The idea of more sleep was tempting. However, she could feel her milk letting down, and her arms longed to hold her son.

"I'm coming," she said, dropping her legs over the side of the bed and hurrying to the nursery. "It's all right. Mummy's here." She lifted the red-faced infant from his crib and held him against her. He quieted and gazed at her. Rebecca wiped tears from his cheeks and kissed him.

All of a sudden he smiled and his face lit up as he chanted, "Dada, da . . . da . . . da . . . da."

"Oh my! You said dada."

"Dadadada . . . ," he prattled.

Rebecca kissed his cheek again. "What a bright boy you are." She held him up in front of her. "Now, how about mama . . . mama."

Joseph planted pudgy hands on her cheeks, then reached and grabbed a handful of dark hair.

"Oh, no you don't," Rebecca said, gently loosening his hold and then pushing her hair back out of his reach. She carried him to the rocker and sat. "One day you'll say mama."

⁂

By the time Rebecca had fed and changed Joseph and dressed and coifed herself, Mildred and Thomas had already finished breakfast. When she walked into the kitchen, they sat at the table drinking coffee. Willa carried a cup and saucer to the sink.

"Mmm, coffee smells good. I think I'll have some rather than tea this morning," Rebecca said.

Thomas stood and pulled out a chair for her. "I'm afraid I brought my coffee habit with me. Gwenn always made the best coffee. I'm afraid she spoiled me."

Rebecca glanced across the table and caught the wince of pain in Mildred's eyes.

She sat and settled Joseph in her lap. "Although I do enjoy my tea, coffee is nice for a change. It's rather fortifying."

"You look rested," Willa said.

"I am. Joseph actually slept through the night." Rebecca kissed the top of his head. "And this morning when I went to get him from his crib, he asked for his dada."

"Why, he's only a little more than four months old!" Mildred reached across the table and took Joseph's hand. "He's very bright."

"Would you like somethin' ta eat, mum?" Lily asked.

"I'm famished. In fact, it seems that since Joseph was born I've developed a man's appetite. Sometimes it's embarrassing."

"It 'as ta do with yer feedin' the bybie," Lily said. "Mothers

128

need more food if they're ta 'ave enough for themselves and the bybies." She smiled. "I made scones, but if ya'd like eggs it wouldn't be nothin' for me ta cook some."

"A scone will be fine." Rebecca settled her eyes on Mildred and Thomas. "So what do you have planned today?"

"Oh, I don't know." Mildred turned to Thomas. "Since you decided to spend the day with me rather than work with Daniel, it seems the choice should be yours."

"I was thinking a picnic and fishing down at the billabong."

"Sounds lovely." Mildred glanced at Rebecca and Willa. "Would either of you like to join us?"

"No. Actually, I've some paperwork waiting for me—documents and such to sort out in Bertram's desk." Willa's voice sounded leaden. "I hate the thought." Swiping at a single tear, she added, "Silly of me, hanging on to his outdated papers."

Those in the room quieted, reminded of the man who had once ruled Douloo.

"I'd be more than happy to help. I used to do that sort of thing for my father when I worked in his law practice," Rebecca said.

"Thank you for offering, but no. This is a task I must see to myself." Willa's blue eyes glistened with tears, but she managed a smile. "I think you ought to picnic with Mildred and Thomas. It's a lovely day."

"I was hoping to take Chavive out for a ride." Lily set a hot scone spread with jam on the table in front of Rebecca. A sweet aroma rose from the breakfast pastry.

"Where were you planning to ride?" Willa asked.

"I'm not sure, but you needn't worry about me. I know my way around quite well these days."

"Yes, of course. I was just curious."

"I might go into town or to Cambria's. And I suppose I

could stop at the billabong for a bite and the opportunity to watch Thomas catch a fish." Rebecca smiled.

"Oh yes, do," Mildred said.

Rebecca thought she detected disenchantment on Thomas's face. "However, I wouldn't want to barge in on you two."

"Don't be silly. Of course you wouldn't be barging in." Mildred glanced at Thomas.

"We'd enjoy your company," he said.

"Are you sure?"

"Absolutely."

Rebecca thought a moment. "I have an idea. Why don't you two join me?"

"You mean ride horses?" Mildred asked with disbelief.

"Yes. You used to ride all the time, Auntie. And I'm ashamed to say that my horse Rena has been neglected since Chavive's arrival. She's long overdue for a ride. She's quite gentle."

"Oh, I couldn't possibly. It's been years."

"Father told me that you were once a fine rider," Rebecca challenged.

"I think it's a splendid idea," Thomas said. "It would be great fun. What do you think, Willa?"

Willa stood in the doorway, arms folded over her chest. "I think it's not up to me. I'm not getting into the middle of this one." She grinned.

Rebecca offered Joseph a taste of jam. He puckered and smacked his lips and then opened his mouth for more. Rebecca gave him another taste.

"Already he likes sweets," Willa said.

"Good taste, I'd say." Thomas grinned. "Who can resist Lily's cooking?"

Rebecca turned to Willa. "Why don't you come riding with us? Daniel told me you were once a very competent horsewoman."

"It's been years. I doubt I'd even remember how. And it's

too painful these days. If I were to go with you, my rheumatism would make me sorry for it." Putting an end to the idea, she pushed her hands into the pockets of her apron and said, "Well then, I have work to do. Whatever you decide, I pray you'll have a grand time of it."

As Willa moved out of the room, Rebecca turned her attention back to Mildred. "So would you join me?"

"Oh, Rebecca . . . I don't know."

"Please. If it turns out to be too taxing, we can always return."

"I'm sure you'll do fine," Thomas said.

Mildred didn't respond.

"Please, Auntie. I know you'll enjoy the outing."

A crooked smile appeared on Mildred's face. "All right. I'll go. But no one's allowed to laugh—it's been a very long while. I don't even have a riding habit."

"If you'd like, you can borrow a pair of my britches and ride astride." Rebecca grinned.

Mildred blanched. "I think not! I wouldn't have the least idea how to ride astride. And it's very unladylike."

"All right, then. You can borrow my riding habit. But you're much more slender than me." Rebecca studied her aunt. "Even so, it should do."

☟

Rebecca placed a foot in the stirrup and swung her leg over Chavive's back. Settling into the saddle, she watched while Thomas led a large gelding and a composed Rena out of the stables.

Thomas studied Rebecca a moment. "I must admit, I'm not used to seeing a woman riding in that fashion. Daniel doesn't mind?"

"Not really. He agrees with its practicality. Of course, if

we were riding in town or with new friends, I would most likely ride sidesaddle."

Thomas nodded, then glanced at the house. "I'm not sure we haven't coerced poor Mildred into this."

"Perhaps." Rebecca smiled. "But I still think it's a good idea. She'll have a tremendous time. You'll see." She studied Thomas a moment. He seemed to be a kind man. She'd wondered about the relationship between him and her aunt, but she'd never felt it was proper to inquire. Curiosity getting the better of her, she asked, "You're quite serious about my aunt, aren't you?"

"That I am." Thomas rested a hand on the gelding's neck. "As a matter of fact . . . I love her. Never knew a finer person. I'd be proud if she'd agree to be my wife." He ran his fingers through a tangled batch of mane. "She refuses to give me an answer. And I can't stay on here at Douloo indefinitely. I have a business to run back in Boston. However, each time I think of returning home without her, the idea seems inconceivable." His horse nipped at Rena, and Thomas tugged on the gelding's reins. "That's enough of that."

Turning his attention back to Rebecca, he said, "I was hoping you might be of help." Thomas patted his horse. "Could you talk to her? Perhaps convince her she ought to marry me?" He offered an embarrassed smile.

"Mr. Murdoc, from what I've seen you're a fine gentleman. And I'd be pleased if my aunt accepted your proposal. But I can't induce her to marry. She must make up her own mind. Only she can know the depth of her affection."

Thomas nodded. "Of course. I apologize for asking, but I must admit to feeling somewhat desperate." He checked the snugness of his saddle by tugging on it. "I was married once. My wife died giving birth to our only child. He died as well." The brown in Thomas's eyes darkened at the painful memory.

"Mildred told me. I'm terribly sorry."

132

"I never thought I'd find anyone else. All these years there has never been a woman who appealed to me. Not until I met Mildred. She didn't strike me right off. She's rather quiet, you know. And she downplays her attributes, so her fine looks aren't immediately apparent."

"I've always wondered why my aunt hadn't married."

"I'd like to believe God saved her for me." His expression turned serious.

"I think she likes you quite well."

"I agree. That's why I don't understand her hesitation. I believe she finds me appealing, and we have many similar interests . . . I don't know what it is that keeps her from accepting my proposal."

"Have you asked her why she won't marry you?"

"She will only say she needs more time, and something about being single." He shrugged. "I think it's something more, but she won't tell me."

"My suggestion is that you persevere, Mr. Murdoc."

"Please call me Thomas or Tom."

"All right, Thomas then. As I was saying, my aunt has never been one to do anything without first giving it careful consideration. I believe she'll come around."

The sound of footsteps on the front porch closed Rebecca's mouth. She and Thomas turned to look. Dressed in Rebecca's black riding habit, Mildred nearly pranced down the front steps and across the yard. "It's too large," she said holding out the loose waist of the riding habit. "I'm surprised it's so roomy. You're quite petite, Rebecca."

"You may be taller, Auntie, but you're much thinner."

Mildred stopped and looked down at the habit. "Is it terribly oversized?"

"No. It will do just fine."

Mildred removed a pin from her small hat, tidied her hair, and then repinned the hat.

"I think it's just fine. And you look quite robust," Thomas said. "Your cheeks have a high color."

"They do?" Mildred asked, brightening at the compliment. She approached the small buckskin mare. "Well now, I'll need a hand up."

"Allow me," Thomas said, quickly moving to her side.

Mildred faced the horse. "It's been so long."

"Just put your foot in my hand and I'll lift you."

Mildred handed him her riding crop and did as he said, then gripping the saddle horn, she allowed him to boost her. However, instead of landing lightly in the saddle, she ended up draped over it. The mare pranced and tossed her head.

"Oh dear. Help me. Please."

Rebecca laughed while Thomas assisted Mildred.

Once she stood on solid ground again, Mildred smoothed her dress and tucked loose hairs back into place. "This is not a good idea. I can't even get on the animal."

"It was only your first try," Thomas said. "I'm sure you'll get it the next time."

"Hmm." She stared at Rebecca. "This humiliation is your fault."

Rebecca grinned and Mildred cracked a smile. "All right. I'll give it one more try."

Once again she planted a foot in Thomas's hand and gripped the saddle, and up she went. This time, although a bit wobbly, she managed to settle herself on the saddle. Awkwardly she lifted her right leg, placed it around the tall saddle horn, and arranged her skirts so as not to reveal her legs. "I'll need my riding crop." Thomas handed it up to her. Sitting very straight and stiff, she said, "I'm ready."

Thomas mounted his horse and then said to Rebecca, "You know the way. We'll follow you."

Chavive had been prancing, ready for a run, but Rebecca

134

held her in. With a light kick, the horse set out at a rapid trot. Thomas and Mildred followed.

"Oh my," Mildred said, gripping the reins tightly and keeping one hand on the saddle horn. "I'm not sure I'll be able to keep my seat."

Rebecca glanced back. Mildred did look a bit unsteady. "We'll walk for now," she said, pulling back on the reins to slow Chavive, who obeyed with reluctance.

The three walked along side by side, Chavive and Thomas's gelding tossing their heads, hoping for permission to run. A soft breeze rippled short grasses and stirred the leaves on the occasional tree.

"It's quite a lovely day," Mildred said. "And I'm enjoying myself immensely. I'm so glad I came. Thank you for convincing me of the idea."

"I knew you could do it," Thomas said, wearing his crooked smile. "You sit a horse very well."

"You think so?" She lifted her chin slightly and rotated her shoulders back just a bit.

Rebecca smiled. "Do you think you're up for a trot?"

"Oh, I don't know." Mildred glanced at Thomas. "Well, why not." She tapped the mare with her riding crop, and the horse stepped into a brisk trot.

The other horses did the same.

"You're doing well, Auntie. I can't believe you and I didn't ride together when I lived in Boston."

"Yes, well, you know how easy it is to get into a rut. I guess I thought it wasn't dignified for a woman my age."

"Your age? You're not all that old. You're barely over . . ."

"It's not proper to reveal a woman's age, Rebecca," Mildred cut in.

"Right. I'm sorry." She offered Thomas a smile. "She doesn't look old at all, does she?"

"Not at all. She's a beauty."

"Go on, now. You're embarrassing me." Mildred's face had turned pink. "I believe a canter is in order," she said, leaning forward slightly and tapping her horse with the whip. Rena broke into a smooth lope. Mildred's face shone and her hair caught in the wind. She actually looked young.

"This is marvelous," she said, moving beyond Rebecca and Thomas.

"Be careful," Rebecca said, kicking her horse and quickly catching up to her aunt.

"It's all coming back now. It's delightful. I think we ought to ride more often."

"I agree," Thomas and Rebecca said in unison.

After sharing lunch beneath a gum tree, Thomas walked to the fishing hole. Rebecca and Mildred put away the lunch items. When they had finished, the two women remained on the quilt, leaning back and resting on their arms. They gazed out over the tranquil greenery of the billabong. The woods were filled with the buzz of insects and the songs of birds.

Rebecca lay on her back and looked up through the sparse limbs of the tree. She could detect the subtle aroma of eucalyptus. For a moment the taste of it was on her tongue, and she was reminded of the tea Lily had made her drink while she'd been ill. Quickly setting the thought aside, she said, "I've really enjoyed myself today. Thank you for joining me."

"It's been my pleasure." Mildred lay beside Rebecca, closed her eyes, and rested a hand on her stomach. "Oh, I think I ate too much." She was quiet a moment, then asked, "Who's taking care of Joseph?"

"Callie." Rebecca took in a breath and slowly released it. "It's a puzzle. I hate to leave him with her, and at the same time I'm grateful. Because of her, I'm allowed times for fun like today. But sometimes I'm afraid Joseph will love her more than me."

"Fiddle-faddle! We've talked about this before, and I think you're borrowing trouble."

Rebecca reached out and took her aunt's hand. "I'm sure you're right."

She watched the slender leaves twirl in the breeze. "I wish Daniel were here. It would be an even better day if he had joined us." She rolled onto her side, placed an elbow on the blanket, and rested her face in her hand. "You're very lucky to have a man like Thomas. He makes time for you."

"Yes. I suppose so."

"He loves you, you know."

"He's said as much." Mildred's tone was reserved, and she continued to stare up at the tree limbs.

"Auntie, why are you shutting him out?"

Mildred turned to look at Rebecca, her eyes wide. "I'm doing no such thing. I'm just not certain what I ought to do yet."

"You're not getting any younger, you know. He's a fine person and you're lucky to have him."

"You think it's so important that I have someone?" Mildred sat up and stared at the water.

"No . . . well . . . oh, I don't know. I just think it would be nice if you did."

Mildred didn't respond for a long moment, then she said, "He doesn't really love me. He's still in love with his first wife. I don't think I could abide that."

"Why do you think that?"

"Oh, he talks about her all the time. Just like this morning when he said how much he loved her coffee."

"Auntie, he spent many years of his life with her. Of course there are things that happened between them that he'll always remember. That doesn't mean he isn't in love with you."

137

Mildred pushed herself up off the ground. "I think I'll have a look and see if Thomas has caught anything." She walked briskly toward the pool.

Rebecca joined her, matching her stride. "Auntie, you can't keep him waiting forever. One day you'll have to make a decision."

"That may be so, but not today," Mildred said curtly and walked down the bank.

A tree had fallen across the water, creating a natural bridge to a small island in the middle of the pool. Thomas stood on the island. Mildred stepped onto the log and started across. Holding her arms straight out from her sides, she moved along carefully.

"Wait, Mildred, I'll come across and help you," Thomas said, setting down his pole.

"Be careful," Rebecca called.

"I'm just fine," Mildred said, glancing back at Rebecca. At that moment, she lost her balance and teetered to one side. Her arms fanned the air. "Oh dear." With a small squeal, she tipped sideways and dropped into deep water. She splashed to the surface. "I . . . I can't swim! Help me!" Her arms flailed and churned the dark waters, and then her head disappeared beneath the surface.

"Oh, Lord! Auntie!" Rebecca ran to the bank.

Thomas sprinted to the water's edge. Without hesitation, he dived in and swam toward the place where Mildred had been. Although built slightly, Thomas had a powerful stroke. It took only a few moments for him to reach the spot where Mildred had disappeared. He dived beneath the surface and a long moment later reappeared without Mildred. Frantically he searched the surface of the water.

"She was right there," Rebecca yelled, pointing at the place where her aunt had gone under. "Please find her! Save her!"

Thomas dived again.

138

Rebecca clasped her hands, holding them against her chest, and prayed.

The dark waters rippled and Thomas appeared, clutching Mildred's arm. He lay his arm across her chest, grasping her around the rib cage. Holding her close, he swam toward the bank.

Rebecca waded into the shallows. Her aunt's skin looked ashen. "Is she alive? Auntie? Oh please, Auntie. Please be all right."

Thomas stood and lifted Mildred and waded toward shore. "She'll be fine. She'll be fine," he said, as if saying it would make it so. "Mildred?" he asked, gently lowering her to the ground. "Mildred. Come on, now. Wake up."

She lay limp and quiet.

Thomas rolled her onto her side and patted her back. "Mildred! Breathe!" He hit her harder. "Come on, now. Breathe!"

A choking cough erupted from the frail woman.

"There you go. That's it." Thomas sat her up, bracing her back against him.

She gulped down air and coughed again.

"I've got you," Thomas said. "You're fine now."

Rebecca knelt in front of her aunt. "Are you all right?"

Mildred took a deep breath, choked, and then gasped. Resting a hand against her chest, she said. "Yes. I think so."

Rebecca hugged her aunt. "Oh, Auntie, you scared me to death!"

"It was so silly of me. I should have been more careful."

"Just so long as you're well," Thomas said, tightening his hold slightly.

Mildred grasped her wet skirt. "My dress pulled me right down. If not for Thomas . . ." She looked at him. "You saved my life. How can I ever repay you?"

12

"I've never been to a horse race before," Mildred said, tugging on her gloves and then lifting the collar of her coat up about her neck. She snuggled deeper into her seat in the surrey. "It's quite chilly, isn't it? Almost reminds me of Boston in the fall."

"The month of May can be quite cool." Willa glanced at Joseph, who slept in her lap.

"I've still not gotten accustomed to the order of the seasons here. It's strange—your winter is our summer, and summer is winter."

"Yes, I suppose it can be rather confusing."

"Do you ever get snow?" Mildred asked.

"Never seen it 'round 'ere," Woodman said, glancing back at his passengers. "I've heard of snow in some of the mountains though."

"And it will get cooler, Auntie," Rebecca explained.

"What about rain? Can we expect more soon?" Mildred's voice held a hint of longing.

"We get most of our rain during the summer, but we can anticipate showers over the winter months." A distressed

140

expression crossed Willa's face. "But of course, this year has been exceptionally dry."

Rebecca looked at Mildred. "Are you considering staying?"

"Not permanently, but I can't bring myself to leave just yet." Mildred's gaze went to Thomas, who rode a few paces ahead of the surrey along with Daniel and Jim. "I need a little more time to sort things out."

Jim said something to his two riding companions, and Thomas laughed heartily.

"Looks as if Thomas has become a regular bloke," Rebecca said, smiling. "Do you think he'll return to Boston soon?"

"He keeps saying that he's leaving, and yet here he is."

Rebecca raised an eyebrow. "He must have reason to stay."

"I suppose so."

"He did save your life."

"That he did. And I'll always be grateful. But I can't count that as a sign that I ought to marry him. Thomas is a fine man and would never turn his back on someone in need, no matter who it was." A soft smile touched her lips, and her eyes warmed as she continued to watch him.

"Oh, Auntie," Rebecca said in frustration. "Why don't you just admit that you care for him and say yes to his marriage proposal?"

Mildred lifted her chin slightly. "And what of his first wife? He still loves her."

"Yes. I'm sure he does. But that doesn't mean he can't love you. When someone dies they're not forgotten, and from all I've seen in the fine people I know, there's always room to love."

"Too right," Willa said. "However, I must admit that I can't imagine ever remarrying."

"See, Rebecca. It's not really possible to get over someone you truly love. I admire Thomas greatly, but I would always feel like the second wife."

"Well, then you best tell him you're not going to marry him and let the poor man return to his home," Rebecca said.

Mildred nodded slightly. "I suppose."

"If you do, it will be a mistake," Willa said softly.

Mildred looked at her. Then as if nothing important had been said, she moved on to another subject. "Tell me about today's festivities. What can I expect?"

There was a pause before Willa explained. "There will be horse races and horse trading. It's a grand time for all. In some ways it's a bit like a carnival. However, there is also serious horse business going on."

Rebecca propped an elbow on the ridge of the surrey and leaned her cheek against her hand. "I'm quite interested in looking at the horses. Some of the finest animals in the district will be here."

"Are there any nice shops in Roma?"

"Some," Willa said with a smile. "But not nearly enough for me. I dare say, I'm ready for a trip to Melbourne. It's a marvelous city."

"Did you hear from your aunt Ada?" Rebecca asked.

"Yes, as a matter of fact. I thought I had told you."

"No."

"Well, she said that any time we wanted to visit we'd be welcome. And that November would be a fine time."

"November seems so far away. I can barely wait to go. From what you say, Melbourne is grand."

"It is."

$\maltese$

The small group from Douloo approached Roma. The settlement wasn't large by any means, but it offered more than Thornton Creek. The surrey moved slowly through the

142

center of town. Woodman expertly guided the horses down a street crowded with traffic and vendors.

Much like a girl on her first outing to the city, Mildred leaned forward, taking in all the activity. "Oh my, there's a curio shop. I'd love to have a look inside."

"Yes. Absolutely. They have some lovely things. We'll set up our picnic spot first and then come back," Willa said.

"If you don't mind, I'd rather go with Daniel." Rebecca smiled apologetically. "I've been anxious to look at the horses."

"That's fine, dear." Willa gazed at the eddy of activity about them. "Bertram always loved this. I wish he were here."

"I wish he were too," Rebecca said, reaching across to Willa and clasping her hand.

❦

Arms intertwined, Daniel and Rebecca toured the corrals. With a smile, Rebecca glanced at Joseph, who was safely settled in his father's free arm. Grinning, the youngster gawked at all the goings-on about him, pointing at one thing or another. Rebecca felt more content than she had in weeks. Today she and her family would enjoy the festivities together. Momentarily she rested her head against Daniel's arm. He smiled down at her. "Thank you for today," she said.

"Can't think of anything I'd rather do." He moved his arm about her waist and gave her a squeeze. Hefting Joseph slightly, he said, "See how he's watching everything. He's truly interested."

"Well, of course. He's bright. He's a Thornton."

Willa, Mildred, and Thomas joined Daniel and Rebecca.

"What do you think of my new hat?" Mildred asked, turning around to show it off. "I found it in a small millinery shop just around the corner."

143

"It looks quite stunning on you," Rebecca said, admiring the stylish maize crepe hat. "It brings out the blue in your eyes."

"Absolutely. You look beautiful," Daniel said with a grin.

"I've told her she's beautiful," Thomas said. "But she doesn't believe me."

"Stop it, you two. It's the hat that's attractive." Mildred smiled. Her eyes looked brighter than usual, and her cheeks glowed soft pink.

The group approached a corral with several horses. "Oh, look there," Rebecca said pointing at a roan mare. "She looks very much like Chavive. Maybe not quite as tall, but still handsome."

"Quite right," Daniel said. "Her coat is the same chestnut color, but don't you think a bit less dappled?"

"A bit," Rebecca said.

Daniel studied the animal. "She's grand though."

"She is at that," said a man dressed in a pinstripe suit. "A real beauty, eh?" He smiled in an overly friendly way.

"I have a mare that looks very much like her," Rebecca said.

"You're lucky, then. There aren't many as nice as this one."

The man extended his hand to Daniel. "Collin O'Neill."

"Daniel Thornton."

"A Thornton, eh? Nice ta meet you. You must be the boss cocky, then." He grinned and turned to Rebecca. "And this is your wife?"

"Yes," Rebecca said. "Rebecca Thornton."

Collin nodded at Willa and Mildred, then looked at Thomas.

"Thomas Murdoc," the middle-aged Bostonian said with a nod.

144

"G'day ta you." Collin turned to Daniel. "Now, what can I do for you? Interested in the mare?"

"Possibly." Rebecca glanced at the horse. "I'd like to take a closer look."

"You won't find any blemishes, I can assure you." Collin chuckled. "My horse trading days would be over if I were to sell animals that weren't sound."

"We're not really interested in purchasing a horse, Mr. O'Neill," Daniel interjected. "Just admiring them is all."

Rebecca wasn't as certain as Daniel seemed to be about not being ready to buy. The station could always use good horses. However, she held her tongue.

"Well then, have a fine day. Enjoy yourselves. The mare's brother will be racing this afternoon. You can't miss him. He looks like her, only a bit more showy."

Rebecca was immediately interested.

It must have been apparent, because Collin settled his gaze on her and said, "You have ta get a look at him. You'll be impressed."

"We'll do that," Rebecca said.

The man removed his hat, revealing straight blond hair with traces of gray. Tucking the hat under one arm, Collin took a card out of his breast pocket. "If you change your minds, get in touch with me, eh? I have some good stock you might want ta have a look at."

Daniel took the card. Rebecca glanced at it. "Thank you, Mr. O'Neill," she said. "We'll make sure to watch for your horse this afternoon."

Joseph let out a cry. "Think he's wanting his mummy," Daniel said, handing the baby over to Rebecca.

She took him and cuddled him, but Joseph continued to fuss. "You certainly can't be hungry. It hasn't been very long since you ate." Doing her best to squelch irritation, she shuffled the lad to her hip and bounced him, but his cries became more intense. Rebecca had counted on watching the races and talking horses with people from around the district. A fussy baby would make a shambles of the day. *Perhaps Callie will watch him*, Rebecca thought and looked about for the servant. She spotted her nearby, setting out snacks on a quilt.

"I'll be just a moment," Rebecca said, and with Joseph resting on her hip, she walked toward the servant. "Hello, Callie."

"G'day. Ya 'avin a good time?"

"Yes. You?"

"Fine, mum."

"I was hoping to speak with some of the traders here, and I can't seem to quiet Joseph. Would you mind terribly watching him for me? He's been fed and changed, but I still can't make him happy."

Callie reached for the baby. "Wal, course I can watch 'im." She smiled at Joseph. "I think he's cutting a tooth." She stuck a finger into his mouth and probed. "Yais, that's it. 'Is poor little gums is real swollen." Rocking from one foot to the other, she cradled him. Still whimpering, Joseph rested his head against her chest. "Ya go on, now."

Grateful and jealous at the same time, Rebecca walked away. As she headed toward Daniel, she spotted Meghan Linnell chatting with him. Immediately her pulse quickened. *What does she want?* Rebecca hurried her steps. She wasn't about to give that vixen one minute more with her husband than was necessary.

As Rebecca stepped up, Meghan flashed her a coy smile. "For heaven's sake, Rebecca. You needn't look so put out. I have no designs on yer husband. I was just giving him a bit of news." With a toss of her mahogany-colored hair and a wave of her hand, she walked off.

"That woman. I can't believe she has the nerve to . . ."

"Rebecca, she hasn't caused us a bit of trouble in months. You'll have to let go of your anger sooner or later."

"Daniel, have you forgotten the horrible lies she told about us?"

"No. I haven't, but we must live with the people in the district, and I still do business with her father. Plus, she's been a longtime friend. Let it go." He rested a hand on her back.

"I know it's difficult," Willa said kindly. "But Daniel's right, dear."

"I suppose so. I just haven't seen her recently and she took me by surprise."

"She's always in church," Thomas said.

"Yes. We avoid each other," Rebecca said. "Too bad she doesn't hear a word of the reverend's sermons."

Daniel gently squeezed her shoulder. "That's not a very good start at forgiveness."

Rebecca nodded, but her insides still shook. Meghan had nearly ruined her marriage. She could never be trusted.

Daniel moved to a fence alongside the track. "That horse you wanted to see is in this race."

Shrugging off her annoyance, Rebecca stepped close to the fence and peered through. The animals were prancing at the starting line. It was easy to spot the stallion. He was larger than the rest and looked so much like Chavive that he could have been a sibling. The air pulsed with excitement as quiet settled over the crowds. An official raised a gun into the air.

A sharp blast penetrated the hush, and the horses lunged forward. For the first several strides, they sprinted in a huddle, almost as one. Then hooves and striding legs nearly tangled as each fought to break free of the pack. The stallion was trapped in the middle and unable to find his pace. His gait wasn't impressive, and yet Rebecca could see restrained power in his shoulders and hindquarters. Expectant, she kept her eyes on him.

"So what do you think of him?" Thomas asked Daniel.

"A bit slow. But we'll have to wait and see, eh?"

As they rounded the first bend, the stallion remained wedged between other contenders. And then a space opened, and he broke through, charging to the outside. Lengthening his stride, he plunged ahead.

"There he goes," Rebecca said, gripping the fence. He was magnificent. His deep chestnut coat gleamed in the sunlight, and he held his tail high like a flag.

"Not a bad looking horse," Daniel said, climbing onto a higher rung of the fence and leaning toward the battle.

The stallion gained on the front-runners, each stride carrying him closer to the lead. By the time he rounded the next turn, he was nearly even with the leader. Kicking up sod, he charged on, his powerful chest heaving. His coat shimmered with sweat. On the final stretch he hurtled past the lead horse. With his neck extended he reached for more ground, his hooves pummeling the soft earth. Crossing the finish line, he raced alone.

Rebecca leaped and cheered, feeling as if the stallion belonged to her. "He's magnificent!" She turned to Daniel and clasped his hands. "I want him! Can we buy him?"

"What? What use do we have for such an animal? We don't race horses; we work them."

"Yes. I know. But he's so beautiful and so much like Chavive. Just think what a beautiful foal could be produced between him and Chavive."

"We don't have to buy him to accomplish that. Perhaps Mr. O'Neill is offering stud service on him."

"We could ask." Rebecca knew her voice sounded whiny. Trying to sound as businesslike as possible, she added, "If we were to own such a horse, we could produce some splendid foals as well as provide stud service." Rebecca gazed at the animal as he trotted around the track. "I've never seen a horse so much like Chavive and so magnificent. Look how he holds his head. He knows he's won, that he's something special."

"No. There's no need for such an animal at Douloo."

"You wouldn't want to ride him?" Rebecca asked, lifting her brows.

Daniel studied the animal and anticipation touched his eyes. "Indeed. That would be a pleasure."

"Daniel, I've been around horses all my life. I know an exceptional animal when I see one." Rebecca watched as the stallion slowed to a walk.

Daniel stared at the horse.

Rebecca stood closer to Daniel and leaned against him. "It would be something to fill the hours when you're gone. Something special that I could do."

"Rebecca, an animal like that wouldn't be content not to race. It wouldn't be right to close him up on a cattle station."

She studied the stallion. "I suppose . . . Chavive is a fine animal, and she's quite content just as long as she's ridden regularly."

Daniel continued to study the horse.

"I could ride and train him, plus the foals he and Chavive will produce." She grasped Daniel's hand. "We'd have some of the finest foals in the district. Most likely *the* finest."

Daniel slowly shook his head. "I don't know, Rebecca. We've been stretched a bit thin. The drought is taking a toll."

"It's just one more horse. What difference can one horse make to Douloo?"

Still watching the stallion, he said, "We don't even know if Mr. O'Neill will sell him."

"We can ask."

He turned and faced her squarely. "All right. It's against my better judgment, but we'll speak to him."

"Oh, thank you!" Rebecca threw her arms about his neck and hugged him tightly. "You're a wonderful husband."

"I'll remind you of that the next time you think I'm not," Daniel teased.

Rebecca smiled broadly. "Can we speak to Mr. O'Neill right away?"

"Slow down, eh?" Daniel grinned. "I'd like to make some inquiries. I know little about him."

"Of course."

Daniel took her hand. "I'm starved. Let's get something to eat. It's way past lunch." He kept hold of her hand as they walked toward the picnic area.

Jim and Cambria sat in the shade of a eucalyptus tree. Cambria waved and called, "G'day. Please come join us." She flashed a warm smile. Removing her bonnet, she said, "It was so cold this morning when we set out. I was a bit concerned it would rain and ruin the day, but . . ." She glanced at a nearly cloudless sky. "It's turned out to be quite nice."

"I wish it *would* rain," Daniel said. "In case you haven't noticed, the rivers are down, way down."

"Yais. I noticed," Cambria said, her voice surly. "But this is a special day, and if it's going to rain, I'd rather it did so on a day that didn't matter."

Rebecca sat and arranged her skirts properly about her.

"Where's Joseph?" Cambria asked.

"Callie has him."

"Oh." A frown creased Cambria's brow.

"Is something wrong?"

"No. I was just hoping ta see him, is all. I'll just have ta search out Callie." She picked up a basket. "Seems Callie has him quite a lot."

"He was fussing, and I wanted to have a look at one of

150

the horses in that last race. Did you see him, the stallion that won?"

"Yes. He was splendid." Cambria held out a picnic basket. "Would ya like a sandwich? We've plenty. I made several of me own, plus yer Lily gave us extra. I'm certain hers are better than mine."

Rebecca and Daniel each took a sandwich. For a few moments they ate in silence. "I didn't realize how hungry I was," Rebecca said.

She finished her sandwich and then folded her hands in her lap. "I have some news. Daniel and I are going to buy that stallion."

"Wait, now. We haven't even talked with Mr. O'Neill. He may not want to part with him."

"Oh, Daniel. There's always a way," Rebecca said. "I'm sure we can convince him."

Daniel didn't reply. Instead, he took another sandwich.

"He's a beaut," Cambria said. "Wouldn't mind owning a horse like him meself."

"What are you going to do with a racing horse?" Jim asked Rebecca.

"He's such a fine animal and looks so much like Chavive, I was thinking we should breed the two of them. And the stallion would be Daniel's to ride."

"I'd like ta ride him someday," Cambria said.

"If we buy him you'll have a turn on him," Daniel said.

"I wouldn't mind taking him out myself," Jim said.

"I didn't say we are buying him." Daniel frowned at Rebecca, then grudgingly said, "If we do, we'll go for a ride and I'll let you have a turn on him."

"Which is when?" Cambria asked. "From what I've seen, ya've no time for anything but work."

"I'm 'ere today, aren't I?" Daniel challenged.

"Right. You are at that."

151

"Before we can do anything, we need to check out Collin O'Neill," Daniel said. "I don't know much about him. He's new in the district."

"Certainly," Rebecca said. "But I see no harm in speaking to him."

"Rebecca, patience is required 'ere. If he knows you're too eager, you'll pay top dollar."

"I'll manage to restrain my exuberance." She leaned back on her elbows. "When can we speak to him?"

13

Callie lifted Joseph out of his crib. "G'day ta ya, lad."

Joseph smiled and cooed.

"I'll take him," Rebecca said and lifted Joseph out of Callie's arms. She held him close, pressing her cheek against his and then holding him away from her. "My goodness, you're wet. I'd say you need a new nappy, young man." She returned him to his bed and removed his wet diaper and quickly replaced it with a dry one.

Wearing a broad smile and chortling, Joseph twisted and kicked as Rebecca tried to fasten a safety pin. "Ouch!" she gasped as the pin plunged into her finger. She pushed it through the heavy material and fastened it. "You little rascal," she teased, standing him up. Blood seeped from the wound.

Callie took the wet diaper.

"He's getting to be a handful."

Callie handed Rebecca a clean cloth for her bleeding finger. "That he is. He's a strong lad too," she said, dropping the nappy into a pail. "One day he'll be a good man like 'is dad."

"Absolutely." Rebecca wrapped her finger in the cloth and lifted Joseph out of the bed. He snuggled close. "I truly think he looks like his father, don't you?"

"Yais, for sure." Callie smiled. "Got those same bright blue eyes and yellow hair. And he's got an agreeable nature too. Gettin' more like 'im every day." She chucked Joseph under the chin. "Wal, I got work ta do."

"Please stay and visit for a few minutes." Rebecca sat in the rocker. She removed the cloth and checked her finger. It had stopped bleeding. Putting Joseph to her breast, she said, "The bigger he gets, the hungrier he is and the more time I spend in this room by myself. I could use some company."

Callie sat in a straight-backed chair, hands in her lap. She didn't much like inactivity. "I'd be happy ta stay, mum. Course, I 'ave ta get ta me work soon."

Rebecca rocked. "What do you think about giving Joseph solid food? Do you think he's ready?"

"Yer askin' me? I got no bybies." Callie studied the infant. "But he's growin' fast. I'd say maybe yais. Ya might 'ave a go at it."

Rebecca ran a finger along Joseph's cheek. "I was thinking of asking Lily to make him a little mush this morning."

"I figure he'd like that well enough." Callie grinned. "From the looks of things, he likes ta eat." She stood as if to go.

"Callie . . ."

"Yais, mum?"

"Daniel and I are thinking of purchasing another horse, a stallion. He'll need some extra training, and I'd like to pair him up with Chavive. That means Chavive will need some extra care, and eventually there will be a foal to look after. I'll need more help with Joseph. Would you mind?"

Callie looked at the baby. "Course not, mum. I'd be 'appy ta care for 'im." She sat in the chair. "Ya sure ya want ta take on more? Bein' a mum and helping Mrs. Thornton is quite a lot."

"I love horses. It won't seem like work at all."

"Ya do 'ave an eye for them, and yer roight good with 'em." She paused and asked, "What does Mr. Thornton think?"

"He doesn't mind. But the horse might be a bit difficult to train. He's been used for racing mostly."

"Ya'd 'ave yer 'ands full, then, eh?" Callie smiled. "But yer a good rider." Her eyes returned to Joseph. "Ya know how I feel 'bout the bybie. Watchin' 'im would be no trouble." She hesitated. "Course, ya might want ta speak with Mrs. Thornton. I still 'ave me duties 'ere."

"Of course. I wouldn't ask for your help if Willa needs you." Rebecca continued to rock. Joseph's eyelids closed. He struggled to open them but finally lost the battle and slept. "I'm excited about the venture. The horse we're buying is a beautiful animal. You'll like him." Rebecca remembered the stallion and how he'd looked on the track.

"If he's a racer, mum, there could be some trouble. Ya be careful, eh?"

"I've dealt with horses a long while. I'll be fine."

The two women sat quietly for a few moments, and then Callie said, "Mum, I been thinkin' . . . there's somethin' I'd like ta show ya."

"Oh, what is it?" Rebecca asked, troubled by Callie's serious tone.

"A special place. No whites 'round 'ere know 'bout it."

"A special place?"

"I can't explain it. I'll 'ave ta show ya."

"All right, then. When?" Rebecca asked, her curiosity piqued. She glanced down at Joseph.

"Wal, if ya 'ave time . . . maybe Miss Mildred or Mrs. Thornton can watch the bybie. And I'll take ya straightaway. It's not far, but probably best if we ride."

"Sounds like fun. I'm sure it'll be no problem finding some-one to watch Joseph." Rebecca slowly rose from the chair and laid the sleeping child in his crib. Her curiosity growing, she hurried downstairs.

☙

As Rebecca and Callie moved across the flats, the air felt cool. A brisk breeze whisked scraps of white clouds across a pale blue sky. As if sensing Rebecca's eagerness, Chavive pranced. Callie's horse, Rena, remained steady.

Callie pulled on the reins and stopped. Studying the open grasslands, she said, "It's not far. Just over that way." She pointed toward a low place in the terrain.

"Why, that's quite close to the house. And you say only blacks know about it?"

"Yais. No whites go there."

"Why is that?"

"Whites ain't interested in such things."

"What things?"

"Ya'll see."

"All right, then." Rebecca gazed at the dry plains and wa-terless clouds. "I wish it would rain."

"Yais. Me too."

"We're having a man put in some wells. That way we can pump water right out of the ground."

"That's good."

"Will the rains come, do you think?" Rebecca asked.

Callie didn't answer right away. Then solemnly she said, "No, mum."

"How can you know?"

She shrugged. "I know, that's all."

"It could rain." Rebecca looked at the place where the

156

blue ceiling touched the earth. "What will we do without water?"

"Can't say, mum." Callie kicked her horse and moved on.

A short time later, what looked like a pile of rocks appeared in the distance. "What's that?" Rebecca asked.

"Gibber."

"I've heard that term before. What does it mean?"

"Oh, big rocks is all, mum. It's where we're going."

Rather than hurrying as Rebecca wanted, Callie continued to move at a slow, steady pace. Rebecca studied her unusual friend. Although she rarely rode, she looked comfortable and confident on Rena's back. Callie always seemed to possess dignity and calm.

"Callie, you and I ought to ride more often. You sit a horse well."

"Ya think so? I like it."

"Well then, we'll ride again . . . soon."

"Yais. Sure."

When they reached the pile of rocks, Callie guided her horse around to the north side, then stopped and dismounted. Leaving the mare tied to a bush, she stepped toward what had appeared to be a shadow. "It's 'ere," she said.

Following, Rebecca could see that an entrance to a cave lay in the shade at the base of the rocks. The boulders looked as if they'd been tossed out and had landed leaning against one another, leaving a dark place hidden beneath the stack.

Callie stepped into the darkness and disappeared.

Apprehensive but eager, Rebecca followed her inside. Blackness closed in around her. It felt cooler beneath the stones. Something scuttled in a distant corner of the chamber. Unsettled at the thought of what might be hidden in the dark, Rebecca remained completely still. "Callie?" Her voice echoed.

"I'm 'ere. Don't fear, mum."

There was the sound of a match being lit, and then a tiny, brilliant light pushed back the darkness. Callie held the flame to the wick of a lantern.

"Was that here?" Rebecca asked.

"Yais. Aborigines 'ave powers, but we can't see without light." She grinned, and her teeth looked very white against her black skin. Lifting the lantern high, she said, "This is what I wanted ta show ya."

Shadows flickered like dancing specters. A lizard darted along a rock ledge, then disappeared into a crevice. Rebecca's eyes moved to a broad, flat wall. It was covered with pictures! "Oh my goodness! What is this?" She moved closer to study the intricate designs. The colors were primarily tawny oranges and yellows. Layers of pictures, some primitive and others complex, were all that remained of the people who had once visited this place.

There were scenes of naked men and women. Some suggested secret ceremonies. There were also pictures of local animals pursued by what appeared to be hunters carrying spears. There was even a drawing of a peculiar-looking fish.

One image in particular was especially striking. A large kangaroo was depicted in vivid red; exceptional detail had been used to create it. She traced the form with her finger. It overlapped another—a very tall person. "Oh my!" Rebecca said, withdrawing her hand as she realized the figure was one of a well-endowed male.

She took a step back from the rock wall and let her eyes follow the images. A hand, fingers extended, seemed to be reaching out to someone or something. The illustration made her feel sad.

Her eyes continued to roam across the painted wall. "What does it all mean?"

"This is the story of me people. Their tales of birth . . .

their lives . . . disease . . . and death. There is much power 'ere." She pointed at a place where a man appeared to be crawling. "This man is dying, and he is crawling up the sickness road."

The image was unclear to Rebecca.

"The people tell how we should live, what we may hunt. And they speak to us 'bout dancing and 'bout loving."

Rebecca's eyes moved from one image to another. "But why pictures?"

"So we can all know the wisdom of the ones who came before. In yer books there are words. If a person cannot read, they cannot understand. But a picture . . ."

"Why did they paint on rock walls?"

"They will be 'ere forever. No one can burn them or throw them away." Callie rested a hand on the figure of a child. "When I came ta Douloo, I was alone. I didn't know people, so I walked. That's how I find this. Woodman became my friend. He knew 'bout the cave. Sometimes he came with me. The power of our spirit ancestors and the strength of the gods makes us stronger."

Rebecca was taken aback by the reverence she heard in Callie's voice, almost as if she were in church.

"The people 'ave always been; we will always be. Creation starts with the land. The gods got up and they walked 'bout. The places where they passed by are sacred. We are from the earth. It is our mother, and one day we will return to 'er arms."

Rebecca gazed at the pictures, trying to fully comprehend their significance. In some places the layers of images made it difficult to make out just what had been painted. "Why are so many of the pictures placed on top of others? I would think it would be better if they could all be seen clearly."

"No. With many there is power. It is better."

Rebecca ran a hand over a part of the wall. "These are

incredible. But it's a shame they weren't created outside in the sunlight so more people could see them."

"This is a good place. The gods were walkin' and they stopped 'ere ta rest and talk. Ya can see that. They leaned close ta each other, so close that they were touching, and they made this cave. Their power is 'ere."

"You believe the rocks were gods?"

"Roight. They are."

Rebecca started to grasp that what Callie was showing her was of great significance. This place was something she would reveal only to someone she considered worthy. "Callie, why did you bring me here?"

"Ya treat me kind and talk ta me. Ya trust me with yer son, and now I share with ya."

Rebecca could feel the sting of tears. "I'm honored." She reached out and grasped Callie's hand. "I think I understand a little better now. I will remember this place."

Callie pointed at a picture of two women. "These lydies are aboriginal like me—they are dancing, they are beautiful." She pointed at what looked like smaller versions of the women. "And their children are 'ere where the mothers watch over 'em." She paused. "Sometimes I wonder if I will be a mum one day. I do not think so."

Feeling the sorrow and resignation she heard in Callie's voice, Rebecca said, "Oh, Callie, I'm sure you will be." Shame touched her. Before this moment, she'd never given Callie's needs or desires much thought.

"I hope yer roight, mum. Family matters more than everything."

Rebecca squeezed Callie's hand. "If that's what you feel in your heart, then I'm certain you'll be blessed with a family one day."

"Sometimes I look out on the land and wonder where me people are—where did I come from?"

"You don't know?"

"No. Just me mum. And she's gone now."

"Then maybe you should find your family."

"It is only a dream, eh? And foolish." She moved toward the cave entrance. "We should go." Callie extinguished the lantern and stepped out into the sunlight, and Rebecca followed. They shaded their eyes against the brightness.

Callie gazed out over the dry land and scrub. "One day I'll go back ta me mother, the earth. That's me family."

Rebecca felt heaviness in her heart. Callie really had no one she could call family. And her creator was mysterious and veiled. Yet Rebecca could feel her reverence for her spiritual roots. She caught a hint of how difficult it would be for Callie to accept the white man's account of a heavenly Father as creator. To believe, Callie would have to turn her back on her ancestors and the knowledge passed down through the centuries—all the stories spoken and visual images given. She would have to turn away from what she knew to be true and sacred.

How could she help Callie see that God was alive—that he wasn't a rock or a piece of ground?

She turned and looked back at the cave where generations had left parts of themselves. It was unfathomable to consider how many remarkable people had stopped here and, after contributing to the hidden canvas, had walked on. And yet she understood that even the greatest artistry, the finest people, all ended the same—they became dust. In the end this magnificent work would mean nothing.

14

Rebecca signed her name and then reread the letter she'd written to Collin O'Neill. It was important that it be done properly. She didn't want to miss an opportunity to buy the stallion.

Finally satisfied that it was professional and reasonable, she folded the letter and slid it into an envelope. As she sealed the envelope, her emotions were a mix of excitement and trepidation. She set it on the desk and stared at it. What if the horse was too much for her? Cambria hadn't been the only one to caution her. Willa and Mildred had both been concerned about her taking on a high-strung stallion. *He might be quite docile*, she told herself, knowing it was unlikely.

With resolve she picked up the letter, pushed back her chair, and hurried downstairs. Woodman would be going into town soon. She needed to get the letter to him before he left. Taking quick steps, her skirt sweeping up dust as she went, Rebecca crossed the yard to the carriage house.

Woodman stood in the shade, grooming one of the Morgans tied to an outside post. He ran the brush across the animal's side and with each stroke followed it with an open hand, kindly smoothing the animal's dark coat.

"Woodman," Rebecca said.

He turned and faced her, resting a hand on the animal's back. "G'day, mum." He smiled, and his plump face creased into deep folds, nearly enveloping his dark brown eyes.

"Thank goodness I caught you. I was afraid you'd already gone." Rebecca patted the horse's neck. "He's a fine animal."

"That he is."

Rebecca offered Woodman the letter. "While you're in town, could you post this for me?"

He took the envelope and dropped it into his shirt pocket. "Roight. No trouble at all." He returned to brushing. "Important letter, mum?"

"Perhaps. I'm writing to that man we met at the races—Mr. O'Neill."

"Yais. I remember him. Seemed like a fine bloke. Horse trader, roight?"

"Yes."

Woodman's arm settled at his side, and he turned a steady gaze on Rebecca. "S'pose we ought ta know more 'bout him if yer thinking of doing business with him. I'll ask 'round if ya like."

"That would be fine. Daniel's already done some checking, and he hasn't discovered anything unsavory about the man."

"Good, then."

"Well, have a fine day," she said and walked back to the house, hoping she wouldn't have to wait long before hearing from Collin.

~

The waiter filled Daniel's and Rebecca's coffee cups. "Anything else I can get for ya, Mr. Thornton?"

"No, we're fine 'ere."

With a nod, the young man returned to the kitchen.

"This is quite good," Rebecca said, taking a bite of chicken. "It would be nice if we could dine out more often."

Daniel chewed a bite of roast beef. His mouth full, he said, "Figure someone will think me a real duffer, eating 'ere when we've plenty at home." He lowered his voice. "Lily's cooking is better. She could give the cook 'ere a few lessons, I'd say." He grinned.

"True, but the food's good. In Boston we used to eat out occasionally. It was considered sociable. And this is nice, just the two of us."

Daniel reached across the table and grasped Rebecca's hand. "I must admit, it is at that."

Rebecca squeezed his hand. She searched Daniel's face. His skin was dark from the sun, and the lines at the corners of his eyes gave him a look of maturity. "I love you so much, Daniel. I want to spend more time together."

"I want that too." A soft smile touched his lips. "We'll come 'ere again."

"That would be nice." Rebecca released his hand and took a sip of her coffee. With a grimace, she held the cup away from her. "But no coffee next time. It's quite strong." She set down the cup. "I heard from him."

"From who?"

"Mr. O'Neill. You know, the horse trader we met at the races."

Daniel nodded. "Right. I remember."

"I wrote to him. And he's invited us to his home."

"It seems he's got a good reputation, but it's quite a trip to Roma. Seems a long way to go for a horse."

"You'd make the trip if you had an interest in a prize bull."

"Right. I would at that." Daniel furrowed his brows. "I don't know that I feel good about you taking on that horse."

"I thought you were in favor of buying him? Is it the money?"

"No. We're good on that count, for now anyway. He's a fine animal, but . . ."

"Daniel, we've already talked about this. I can train him to work the cattle." Rebecca moved her plate aside and rested her arms on the table. "And can you see us—you on the stallion and me on Chavive? We'd be a striking pair. And any foals they produce will be grand."

"You sure it won't be too much for you? Taking care of the baby and working with the horses? You've already got quite a lot to do."

"No. Of course not. It would be fun. I don't think I'd be putting in much more time than I do now."

"Right." He looked down at his hands, which rested on either side of his plate. "It's probably not a good idea to buy stock right now. The drought's getting worse."

"He's not just stock. He's special."

Daniel picked up his knife and fork and sawed at his meat. "You're being stubborn, Rebecca. I'd like to buy him, but sometimes we've just got to be reasonable."

"Are you saying I'm not?"

"No. But what are you going to do if we have to sell off the stock, including the stallion?"

"It won't come to that. I'm sure of it."

Daniel rested serious eyes on Rebecca. "You haven't been through an Australian drought. You haven't seen what it can do."

"That's true, but I know God will take care of us no matter what we have to face."

Daniel let out a long breath. "And sometimes he just wants us to be practical."

Rebecca held her breath and waited, then finally asked, "So can we go and look at the stallion?"

"Yes, but I'm not promising anything."

"You already promised." Rebecca folded her hands in front of her, fighting for calm.

"I didn't."

"Yes, Daniel, you did. When we saw him at the track, you told me we could buy him."

Daniel studied her. "If you recall, I never said we'd buy him, only that I would consider it. I want to have another look at him. It's never wise to make rash decisions."

"I seriously doubt that waiting for weeks would make this a rash decision. You and Woodman have looked into Mr. O'Neill's character, and we've already seen the horse. I'm going to buy him."

Daniel squared his jaw and in a loud voice said, "We'll buy him if I say we can."

People turned to look.

Rebecca glanced about the café and then stared down at her hands. Controlling her own temper, she said, "Please, lower your voice. People are staring."

Silence hung over Daniel and Rebecca. Daniel returned to eating. Rebecca sipped her coffee, now unaware of its bitterness.

Finally Daniel said, "We must make important decisions together."

"All right. We'll have a look at him and then decide."

Daniel set his fork on his plate. With a shake of his head, he said, "I don't know . . . I have a bad feeling, Rebecca. Something's not right."

⯁

Nerves on edge, Rebecca climbed into the surrey. Daniel followed and sat beside her. Thomas and Mildred were already seated in the back. Today the four would travel to Roma, where Daniel and Rebecca would meet with Collin O'Neill and take another look at the stallion.

Seated so she could look into the backseat, Rebecca said, "I'm so glad you two are coming with us."

Thomas smiled. "It makes for an adventure." His brown eyes settled on Mildred. "I'm all for adventures."

"When we get to Roma, I'd rather do some shopping than look at horses. Do you mind if I stay in town while you go out to Mr. O'Neill's?" Mildred asked.

"No, Auntie. Not at all. But I don't want you out on your own."

"I'll be more than happy to escort Mildred about town," Thomas said.

Woodman flicked the reins and clicked his tongue, and the horses set out. Rebecca looked at the porch where Willa stood, Joseph in her arms. It had been decided that the baby would stay. Rebecca felt a pang of regret but managed to smile and wave. "Good-bye. I'll be back tomorrow," she called.

Willa lifted Joseph's arm and waved for him. "Say bye-bye."

Rebecca held on to her smile, then finally turned and settled back in her seat. *Sooner or later he must get used to me being gone*, she told herself. *He'll be fine.* She looked at Mildred. "I think I miss him already. I've never left him before."

"I'm sure it's not easy for you, but I'd say it's good for a mother to get out without her children now and again." She looked at Daniel. "Don't you think so, Daniel?"

"Right. They'll both be better for it."

"I suppose," Rebecca said, unconvinced. She watched him as the surrey moved away. "Maybe we should bring him."

"Nonsense," Mildred said. "The trip will be tiring for him. He'll be much happier at home."

Daniel put an arm about Rebecca's shoulders and pulled her close. "It will give us a bit of time alone, eh?"

Rebecca nodded and leaned against Daniel.

"I really must visit the millinery shop in Roma," Mildred said. "They have some lovely hats." She smiled. "Roma's not a bustling city, but it does offer more than Thornton Creek. You don't suppose they have an orchestra, do you?"

"No, Auntie. I'm sure not. But perhaps a minstrel show." She gazed at her aunt. "You're missing Boston, aren't you?"

"I must admit, I am." Mildred glanced at Thomas and then turned her gaze to the empty countryside.

For a while the foursome traveled in silence.

Growing bored and uncomfortable, Rebecca convinced Woodman to allow her to drive. Sitting beside him, she remembered how she'd tricked him into teaching her to handle a team when she'd planned her escape from Queensland and a return to America.

The feel of the reins in her hands and watching the muscled hindquarters of the Morgans brought back the morning's events of the day she'd attempted to flee—that horrible moment when Bertram had fallen and been trampled. Rebecca closed her mind to the dreadful incident and concentrated on driving and on the countryside. Rain still had not come to the flats, and each passing mile revealed more of the drought and its cost—dry riverbeds, vultures feasting on dead livestock, sparse grass, and even gum trees that seemed withered.

Maybe Daniel's right. Perhaps it's not a good idea to buy a horse right now. She glanced back at her husband. His eyes were closed. He'd fallen asleep. "Woodman, you've never said a thing about our buying the stallion."

"Not me business, mum." He kept his eyes forward.

"I'd like your opinion."

"It's not for me ta say. This is yers and Daniel's decision."

He picked up a canteen of water from the floor at his feet. "Daniel knows what he's doing," he said, unscrewing the lid and taking a drink.

Silence settled between the two. "I convinced him to have a look. And I'd like to know your opinion."

Woodman took another drink, replaced the lid on the canteen, and set it back on the floor. Glancing at her, he rested his arms on his thighs. "Not a good time to buy a fancy horse, mum."

"How so?"

"Drought gonna be bad."

"How can you know?"

"Just do."

Rebecca wanted to throttle Woodman. He always seemed to "just know." If she listened to him, she was certain someone else would buy the stallion. "It's just one horse," she finally said.

"Roight. But ya'll 'ave a lot of time inta trainin', and then when things get bad ya'll 'ave ta let 'im go . . . if ya can find someone ta buy 'im, that is. It'll be hard on ya." He went silent a moment, then continued. "And a horse like that needs a strong 'and."

"I can be strong."

Woodman smiled down at her. "I s'pose ya can be at that, mum."

✿

Midday, the group stopped to eat among a grove of acacia. A small stream cut across the open landscape and wound through the trees before trailing off through the grasslands.

"Not good," Woodman said.

"What's not good?" Mildred asked.

"This 'ere is usually big water." He gazed at the rivulet. "Soon it'll be dry." He returned to eating his tucker.

"Are you certain?" Mildred asked.

"Certain as a man can be."

Daniel drank from a canteen, washing down a bite of bread. "Never knew you to be wrong."

Woodman settled his gaze on Mildred and Thomas. "Ya might want ta begin thinking 'bout takin' that big boat back ta America. It's gonna get mean 'round 'ere."

All eyes turned to Mildred.

She fiddled with her collar. "I don't know. I rather feel as if I belong here."

"I'll be staying on for a while," Thomas said. "Some of the gentlemen in the district wanted me to have a look at their accounts. And I'm not afraid of a drought."

"Do as ya please." Woodman stood and grabbed the horses' reins and led them to the stream.

Daniel walked along with him.

"I think I'll freshen up a bit," Mildred said, standing. She walked to the creek, knelt down, and dampened her handkerchief, then used it to pat her face and neck.

Wearing a frown, Thomas watched her. "I suppose I should go back to Boston. I don't really belong here. But I keep hoping she'll come around."

"I thought things were better between you," Rebecca said.

"Better, yes. But she's still not given me an answer." Thomas plucked a piece of dry grass. "How long should a fellow wait?" He looked at Rebecca, unable to disguise the pain he felt. "Mildred's caught hold of my heart."

Rebecca nodded slightly. "You must tell her, Thomas."

"I have."

"Tell her again."

"I'm beginning to think she'll never return to Boston.

And . . ." His gaze roamed over the desolate countryside. "I don't fit here. And I like Boston." He nodded at Daniel and Woodman. "I'm not like them. They know this place. Sometimes I believe Woodman can hear the earth speak to him."

"I believe he does." Rebecca leaned back on her hands. Her eyes wandered to Mildred. "I don't think you have to worry about Mildred staying. She loves Boston too. She'll return in due time. Although I wish she'd stay."

"I have a business in Boston . . . and limited finances. Soon I'll be forced to return." He studied Mildred as she knelt and ran a hand through the stream. "She's a fine woman. I love her," he added, his throat sounding tight. Glancing at Rebecca, he continued, "I've actually considered closing my business and remaining here . . . if that's what she wants. I'd do it for her." He shrugged. "But she won't tell me what she wants."

"You need to talk with her again. Perhaps she can tell you what she's afraid of. I know she thinks highly of you."

"I'll give it a try," he said, sounding discouraged.

⤻

Hat in hand, Collin O'Neill walked across the lobby of the Roma Hotel. He carried himself with confidence, giving the impression he was a bigger man than he actually was. Wearing a broad smile, he approached Daniel, extending a hand. "G'day. I hope you had a satisfactory journey."

"It was fine."

Collin turned to Rebecca. "And good to see you. I must say, I was surprised to receive your letter. It's been a while since the races, and I figured you'd given up on the idea of buying Noble."

"That's a fine name," Rebecca said.

"Right from the start the name fit him. He knew he was special. Stood up faster than any colt I've ever seen and was moving about his stall and meeting his admirers right off." He smiled. "He's a fine one." Collin spat tobacco juice into a spittoon. "I've a few other horses you might be interested in—good, solid stock."

"No," Daniel said. "We're just here to look at the roan."

"Right, then. Shall we go out to my property and have a look? It's not far."

Collin's home was like many in Queensland. It sat alone, huddling in meager shade provided from sparse shrubs and trees. Long and low-slung, it had a broad veranda that wrapped around two-thirds of the house. Corrals and barns were scattered over the dry acreage.

Collin moved toward a nearby paddock. "I've a fine mare 'ere."

"We're interested in the stallion," Daniel said, irritation in his voice.

Ignoring Daniel's comment, Collin stopped at the paddock where a handsome bay mare stood at a watering trough. "Name's Miss. Good, solid mare—always been quite proper. She's ready to foal in a month's time. The sire's a sturdy working horse. Won't find a finer animal. As you can see, she's powerful. Right good stock."

The mare trotted around the enclosure as if she knew she was on display. Her gait was smooth and balanced.

Rebecca stepped up to the railing. "She's a beauty." The mare moved to Rebecca and rested her head against the top rung of the fence. Rebecca scratched the area between her ears and then smoothed the hair down the front of her face. Glancing at Daniel, she said, "Did I hear you tell Jim we needed a good cutting horse?"

"Yeah. We do, but that's not why we're 'ere."

"I know, but she's lovely and quite powerful looking. She

and the foal would be fine additions. I can help train her and take care of the foal."

Daniel leaned close to Rebecca and said quietly, "You have enough to do now. I really don't see that—"

"I can do it. Please. She's a fine horse."

Respectfully Collin stepped away, allowing Daniel and Rebecca privacy.

"You want to buy her instead of the stallion?"

"No. In addition to."

Daniel blew out an exasperated breath. "Rebecca, the drought. You know the trouble we're facing."

"One more horse won't make a difference."

"Two more."

"If we have to, we'll sell them. You said we could do that, right?"

"Right. Yes." He rubbed the back of his neck. "All right." He smiled his surrender. "As you wish. I hope it won't be too much for you."

Collin rejoined them. "So have you made a decision?"

"We'd like to include the mare in our purchase." Rebecca caught Daniel's eye. "That is, if we buy the stallion."

"Good choice." Collin smiled. "The stallion's in the paddock back 'ere." He led the way.

Rebecca's nerves fairly popped. She'd admired the stallion since the first moment she'd seen him. It would be incredible to own him.

They walked to the enclosure. Rebecca's excitement climbed when she got her first glimpse of the chestnut-colored roan. He was well muscled and balanced, obviously in top condition. "He's a bit heavier than most race horses," she said, trying to disguise her enthusiasm.

"Right. But it hasn't slowed him down a bit. You saw him race."

"He was fast, all right," Daniel said. "But we're looking

for a horse that can do more than run. He's got to be smart and hold up to a day's work."

"This isn't a workhorse, Mr. Thornton. You don't mean to put him in a harness do you?"

"No. But I'll be riding him, and the station's large. Also, we drive herds south for sale. He'll need stamina."

"He's got that, all right."

Collin grabbed a handful of grain from a bin and extended it in his hand. "Noble. Come on, lad." The animal trotted toward Collin. His gait was balanced and light. He pressed his nose into the outstretched hand and, with a smacking of his lips, licked up the grain.

Rebecca squeezed between the corral boards and leaned out to pat him. He shied slightly. "Steady, boy." She ran a hand over his neck. He quieted. When the grain was gone, he sniffed her arm. Rebecca caressed his silky nose. He nickered and then nuzzled her. "He's quite friendly, isn't he?"

"Right, but he's got a lot of spirit."

"Can you lead him out?" Daniel asked. He stood tall, his arms folded over his chest.

Collin stepped into the paddock, clipped a lead on the stallion's halter, and led him out of the gate. The horse flicked his tail, moving nimbly.

Rebecca studied him. He had good lines. Running a hand along his side, down his flanks, and then along his legs, she noticed he remained calm. She detected no weaknesses.

"Could you lunge him for us?" Daniel asked.

"Right." Collin got a lunge line, and the horse galloped around the arena.

Rebecca was more convinced that she wanted him. His gait was smooth and uniform. She looked at Daniel. "What do you think?"

"He's a fine animal," Daniel said, admiration lighting his eyes.

Rebecca knew Daniel had been won over.

He took the lunge line from Collin and worked with the horse a few minutes, then brought him to a walk and approached the animal. Running a hand over his glistening coat, he said, "You're a fine one, all right." He patted his neck. "How much you want for him?"

15

Daniel leaned on the table and stared down at his plate of eggs. He was nearly too tired to eat.

"Is there somethin' wrong with the food?" Lily asked.

"No. It's fine." Daniel took a bite of egg. "I'm just a bit weary is all."

"You're working too hard," Willa said. "You ought to slow down."

"I will . . . soon." Daniel didn't know how or when that might happen. There was so much that needed to be done. The responsibility felt overwhelming.

Rebecca pushed away from the breakfast table. "I've got a mare that needs to be checked. Today could be the day."

"The foal?" Willa asked.

Rebecca carried a plate to the sink. "Yes. Miss has been acting restless and her milk is in. I'm sure the foal will be here any time. But I think Miss is waiting until she's alone. It seems horses prefer solitude for foaling." She washed her hands. "I'd best go out and see if she's all right. Can you watch Joseph for me? He's still sleeping but ought to be up any time. If I'm not back, a bit of mush should satisfy his hunger."

"I'll go up and check on him, then," Willa said.

"I'll be out after I finish eating," Daniel said.

Rebecca moved to the table and leaned down and kissed him.

He gave her a crooked smile. "You must be more tired than me. You barely slept."

"Actually, I'm not tired at all. I think it's the anticipation." She smiled and took a deep breath.

Daniel squeezed her hand. "If you need help come running, eh?"

"Is Mildred still sleeping?" Willa asked.

"Yes," Rebecca said. "She seemed especially tired last night."

"And where's Thomas?"

"I expect he's still sleeping too," Daniel said. "He's the reason Mildred was up late. They sat in the kitchen visiting until late."

"You don't suppose they have decided to get married, do you?" Willa asked.

"If that were so, I doubt Auntie would still be asleep. She'd have been up with the chickens to tell us all." Rebecca smiled. "I'm sure an announcement will come . . . eventually. My aunt just needs to say yes."

"You think she will, then?" Willa asked.

"I do. She's just a bit confused right now. I know she cares deeply for Thomas, and he obviously loves her." Rebecca retied a ribbon that held back her dark hair and then turned and headed for the kitchen door. "I've got work to do," she said brightly, stepping onto the porch.

Feeling a disquiet he didn't quite understand, Daniel watched Rebecca through the kitchen window as she walked toward the barn. She swung her arms freely and her step was light. She seemed to possess an abundance of confidence and trust. His faith felt feeble compared with hers.

A cup of tea in her hands, Willa sat across from Daniel. "Are you all right? You look worried."

"I'm fine." Daniel offered what he hoped was a confident smile.

Willa sipped her tea. "I barely see you these days. And I dare say, you see little of your wife and son." She watched as Rebecca disappeared inside the barn. "You need each other, especially in these hard times."

"It's the way of things, Mum. Don't fret."

"How bad are things, Daniel? Really?"

Daniel didn't answer right away.

"Your father used to share troubles with me, and we'd pray together. Now I feel ignorant of our circumstances."

"We've a rough patch ahead, but we'll be fine."

"Really?" Willa met his gaze. "That's not what I see in your eyes."

Daniel turned his attention to the barn. "The drought's bad. But we'll make it. We always have."

"How bad? What about the wells?"

Daniel pushed his plate aside. "The main river's real low; the other streams are drying up. But the man who's drilling the wells will be 'round soon. He's working for another bloke right now, but he said it wouldn't be long until he gets to work 'ere." Daniel picked up his cup of coffee and took a sip. It was cold. He set down the cup. "Wish Dad were 'ere. And I could sure use Elton."

Sorrow touched Willa's eyes. "I miss them. And I'm so sorry this trouble has fallen on your shoulders."

Daniel didn't speak. He stared down into his nearly empty cup. What would they do if the rains didn't come? How would they survive?

Willa reached across the table and lay a hand over Daniel's. "Everything will work out. You'll see."

Daniel nodded. "I think about how Grandfather settled 'ere. He had a vision of what Douloo would be one day. He worked hard, and then Dad made Douloo even grander. Now it's my responsibility and . . . and I'm afraid I'll lose it all."

"No. Never, Daniel. That won't happen." Willa offered an encouraging smile. "We'll manage . . . all of us, together."

"That's roight, mum," Lily said, as she scrubbed a cast-iron skillet. "Douloo is like the land. It'll stay put."

"I pray you're right." Daniel reached for his hat sitting on the end of the table and settled it on his head. "I better see if Rebecca needs me."

"A new life's 'bout ta come inta the world," Lily said. "That's a good sign, eh?" She smiled broadly.

"That's right," Willa said. "It's the best sign."

"Rebecca's happy." Daniel ran a finger along the brim of his hat, then looked up at his mother. "She has no doubt things are going to be all right. I'm the one who lacks faith. Sometimes I wonder what it's about, the struggle."

"It's the struggles that make us strong," Willa said. "And here on the flats, that's important."

"Right." Daniel opened the door. "Well, if there's a foal being born, I might be needed."

Feeling a bit more optimistic, Daniel joined Rebecca. "How's she doing?"

"It'll be soon." Rebecca moved close to Daniel and leaned against him. "I'm glad you're here."

Woodman, who had been examining the mare, stepped out of the stall. "That foal will be 'ere in no time."

179

Over the next few hours, Rebecca and Woodman waited and watched. Daniel was in and out of the barn, leaving most of the responsibility in Woodman's and Rebecca's hands. He managed to be there just before the foal made its appearance. In active labor, the mare lay down. Grunting, nostrils flaring, she pushed. Rebecca knelt beside her and ran a hand over her abdomen. In a soothing tone, she said, "It's all right, Miss. You're doing well."

The horse looked at Rebecca, eyes wide. She dropped her head to the hay bed, then acted as if she might rise when the next contraction hit. She whinnied softly and pushed again and again. A hoof appeared, then another. Finally a nose emerged. With a blast of air from her nostrils and a heavy grunt, the mare pushed, expelling a foal covered in a transparent cocoon.

Immediately Rebecca worked with Woodman to release the baby from the bag of waters and to clear its nostrils. The new arrival took a breath and then lay on its side. Rebecca rubbed down its coat. "It's a colt!"

"He's a handsome one," Daniel said, smiling broadly. "A bay just like his mum."

"He's a beaut, all roight," Woodman said.

Rebecca stood beside Daniel and watched the mare and her foal become acquainted. Miss stood and started licking her baby. For a long while the colt lay quietly in the hay, but finally he stuck his front feet straight out in front and then tried to lift a quaking hind end. He tottered there for a moment and then fell.

"Ah, there he goes," Woodman said.

The colt lay in the hay, panting. A few moments later he tried again to stand. This time he managed to make it up on all fours, but he'd planted his front legs wide apart, and when his mother licked him, down he went. Not to be defeated, he tried once more.

"Persistent, eh?" Daniel chuckled. "I figure he'll be a determined one, then."

The colt got to his feet, and this time mother and son nuzzled each other. The foal searched for a meal and found it, his tail flicking in delight as he took his first nourishment.

Rebecca cuddled under Daniel's arm. "He's beautiful, isn't he?"

"Yes. Fine indeed. He'll make a good addition to our stock. Course, you might be able to get a fine price for him if you're willing to sell him."

"Let's not talk of selling right now." Rebecca studied the colt. "He's quite spectacular. I would like to keep him."

Daniel draped an arm around Rebecca's waist and gave her a squeeze. "You have to be practical, luv. He ought to be worth a fair bit. We'd be foolhardy to hang on to him. Douloo will likely need the money. We've lost some stock to the drought already. And we'll be spending plenty on the wells."

"Have you ever considered selling off a portion of Douloo?" Rebecca asked.

Instantly angry, Daniel stared at Rebecca. "You think I'd do such a thing? Not a piece of this ground will be let go while I'm running this station."

"But we have so much. We could sell a section and it would never be missed."

"No! I'll not sell any part of my grandfather's heritage."

"But it makes sense, Daniel."

"Enough." Shocked and angry, he stared at her. Without another word, he turned on his heel and stalked out of the barn.

Willa stood just outside the door. She leveled a questioning look at her son.

"How can she not understand?" he muttered, glancing back at Rebecca. "I'll let none of it go. I'll keep this station in fine shape. Just have to work harder is all."

181

"Daniel, there's a limit to what a man can do. If it's God's will that we preserve Douloo, then he'll see to it. This is bigger than just one man. You can't rely on *your* strength only."

"And what am I to do, then? Throw up my arms and say, 'Do it for me, God'? No. I'll have to work for it. It'll take more than a bit of faith to hold on to Douloo." He pulled off his hat and swiped a hand through his hair. "And where is God? Already we've lost a portion of the herd."

"Daniel," Willa said, grasping her son's arm.

Daniel took a deep breath, blew it out, and then continued more calmly. "Everything will be fine. Douloo will be fine. Please don't worry. I'm sorry for my outburst."

"I'm all right, but it frightens me to see *you* losing heart."

"I'm just frustrated." He turned and faced the barn, folding his arms over his chest. He truly didn't know what to do other than to keep going one day at a time. Finally, he turned and looked at his mother. "We've a fine new foal, reason to rejoice, eh?" He managed to smile. "And that's what I'm going to do."

Daniel and Jim rode toward the southern edge of the station. Cattle had been spotted wandering beyond its borders, and they needed to be rounded up. Daniel's mind, however, wasn't on the misplaced stock but rather on his mother's words of faith. He'd acted as if he agreed with her, but in truth he'd been tussling with God. Why did hardship touch the faithful?

I've done nothing to deserve your reproof, Lord. I'm not fault-less, but I've done my best to obey you and to trust you. I've worked hard. I've watched over my family and Douloo. And I've not missed church nor forsaken my prayers.

Daniel gazed at withered grasslands, his mind turning to

182

a Scripture that taunted him. "He maketh his sun to rise on the evil and on the good, and sendeth rain on the just and on the unjust." Daniel knew he possessed no guarantee of protection from hardships.

"Hard to know just what you're getting with scrubs," Jim said. "Could be someone else's cattle."

"No one grazes that area. Wild or not, I figure they're ours."

"They're liable to give us trouble."

"And if we leave 'em, we'll be facing poddy dodgers."

"S'pose you're right. Better to deal with a rowdy scrub today than be forced to run down thieves tomorrow." Jim grinned.

"Right." Again, the words "He maketh his sun to rise on the evil and on the good, and sendeth rain on the just and on the unjust" rolled through his mind.

"Everything all right?" Jim asked.

"Yeah. Fine."

"You've just been quieter than usual."

"Been thinkin'. There's a lot needs to be done." Daniel lifted his hat and smoothed back his hair. Squinting into the sun, he studied the empty plains. "We ought to come across that mob any time."

"I'll wager they're down at the creek."

"Not much out 'ere for them. Even the cool weather doesn't help, not without rain. I was out at the billabong yesterday. Even it's drying up." Daniel replaced his hat. "We'd better find water in the boreholes."

"Drilling going on yet?"

"Soon." Daniel's eyes settled on a grove of gum trees huddled together as if seeking shelter from promised winter storms. "Time for a rest, eh?"

As if understanding his rider's words, Daniel's horse picked up his pace and headed for the grove. Daniel and Jim dismounted, tied the horses, and sat on a log in the sunshine.

After gulping water from a canteen, Daniel screwed the lid back on and rested his arms on bent knees. "The horses will be needing a drink too."

Jim sat on the ground and leaned against a downed tree. "I feel as parched as the land. Sometimes I dream of rain. When I was growing up back in New York, seemed we always had more than enough of the wet stuff. A summer storm was a playground for us kids. The wetter we got, the more we liked it."

Daniel nodded and gazed at a hazy sky.

"Got to admit, at times like this I wonder why I stay."

"You thinking about going back to the States?"

"Nah. Not really. Been here too long." Jim took a drink. "Don't have anyone there anyway."

"Right. And Cambria's 'ere, eh?"

"That she is," Jim said lifting a brow.

"When're you going to ask her to marry you?"

Jim screwed the cap back on his canteen. "Don't know that she'd have me."

"Come on, now. She's smitten. And you know it."

"Maybe. But I can't ask her until I have a piece of ground to call my own."

"'Round 'ere don't know that you'd want any, not just now anyway."

"The drought will see its last day."

Daniel nodded, then turned his attention to something rustling in the nearby brush. "What you think we have there?"

"S'pose we ought to find out," Jim said, pushing to his feet.

Daniel stood.

The horses nickered and fidgeted. "It's got them nervous,"

Daniel said, grabbing the rifle from his saddle and cautiously moving toward the brush. Jim did the same and followed closely.

Rifle cocked, Daniel walked alongside the scrub and peered into the shadows. Jim moved toward the far end. All of a sudden a dark blur broke out of the brush and hurtled itself straight at Jim. With an angry squeal, a boar hit him below the knees, burying a tusk in his left leg. Jim howled and brought the butt of his rifle down on the animal's head. The boar squalled and then trotted off. Grabbing his leg, Jim fell to the ground.

Daniel raised his gun and fired. He missed. Knowing the boar wasn't done with Jim, Daniel reloaded and ran toward his friend. He needed to get between the drover and the angry boar. "Go on! Get!" he hollered.

The animal turned his foul temper on Daniel and rushed him. Daniel leaped to one side but didn't completely avoid a tusk. It tore into his pant leg and grazed the skin on his calf. Daniel glanced at the wound. Blood oozed through his dungarees, and he could feel it trickle down his leg.

The enraged boar turned and headed back at Daniel. Taking a calming breath, Daniel rested his rifle on his arm and took aim. He couldn't afford to miss. Over the years, he'd known more than one man killed by a wild boar. Holding his arm steady, Daniel didn't breathe as he squeezed the trigger and fired. With a thud, the animal fell. He didn't move.

Daniel ran for Jim. "You all right?"

"Yeah. I'll live," Jim said, wincing as he tried to stand.

"Stay put." Daniel leaned over him. He pulled out a knife and cut open Jim's pant leg. "He got you pretty good," he said, inspecting an angry wound. The boar had managed to sink a tusk into Jim's calf and had torn it wide open, laying back the flesh clear to the bone.

"Looks bad. We'll get you back to the house and let the doc have a look at it. He'll make it right as rain in no time."

"And what about you?" Jim asked, nodding at Daniel's bloodied pants.

He pulled up the leg of his dungarees and took a quick look. "It's nothing more than a scratch." He shoved down his pant leg and put an arm around Jim. "Can you manage?"

"Yeah. Think so," Jim said, pushing off the ground. He sucked air through his teeth and closed his eyes but managed to hobble to his horse. "Wish it was my right leg," he said, eyeing the stirrup. "Make it a lot easier."

"Mount from the other side. I'll give you a hand." While Jim grabbed hold of the saddle horn, Daniel pushed. Jim managed to settle into the saddle but had to leave the injured leg free of the stirrup. Blood dripped from his wound.

"Hold on a minute. That's bleeding pretty good," Daniel said, taking off his bandanna. "Hold tight. This'll hurt." He tied the kerchief tightly around the wound. "That ought to help." Jim had broken into a sweat, and his skin looked pallid. "You gonna be all right?" Daniel asked, handing him the reins.

"Yeah, but we better get moving. Don't know how long I can ride."

"Right," Daniel said, his mind returning to the question he had for God. Why? Why the hardships? What good could be served by allowing Jim to be injured? Wasn't life hard enough?

16

Daniel favored his injured leg as he and Rebecca moved toward the barn. His encounter with the boar had left a badly bruised and swollen calf.

Still anxious over what had happened, Rebecca kept a hand on Daniel's arm. "You're sure you're all right? You ought to stay off that leg."

"No worries. It'll be fine."

"You and Jim could have been killed."

"Right. But we weren't. It's little more than a scrape."

"It's much worse than that. It looks ghastly."

"Dr. Walker stitched it up and said I'll be fine." Reassuringly Daniel pressed his hand against Rebecca's back.

"And Jim, what of him? His injuries are quite serious."

"It'll take him some time to come around, but the doctor said he'll mend."

"I must say, Cambria took it all quite well."

"She's lived 'ere all her life. Troubles come to everyone. She knows that, and she's seen worse." Daniel tried to sound nonchalant, but Rebecca wasn't convinced. He picked up his pace slightly. "So what have you got planned for the day?"

"I was thinking of spending some time with Noble. He's coming along quite nicely, but he needs more training."

"Sorry I haven't given him more time."

"You've been busy."

"Make sure someone's out 'ere with you. Don't want any accidents."

Rebecca pulled her coat closed. "Chilly this morning."

"That it is."

"What are *you* going to be doing today?"

"I'm meeting with the bloke who's putting in our wells. He said there's no reason not to get started straightaway."

"What happens if we don't find water?"

"No worries. Jessop's good at what he does. He'll give it a fair go." Daniel gave her arm a squeeze. "He'll find water."

"How long do you think it will take?"

"Don't know. It'll depend on how deep we have to go and whether he hits rock or not." Daniel stopped. "I've got to go to the carriage house," he said, kissing her lightly. "Have a good day, eh?"

"You too." Rebecca walked toward the barn and headed straight for the stall with the new colt. Today he'd get his first look at the world.

"How are you doing, young fellow?" she asked when she reached the stall door. The mare lay in the hay; the foal stood in a corner. "Miss?" Feeling a pulse of apprehension, Rebecca opened the stall door and stepped inside. "Miss," she said more insistently and dropped to her knees beside the mare.

She ran a hand over the animal's neck. She was damp. The mare's eyes were wide and her nostrils flared, but she didn't lift her head.

"Daniel! Woodman!" Rebecca yelled, startling the colt. He bolted to the other corner of the stall.

Rebecca ran out of the barn and into the yard. "Daniel! Woodman! Please come quickly!"

The two appeared almost immediately. "What is it?" Daniel asked, running toward her, his limp slowing him down only slightly. "What's wrong?"

"It's Miss. She's sick or something!"

Woodman didn't ask any questions. He headed straight for the stall. Rebecca and Daniel followed.

⁂

"Yais, yer fine," Woodman said gently, kneeling beside the downed horse. Looking her over, he felt her face and neck. "She's sweating—fevered. And 'er panting's not a good sign." When he finally stood he said, "I've seen it before."

"Is she going to be all right?"

Woodman didn't answer right away. "Probably not, mum." He looked at the frightened colt. "Ya'll 'ave ta see ta him. His mother won't be lookin' after him."

"Are you sure? There must be something we can do."

"No, mum. Sorry."

Rebecca couldn't stop the tears as she pressed her forehead against Daniel's chest. "I know that things can go wrong, but why Miss?"

Daniel caressed her hair.

"Ya'll 'ave ta hand-feed the colt, mum. He must be hungry."

Rebecca straightened and swiped at her tears. "Yes. Of course." She walked into the stall and laid a hand on the colt's neck. He whinnied and tossed his head. "It's all right. I'll take good care of you," Rebecca promised, gently running a hand over his withers and along his back. Her eyes went to the sick mare and she thought of Chavive. She'd hoped the mare was pregnant. What if something like this happened to her?

"Woodman, could you get a halter for him, please?" she asked, trying to sound composed.

Carrying a bottle of milk with a nipple, Woodman approached the colt. "It won't be hard on ya," he said, and the youngster bucked and ran to an opposite corner of its new stall. "Come on, now. Ya'll like this." Woodman's voice was soothing as he moved closer to the young horse.

The colt stood still, staring at the man. When Woodman got close enough, he stroked the colt's neck. "Ah, that's a good lad. Yer a good fella. I'll bet yer hungry, eh?" He worked the nipple into the foal's mouth. At first the colt resisted, pulling away and tossing his head. Finally the taste of sweet milk changed his mind, and the foal started to suck. He tugged on the bottle as he ate, unconcerned about the milk dribbling from the corners of his mouth.

Woodman chuckled. "He likes it all roight." With the colt still sucking, Woodman handed the bottle to Rebecca. "Hold it up so the milk flows."

The colt pulled so hard, Rebecca had to grasp the bottle with both hands. "My goodness, he's hungry."

"Yais, a healthy animal." Woodman grinned, but his smile faded as his eyes moved to the stall that held the mare. "We ought ta end her misery, mum."

"You're certain there's no hope?"

Woodman shook his head. "I seen it before. She's suffering."

Rebecca hadn't even considered the possibility of having to destroy one of her horses. She should ask Daniel. *No. He has enough responsibilities. This is up to me.* She kept her eyes

190

on the colt. "All right. But let's give her a couple more hours. If she's no better then, we'll do what we must."

About the time the foal emptied the bottle, Daniel walked up. He hooked a lead onto his halter. "I'll take him outdoors. Might be good for him to get some air and have a bit of a run." He tried to lead the young horse, but the colt wouldn't budge. "That's the way, eh? Come on, now." Daniel looped a part of the lead around the foal's hindquarters and coaxed him forward toward the yard.

Rebecca walked beside him. "Thank you, Daniel."

"Wish I knew how to help the mare."

Rebecca rested a hand on the foal's back. "I wish life were kinder."

"Sometimes it seems we've nothing but trouble."

Daniel and Rebecca walked the colt across the yard and down the drive before returning to the barn. "I've got to meet Jessop. You'll be all right, then?"

Rebecca took the foal's lead rope and nodded.

"Everything will be all right," Daniel said.

"I pray you're right." She managed a small smile.

After leading the colt to its stall, Rebecca returned to Miss. She was still prostrate, puffing, and lethargic. Rebecca dropped to her knees beside the mare. "Oh, Miss, I'm sorry," she said, stroking her neck. She heard the rustle of hay behind her and turned to see Woodman standing just inside the gate.

"Is she in a lot of pain, do you think?" Rebecca asked.

"Yais. Most likely." His eyes rested on the horse.

"Will it be long before she dies?"

"Can't say, mum. Could be soon." He leaned on the railing. "Ya want me ta end it for her?"

Rebecca let her eyes rest on the struggling horse. She'd

been so beautiful. She lay her hand on the animal's neck and managed to nod yes to Woodman's question. Without speaking, she stood and walked out of the barn.

Rebecca headed for the garden. She knew Mildred and Willa had been working there. Maybe she could help. Gardening might take her mind off what was happening in the barn. She'd always enjoyed working with plants. It quieted her.

Joseph sat in a playpen talking to himself and banging a toy against wooden slats. Rebecca bent and planted a kiss on the top of his blond head. "Hello, sweetie."

He looked up at his mother, his face happy and expectant. Babbling nonsense, he reached out and touched her cheek. Rebecca grasped his hand. "You're in a fine mood today." With a butterfly kiss to his hand, she straightened and stepped toward the garden, her mind still with Miss. When would Woodman do it? *Lord, please don't let it hurt.*

"Would you mind if I helped?" she asked.

"We'd love your help," Willa said. She stepped up to Rebecca and circled an arm around her waist. "I'm so sorry about Miss. She's a fine mare."

"Woodman's seeing to her now."

"Can he help her?" Mildred asked.

"No. He's going to . . . put her down."

Mildred blanched. Willa's face showed acceptance.

"I couldn't stay." Rebecca offered a weak smile. "You two and the moist earth have always been the best things for me."

"Are you all right, dear?"

Rebecca shook her head no. "But I will be."

"Sometimes these kinds of things can't be avoided," Willa said. She steered Rebecca toward the garden.

"I know. I just wish it had turned out differently."

With a sigh Willa looked over the plants and flowers. "I'm afraid my garden patch is suffering from this awful drought.

I've barely been able to keep the plants alive. We'll probably have to replant when the weather changes." She blinked back tears. "Bertram always acted as if he was doing me a great favor by providing me with water for the garden, but I think he was just as proud of it as I was."

"It will rain," Mildred said. "It has to sooner or later." She dropped her sunbonnet back onto her shoulders. "Thomas is a wise man and he's certain of it."

"Oh, it will come, eventually." Willa shrugged.

Rebecca took a hand shovel from a bucket jammed with garden tools. "I think I'll work on some of these weeds." She knelt and pushed the shovel into the soil next to a bushy green plant.

Willa rested her hands on her hips and looked beyond the yard toward the west. "I was thinking we ought to plant some cane grass. It will shield us and the garden from hot winds."

"What's cane grass?" Mildred asked.

"It's a plant that looks something like grass, but it grows quite tall. You'd be surprised how well it works."

"In that case, I think it's an excellent idea."

Willa placed a gentle hand on Rebecca's shoulders. "I remember when you first arrived—all the hours we spent together working in the garden. We haven't done so for a while now."

"I know. I miss it too. But the horses have needed me and . . ." She felt a rush of tears. Forcing them back, she said, "Miss is such a fine mare."

Mildred rested a hand on Rebecca's back. "You look quite done in. Perhaps a nap is in order?"

Rebecca's eyes roamed toward the corral that housed Noble. "I think I'll spend some time with Noble. He needs more training, and I'd rather keep busy."

Willa crouched beside a plant and sat back on her heels. "That makes absolute sense."

"You've seemed a bit tired recently," Mildred said. "The baby keeping you up?"

Rebecca pulled a weed and shook the dirt free. "Most nights he sleeps well." She dropped the weed into a bucket. "But even when he does get me up, I don't really mind."

"You're a fine mother, Rebecca," Mildred said.

"Thank you, Auntie, but I'm afraid you're inclined to see only the best in me. Sometimes I feel completely incompetent."

"I did too. Still do sometimes," Willa said.

A shot reverberated from inside the barn.

"Oh." Rebecca pressed a hand to her chest. She felt as if the wind had been knocked out of her. Her eyes went to the barn. Whispering grasses moving in the wind were the only sound. She stood.

"I'm so sorry, Rebecca," Willa said.

Rebecca nodded. "I think I'll spend some time with Noble." She walked toward his corral, blinking back stinging tears.

$\mathcal{D}$

Rebecca moved the powerful stallion through a small herd of cattle. She needed him to cut a bullock out of the rest of the mob. One was balking, so she moved toward it. Noble seemed to know what to do. He'd learned quickly.

The calf bolted away, and Noble cut him off. Rebecca kept her hands lightly on the reins. He would need to learn to do this kind of work automatically.

Noble walked toward the young bull and then guided him toward a corner. *Good, very good*, Rebecca thought. And then once more the calf darted away and managed to get past her and the stallion. She leaned over and patted his neck. "That's all right. We'll get him next time."

She maneuvered the horse back to the herd. They waded into a mass of swishing tails and dust. A flash of horns moved past, very close. Noble shuddered. With a shrill neigh, he reared. Rebecca leaned forward, grabbing for the saddle horn, but she missed it. She felt herself slipping.

Noble came down stiffly on his front legs and then bounded into the mob. Rebecca dropped from his back and hit the ground hard. All she could see were hooves and dust. She pulled her legs in close to her stomach and put her arms over her head.

Something thumped her hard in the back of her head, and an explosion of pain and light spread through her skull. She pushed to her hands and knees and tried to stand, but there was a melee of panicked, mooing animals all about her. Her head pounded and the world tipped. She fell.

Strong arms lifted her. "Mum? Mrs. Thornton!"

She looked up at a broad, brown face lined with concern.

"Ya all roight?"

"I think so." She blinked, gritting her teeth against the pain in her skull.

"Yer bleeding. I'll get ya ta the house."

Rebecca wrapped her arms around Woodman's neck and rested her head against his shoulder. When they reached the porch, she was only partially aware of concerned voices. Woodman lay her on the settee in the sitting room.

Willa leaned over her. "Oh, they've gotten you good," she said, carefully examining the back of Rebecca's head.

Mildred hovered, her face lined with worry.

Rebecca tried to smile to reassure her aunt, but as Willa probed she winced.

"I'm sorry. I don't want to hurt you. But we've got to get

this cleaned out. It seems your hair has done you a bit of good. It's so thick I dare say the animal's hoof only caused modest damage."

Lily handed Willa a bowl of water with a washcloth and a towel. "She'll 'ave a headache though, that's for sure." She smiled. "Ya scared us, mum."

"I'm sorry," Rebecca said, pushing herself upright. Her head throbbed. "I was working with Noble and I think a horn grazed him. He startled and reared. The next thing I knew, I was on the ground."

"Well, it will be the last time you do that," Mildred said sternly. "A woman wasn't meant to train horses. I knew all along this wasn't a good idea."

"Auntie, men have their share of mishaps as well," Rebecca said, grimacing as Willa continued her ministrations.

"I must agree with Mildred," Willa said. "You've taken on too much. Noble is a fine horse but a bit skittish for a woman." She straightened. "Now, I'm sure Dr. Walker would advise you to remain indoors for a couple of days and remain quiet." She returned to cleaning the wound.

Thomas stepped into the room. He glanced at the drops of blood on the floor and then at Rebecca. "Are you all right?"

"Yes. I'm fine."

"I wondered what all the fuss was about down here." He moved to Mildred's side.

"These women are making too much of a fuss," Rebecca said.

"Ya could 'ave been hurt real bad, mum. Ya weren't ta work the horse without someone ta help," Woodman said.

"Yes. I know. I'm sorry. It won't happen again."

"That's right, it won't. I'll see to it," Mildred said, her hand resting against the base of her throat. "You nearly scared me to death, Rebecca."

196

"I'm sorry, Auntie. But accidents happen."

"That doesn't mean one shouldn't be more careful. It's as if you're asking for trouble."

"Why would you say such a thing? Of course I'm not."

"We know," Willa said gently. "All right now, I think the bleeding has stopped, and I've managed to get the dirt out. You ought to rest for a while, dear. I don't know what Daniel will say when he finds out."

"Seems we've had a rash of accidents lately," Mildred said.

Rebecca suddenly felt dizzy. "I think I ought to lie down." She pushed up on shaky legs.

Rebecca allowed herself to be helped up the stairs to her room, where she lay on her bed and closed her eyes. She knew Daniel would be shaken by the accident. *It was nothing but carelessness on my part,* she told herself. But she couldn't help but think of her aunt's statement about a rash of accidents. The troubles had started with the fire and then her getting sick. And since then it seemed there had been a spate of difficulties just as her aunt had said.

Rebecca rolled onto her side and stared at the window. Apprehension welled up. What would be next?

17

Daniel loaded the last bag of feed into the back of the wagon. "Ready to go, then?" he asked Rebecca.

"I suppose." She glanced about the town, her eyes falling on Elle's Dress Shop. "I had a good visit with Elle."

"And how is she?"

"*She's* fine, but business is down. The drought's forced people to choose between what's truly necessary and what isn't. I guess clothing fits into the isn't category." Rebecca looked east at heavy clouds building. They seemed to tumble across the flats toward Thornton Creek. "But it looks like there's a change coming."

Thunder rumbled over the grasslands. "Yep. Looks like we're in for a bit of weather." Daniel gave Rebecca a hand onto the seat, then climbed up and settled beside her. Lifting the reins, he said, "Glad you came along. Nice to have good company." He grinned.

"We ought to do this more often. I've enjoyed myself. Perhaps we can find more time for days like this."

"Sounds good. I'll be making another trip in a couple of weeks."

Rebecca knit her brows. "Perhaps we can ride—you on Noble and me on Chavive. Woodman could drive the wagon."

"Sounds nice." He smiled at her. "You sure you have the time?"

Rebecca felt a flutter in her chest as his roguish eyes swept over her. "Of course." He still had the power to stir up her emotions.

Daniel dropped a quick kiss on her lips. The rumble of thunder resonated from the distant storm. "We better be off, eh?" He slapped the reins, and the horses plodded forward.

"I can hardly wait until Chavive foals."

"You've another ten months to wait, luv." Daniel grinned and his dimple emerged.

"I know. I wish it didn't take so long." Rebecca couldn't help but think about Miss and what had happened to her. Pushing aside her anxiety, she said, "Chavive will have a splendid baby. I hope it's a filly."

"She'll add some height to these scrubby Australian breeds for sure."

"They're not scrubby at all. They're fine, solid animals."

"So they've won you over, then?"

"I admire any horse that's sturdy and spirited. And Noble's not scrubby. He's nearly as tall as Chavive. He's quite grand. The combination of the two should be impressive."

Daniel grinned and flicked the reins. The horses picked up the pace. Thunder growled. "I've been praying for rain, but I hope we make it home before the storm hits."

"Do you really think it's going to rain? The clouds have promised so many times . . . and then left us nothing."

Daniel studied the sky. "Yeah, it'll rain. The smell of it's in the air."

Rebecca sniffed. "Yes. I *can* smell it." She smiled. "We need it so badly. I pray it puts an end to the drought."

"We can hope."

"Will Jessop continue to drill for water?" Rebecca asked.

"Yeah."

"How is the drilling going? You've said very little about it."

Daniel blew out a breath. "It's slow. But Jessop's determined, and he's certain we'll find water soon. You should come out and have a look. We've hit rock, and the auger that's cutting through isn't breaking up the stone very quickly, but it's interesting." He clicked his tongue and snapped the reins. "Come on, now, we need you to go a bit faster than that," he told the horses, glancing at the darkening sky. "Looks like we're going to get wet."

Light exploded, its force crackling across the sky. Thunder boomed. The light breeze that had accompanied them into town was strong now. It buffeted short grasses and bent trees. Rebecca held her hat so it wouldn't blow away. "Is it safe to be out here?" Pillars of dust whirled into the air.

"We'll be fine."

"It looks fierce."

"Right. It does at that. And it's probably carrying a lot of rain." He gazed at the approaching clouds. "Have a look at that, will you." He pointed at a sheet of gray, cutting from sky to earth. "It's really coming down." His eyes moved over the dry land. "Might well be too much rain."

"What do you mean? How could we get too much?"

"If it comes down fast and hard, the land can't soak it up quick enough and there'll be flooding."

"You mean here, right away?"

"Maybe." He grabbed the whip and laid it out over the horses' backs. "Better hurry."

Rebecca gripped the side of the wooden seat. "Perhaps we should return to Thornton Creek?"

"We'll be fine. Might get a bit wet though." Daniel smiled at her, offering reassurance.

Rebecca felt only slightly better. Anxiety jabbed at her. "What about the dry creek bed? If the rain gets here quickly, will water be running through it?"

"Yeah, but I plan on beating the rain. If we don't, well, we'll just go farther upstream and take the bridge." He whipped the horses again, and the pair pulled strong.

The gray sky turned black. Large drops splattered dry ground, leaving damp dimples. Rebecca turned her face up, allowing droplets to wet her cheeks and eyelids. It felt wonderful. "Rain! Precious rain!"

Moments later the drops became a deluge, and wind swept the downpour sideways. In minutes Daniel and Rebecca were soaked through. Rebecca huddled inside her cape. Smiling, she yelled, "All right, that's enough! God, you can turn off the spigot now!"

"The surrey would have done a better job of keeping us dry," Daniel said, pulling up the collar of his coat and resting his arms on his thighs. "It wouldn't do well in the wind though." He glanced at the back of the wagon bed. "Hope the supplies aren't ruined." He turned his attention back to the horses, now stepping through water and mud. "Don't know that we'll be able to cross the riverbed."

"Are we almost there?" Rebecca hollered over the wind. The storm was on top of them. Lightning blazed, slicing toward earth. Thunder bellowed. She flinched at the sudden bombardment.

"Almost."

Before they reached the riverbed, both Daniel and Rebecca knew they'd not be crossing; nevertheless, they pushed on.

When they reached the river, muddy water gushed. Daniel turned the horses north. "We'll use the bridge."

Dry ground became a muddy quagmire. Wagon wheels encased with black mud made the horses fight for every step.

"Daniel, what are we going to do? Maybe we ought to go back."

"Too late for that." He gave Rebecca a reassuring look. "No worries. We'll be all right." He flicked the whip. "Hah, get up there." The horses leaned into the harness and labored forward. "We'll go to the Donnellys' place. They'll put us up until the storm passes."

Rebecca nodded. She was cold and couldn't stop shivering. "Is it far?"

"No. We'll be there in no time."

Thank goodness I didn't bring Joseph with us, Rebecca thought, remembering how she'd nearly decided to include him on their outing. She snuggled close to Daniel.

He glanced down at her. "I'm sorry, luv," he said. "Didn't expect this."

"I know. It's not your fault." She shook her head in wonderment and wiped wet tendrils of hair off her face. "This country of yours is so unpredictable. One moment it's withering from the dryness and the next it's saturated."

"Queensland is never boring." Daniel grinned.

They moved alongside the now furious river. Muddy water, swirling with broken limbs and debris, rose toward the top of the bank. In some areas it had reached beyond the river's edge and washed across the land.

"It's still rising, Daniel. What should we do?"

"We need to find higher ground." He peered through the downpour. "There it is—the Donnellys'." With a look of disbelief, he reined in the horses.

Terror rolled through Rebecca.

The filthy river surrounded the Donnelly home, its waters

reaching for the windows. The family huddled on the rooftop. Mrs. Donnelly clutched her infant son, and Mr. Donnelly held on to their two other children.

"Oh, my Lord," Rebecca said. "What will they do?"

"They'll be fine if they stay put and wait it out. The storm will pass and the waters will subside." He stared. "Never seen it this bad before." He raised his arm and waved it back and forth. Mr. Donnelly waved back. "Hang on, eh? You'll make it," Daniel shouted.

Mr. Donnelly nodded.

Daniel patted Rebecca's leg. "We'll move up onto that hill there." He nodded toward a slight rise more than a hundred meters from the house.

A chunk of fencing broke loose and was swept away with a batch of squealing pigs. Rebecca closed her eyes to their plight. Thunder crashed and shuddered through the wagon. A horse enclosed in a small corral let out a high-pitched neigh. Rearing, it thrust its front legs out of the water, then dropped back to the ground and plunged forward, half swimming and half galloping across the enclosure.

"Daniel! We have to help him! He'll drown! Someone's got to open the gate!"

"There's nothing we can do. The water's still rising. Either one of us sets foot in that and we'll be dragged away."

With the water rising, Daniel turned the team toward the hill. By the time they stopped at the top of the rise, it had become a small island. Rebecca shivered. Rivulets of water ran down her face. She brushed aside wet hair and stared at the family clinging to the rooftop.

Mr. Donnelly waved again. He didn't look frightened.

"Are you sure they're safe?" Rebecca asked.

"Yes," Daniel said, but he didn't sound convinced. "This squall will pass. They'll be fine."

Rebecca and Daniel climbed into the back of the wagon

and huddled together, pressing their backs against the side boards. With a deafening boom, lightning splintered a nearby tree. Rebecca screamed. An acrid smell permeated the air as she stared at the charred and burning shell. Looking like a blackened corpse, it stood boldly amidst the deluge.

The rain didn't let up, and the water continued to rise. With a loud snap, the corral fence broke away. The flood carried the terrified horse downstream. Fighting to keep its head out of the water, the animal slashed out at the torrent with its front legs. Rebecca watched until it disappeared, her stomach aching. She turned and stared at the Donnellys. The two older children clung to their father and pressed their faces against his chest.

"Daniel, the rain's not slowing down at all."

"It will." He hugged Rebecca more tightly.

Rebecca rested her head against his upper arm. She could never remember feeling so cold, not even on the coldest winter day in Boston. Daniel shivered.

A loud pop followed by the sound of splintering wood pierced the din of the storm. Horrified, Daniel and Rebecca watched a corner of the Donnelly house break away and slide toward the water. Mrs. Donnelly screamed, clutching her baby. Her husband scrambled toward her, but as the house pitched he fell backward and tumbled toward the swirling deluge. His fingers found a ridge, and he managed to cling to the rooftop while the portion of house with his wife was ripped away. Her face etched with terror, Mrs. Donnelly huddled with her infant on the wedge of roof. She gazed at her family as she and the baby were carried from sight.

"No! No!" Rebecca screamed.

Daniel folded her in his arms and held her close.

"Oh, Daniel," Rebecca sobbed, clinging to him.

With a ripping sound, what remained of the house was lifted away. The roof slanted downward into the water and bounced. In spite of the tossing, Mr. Donnelly managed to hang on to his children and maintain his perch. The structure pitched and turned in the brown water, and the swirling deluge carried away the rest of the house and the Donnelly family.

Rebecca stared after them in horror. "God, help them!" She clutched Daniel's coat.

"They'll make it. You'll see. Queenslanders are right tough." He pulled her close and stared at the muddy waters. There was no sign that a home had even existed.

"Daniel, we should have helped them."

He didn't answer right away. Then, his voice heavy, he said, "There was nothing we could do. Nothing."

Rebecca looked at the water—it was still rising. Would their island disappear beneath the flood?

Daniel pressed Rebecca's cheek against his chest. "Rest."

She squeezed her eyes shut, taking refuge in the warmth of Daniel's coat and the smell of wet wool. When she heard the mewling of a frightened calf as it was swept past, she didn't look up. She couldn't endure it. Pressing closer, she kept her eyes shut and tried to think only of Daniel's strong arms and the warmth of his body.

᪥

Finally the rain stopped, and shafts of sunlight burst through thinning clouds. Exhausted, Daniel and Rebecca slept, marooned on their tiny island.

Hours later they woke to clear skies and mists hugging the earth. It seemed peaceful.

Unsteady, Rebecca pushed to her feet and looked about. She and Daniel were stranded in the midst of a muddy lake. The storm had passed, leaving behind a fouled river and mud littered with plants and animal corpses. Their tiny piece of

205

earth had already started to dry up and warm beneath the sun. Rebecca removed her wet cloak and draped it over the side of the wagon.

Daniel stood and wrapped his arms about her. He rested his chin on the top of her head.

"Life can change so quickly, Daniel. It's frightening." Rebecca's mind carried her back to the moment the house had broken apart and carried away its family. She closed her eyes, hoping to blot out the memory.

Daniel tightened his hold and kissed her hair. He let out a slow breath. "I've lived 'ere all my life and never seen such a flood."

"You don't think our home . . ."

"No. It's on high ground. But I expect Thornton Creek is in a bad way. We probably got out of town just in time."

"You think it was washed away?"

"Probably not. The town's had its share of floods. It's always survived. But it's probably a real mess." He turned Rebecca around so she faced him. Smoothing her damp hair back from her face, he searched her eyes and then tenderly kissed her forehead. "I love you."

Rebecca burrowed against him. "We could have died. We could have been like the Donnellys. And what would have happened to Joseph if he'd been with us?"

Daniel gazed about, a hard look in his eyes. "We're alive. And Joseph is fine."

Rebecca wrapped her arms around Daniel's waist. "A person never knows when their final day will be." She hugged him. "I love you so much. I never want to lose you."

"You won't. I'll always be 'ere for you."

Exhausted, Daniel and Rebecca lay back down and huddled together. Rebecca forced herself to think practical thoughts. There was so much to be done, especially now with the damage from the storm.

✍

"Hello!" someone called.

Rebecca pushed up on one arm and looked over the walls of the wagon. It was Mr. O'Brien from the Thornton Creek Mercantile. He smiled and waved.

"Daniel! Daniel! It's Mr. O'Brien!"

Daniel stood. "Patrick. Good to see you." He smiled broadly.

"I knew ya probably got caught in it. Thought I ought ta come have a look. Ya all right?"

"Yeah. We're fine. But the Donnellys . . . well, they didn't fare well."

Mr. O'Brien's eyes moved to the place where the house had stood. "Bad one. Seems to me they were advised not to build in this spot." Mr. O'Brien brightened. "They're all right though. It was a downright miracle."

"They made it?" Daniel asked.

"Right. All of them, even the baby."

Feeling a mix of sorrow and gratitude, Rebecca scanned the ruined property. "What would we do if we lost everything?"

"The Donnellys didn't lose everything. They have their lives." Daniel gave Rebecca a squeeze. "Time we went home, eh?"

18

Daniel trudged up the front steps of the house. Removing his hat, he sat on the top step and rested his arms on his thighs. "Murderous hot, eh? Even for October."

"Quite," Willa said. "Too hot for this time of year."

Daniel gazed beyond the yard to the open parched land. Waves of heat rose from the earth. He resettled his hat on his head, tipping the brim down slightly in front. "I'd hoped that big storm would set off a change." Shaking his head, he added, "Can't even tell it rained."

Rebecca pushed out of her chair and crossed to Daniel, her shoes clapping hollowly against the wooden porch. Standing behind him, she rested her hands on his shoulders. "You look tired."

Daniel glanced up. "Old Jessop says there's no water where he's digging. He's going to try another spot."

"Where?"

Daniel shrugged. "He said he'd find the right place . . . might take a few days though." He stood. "I've got a thirst to take care of, then I'll clean up. Jim asked if we'd join him and Cambria for a musical performance in town."

"A performance? What kind of music?"

"Didn't say."

Rebecca suddenly felt energized. "It'll be fun, no matter what kind of music it is. Just getting out with friends will be a pleasure."

"It's high time you two got out." Willa rested her hands on the arms of her wicker chair. "Indeed, it's been far too long."

"Too right," Daniel said with a smile. "Woodman will bring the surrey 'round in about an hour."

Rebecca dropped a kiss on Daniel's cheek. "I haven't much time, then." She hurried inside, stopping by the kitchen. "Lily, Daniel and I won't be here for supper. We're going into town."

The servant looked up from a slab of meat she was cutting. Raising an eyebrow, she smiled. "Wal, good fer ya. 'Ave a fine time, eh?"

"Thank you. We will." Rebecca pranced out of the room and up the stairs. She searched through her gowns and finally settled on a pale blue cotton. After dressing, she stood in front of the mirror. In Boston the practical cloth would have been considered shoddy, but she rather liked the color and the lightweight fabric. In the heat, anything more would be too much.

$\mathcal{D}$

Hands clasped in her lap, Cambria sat beside Jim in the surrey. She looked especially pretty in a yellow dress. Its princess neckline acted as a frame for her fresh looks and golden hair. Her blue eyes sparkled with delight.

"I love your dress," Rebecca said.

"Aunt Elle made it."

"I thought as much. She's a fabulous seamstress."

"I'll tell her ya said so." Cambria smiled. "Aunt Elle saw the performance a few days ago, and she said it's spectacular. I'm so looking forward to it and glad you and Daniel could join us."

Rebecca leaned against Daniel. "It's nice to be out with friends."

The surrey moved along the main street of Thornton Creek. The heat was crushing, and Rebecca looked forward to night-fall and its cooling temperatures.

"Things are quiet," Jim said.

Two men dozed in chairs they'd leaned against a storefront, and a sturdy-looking woman with a baby in her arms and a youngster trailing behind her crossed the dusty road. Other than that, the street was empty except for a horse standing at a hitching post in front of the pub. He swished his tail persistently, swiping away flies. Occasionally he'd shudder, momentarily shaking free of the pests. A draft of air lifted dust and swept it down the empty road.

"The heat must 'ave kept everyone home," Cambria said. "If not for the show, I'd be at home resting on the porch meself."

Woodman stopped in front of the small theater house at the center of town.

"Right, then. Here we are," Daniel said, stepping down from the surrey. He offered his hand to Rebecca, helping her out, and then assisted Cambria. Jim stepped out last.

"I'll be at the stables," Woodman said.

"Right." Daniel took Rebecca's arm and moved toward the theater door. Jim and Cambria followed as Woodman coaxed the horses down the street.

The theater was nothing like the show houses in Boston, but Rebecca found it respectable enough. The floors were made of finished wood and had been polished to a high sheen. A doorway leading into the theater was framed with velvet draperies, pulled aside to allow for passage.

"It's much cooler in here," Rebecca said, feeling a prickle of excitement as she stepped through the door and started down an aisle. Rows of chairs were already filled with spectators. Daniel spotted a group of four empty seats and steered Rebecca toward them. She moved to the third one in and Daniel stepped around her, which allowed Rebecca and Cambria to sit side by side. Jim took the aisle seat.

"This is so exciting," Cambria said. "I've never been to the theater."

"Really?" Rebecca asked in amazement.

"Truly. I've never been. Dad always said it was an unnecessary luxury. And the Taylors aren't ones ta waste money on luxuries," she said, mimicking her father's voice.

Rebecca giggled. She opened up an ornamental fan and cooled herself. "I've always loved the theater, but I must admit, I've never been to a variety show."

"What did ya see at the shows in Boston?"

"We had the opera and ballet. But what I loved most was the symphony." She smiled at the memory. "It was marvelous. I guess I still miss it."

"We went there together while I was in Boston," Daniel said. "The orchestra played music like none you've ever heard."

"Sounds thrilling. Maybe one day if I go to Brisbane or Sydney, I'll get ta visit a theater with an orchestra." Cambria settled back in her seat and gazed at a stage raised several feet above the floor so that those in back could see. "Do you miss it terribly, Rebecca?"

Gazing at the small stage and the shabby drapes, Rebecca had to admit to a yearning for the magnificent performances of Boston. "I miss the wondrous music and the grand plays. It all seems quite glamorous now. But mostly it was a lot

211

of high-society types promenading for one another. I don't miss that."

A small man with a tiny mustache stepped through the heavy draperies onstage. He moved closer to the audience. "Welcome. Welcome. Glad ta see so many good folks. We have a real fine show for ya."

Rebecca felt like giggling. This was definitely not Boston, but surprisingly, she was happy it wasn't. Her anticipation peaked as the heavy curtains were pulled back, revealing a group of musicians. Three men stood alongside an upright piano. One held a violin, another a viola, and the third a banjo. A woman sat at the piano, her hands resting on the keys, and another woman stood a few steps away, hands clasped in front of her. The men were dressed in identical blue-striped suits, and the women wore rose-colored satin gowns.

Daniel took Rebecca's hand and settled back in his seat. Feeling content, she nestled close to him.

⟡

The crowd clapped and whistled their enthusiasm as the curtain opened once more and the performers walked out hand in hand and took their bows. "That was grand!" Cambria bubbled. "I think I liked the opera singer the most. Her voice reminded me of the songbirds that sing first thing in the morning."

"I must admit, she was quite good," Rebecca said, realizing she hadn't expected proficiency from a troupe of entertainers on the flats of Queensland.

"I can't remember hearing better," Jim said.

The foursome wandered out of the theater and down the street to a small café.

As they stepped inside, Rebecca asked, "Is there a necessary?"

"Of course. We're not all that primitive," Cambria said.

"I know. I didn't mean . . ."

"I'm only teasing ya." Cambria grinned. "Come on, then. I'll show ya the way." She walked toward the back of the eatery.

"I feel as if I'm going to melt," Rebecca said, gazing into the mirror. "Look at my hair. It's an absolute mess. It's sticking to my face." She lifted a damp strand and tucked it back into place.

"I think it looks nice, actually."

"It's awful. Sometimes I feel as if my hair looks like a wild horse's mane." Rebecca turned and faced Cambria. "It's nothing like your silky blond hair."

"I wish mine was thick and curling like yours." Cambria lifted a strand. "It's flat and dry."

"No. It's lovely." Rebecca turned back to the mirror and stared at her reflection. "I don't know that I can tolerate another summer."

"It always seems extra hot when the heat picks up quick like it has. Give yerself time, eh?" Cambria leaned closer to the mirror and pinched her cheeks. She grinned at Rebecca. "Got to keep up me looks for Jim."

Rebecca stepped back. "Cambria, are you and Jim serious about each other?"

"I'm not sure what we are. I care for him and I quite like his company. I think he likes me well enough. Otherwise why would he keep asking me to go on outings with him?"

"He's not said anything about marriage?"

"No. Not a word. I'm beginning to wonder at his intentions."

"Would you like Daniel to speak to him?"

"Oh no. If it comes to that, me father will sit him down.

213

But I pray not; that would be absolute humiliation. Please don't say a word."

"I won't." Rebecca folded her arms over her chest. "What will you say if he does ask you to marry him?"

"Yais, of course. He's a fine bloke and would be a grand husband and father." Cambria blushed. "I'm quite fond of him."

Rebecca circled an arm around her friend's waist. "I agree. He's a fine catch." She gave Cambria a quick hug. "I suppose we ought to get back."

"We ordered for you. Hope you don't mind," Daniel said, standing and pulling back a chair for Rebecca.

She sat, thinking she'd have preferred ordering her own meal. Not wanting to spoil the occasion, she said, "I'm sure whatever you ordered will be fine."

Jim seated Cambria just as a waiter carried a tureen of beef and vegetable pie to their table, along with a platter of bread. "Why, we've all got the same thing," Cambria said.

Jim laughed. "It's all they've got."

"Oh, and 'ere I thought ya'd taken care ta order me something special."

Rebecca leaned on the table and smiled at Daniel. "You are a sly one."

He grinned and then held out his plate while Rebecca spooned a mix of meat and vegetables onto it. After that she served everyone else.

Daniel took a bite and chewed thoughtfully. "Good. Not as good as Lily's, but it will do."

The foursome settled down to their supper, and for a few minutes nothing was said while they ate and sipped tea. Jim drank coffee.

"Can I have a taste of yer coffee?" Cambria asked. "Me mother always makes tea. I'd like ta try it."

"Sure." Jim handed her his cup.

Holding it between both hands, Cambria sipped, then grimaced. "Oh. It's bitter."

"I didn't think you'd like it much," Jim said, reaching for the cup.

"No. Wait. I'll try again." Cambria took another taste, holding it in her mouth a moment before swallowing. Returning the cup to Jim, she said, "I suppose I could get used ta it."

Jim made a point of taking a big gulp, then set down the cup and leaned on the table. "We ought to go out more often."

"I agree." Daniel speared a chunk of potato and put it in his mouth. "But if the drought continues, there'll be no money for such outings."

Silence settled over the table. Finally Cambria asked, "Do ya think it will come ta that? I know me father's worried. Worse than I've seen. I hear him and me mother talking at night. And I know they're scared."

The food suddenly lost its appeal, and Rebecca set down her fork. "I'm sure we have nothing to worry about."

"Wish I were so sure," Daniel said. "Figure if God chooses he'll bring the rains."

A soft knock sounded at Rebecca's door. She set down her brush. "Come in."

Mildred opened the door and stepped inside. Her face looked flushed, and her eyes were red rimmed. She gripped a handkerchief.

"What is it, Auntie? What's wrong?" Rebecca crossed to her aunt.

"Thomas is returning to Boston," she said, struggling to maintain a brave demeanor. However, her eyes shimmered. "I'll miss him terribly." Her chin quivered, but she didn't give way to tears.

"Oh, Auntie, I'm so sorry. When is he leaving?"

"Soon, but he still has to make arrangements."

Knowing she was stepping onto forbidden ground, Rebecca asked, "Why don't you marry him? It's obvious you care for him."

"I do . . . but I've been independent far too long. I can't change now. Love is for the young and naïve. I've seen too much in my years to be easily swept away by emotion." She sniffed and then blew softly into the handkerchief. "I'm not young anymore. I can't imagine myself a bride, a wife. It's absurd."

"Why absurd? Thomas is a fine man who loves you. And you love him too . . . don't you?" Rebecca challenged.

Mildred stared straight ahead. She didn't answer for a long while. Finally with a sigh she said, "Yes. I love him."

"Then tell him."

"I want to, but I know he still loves his first wife. I can't compete with a ghost."

"How do you know if you don't talk about it?"

Mildred's brows creased and tears filled her eyes. Pressing the handkerchief to her nose, she sniffled.

Rebecca sat on the bed and pulled her aunt down beside her. "I love you, Auntie, and I hate to see you leave Douloo, but I think it's time you returned to Boston and married Thomas."

Mildred blew softly into the handkerchief. "How do I talk to him about how I feel? I've never done such a thing."

"Just be honest and straightforward."

Mildred nodded ever so slightly.

"Auntie, Thomas may not be willing to wait until you get up your courage. Please, speak with him."

D

Mildred stood at the front door, her hands clasped. Thomas stood at the railing, gazing at the open plains drenched in gold. They soaked up the last rays of light as the sun descended toward the horizon. Taking a steadying breath, she pushed open the door and stepped onto the porch.

Thomas looked at her. Mildred could see sadness in his eyes. "Evening, Mildred. Lovely, isn't it?" He gestured toward the panorama.

She moved to the balustrade and stood beside him. Too afraid to look at him, she allowed her eyes to roam the open flatlands. "It's quite beautiful, especially at this time of the evening. It's almost as if the earth is holding its breath. Everything becomes quiet and still."

Thomas turned his back to the scenery and leaned against the railing. Folding his arms over his chest, he looked down at the floorboards. "I made arrangements."

"Arrangements?" Mildred asked, knowing full well he was referring to his trip home.

"Yes. I purchased a place on the stage, and I'll be catching a ship in Brisbane the first week of November." His brown eyes were warm as he looked at Mildred. "Forgive me for asking again, but I wish you would reconsider and go with me."

Mildred fiddled with a button on her cuff. "Oh dear. This is loose. I'll have to repair it."

"Mildred, I don't care about your button. I want to know why you won't marry me."

Her stomach tumbled, and Mildred wondered why she'd thought she could do this. Never in all her life had she openly

217

expressed her feelings to a man. She forced herself to look at Thomas.

"I know I'm not young," he said, "but I'm not ancient either. And I'm not much to look at, but . . ."

"No. That's not it," Mildred cut in. "You're quite handsome, Thomas. And you're a fine man, gentle and kind. I know of no one finer."

"Then why? Is it that you don't love me? There are many successful marriages that aren't based on love." He moved closer to Mildred. "I love you, but I could be satisfied if all you felt for me was respect and friendship."

"I do respect you, and I consider you a true friend . . . and . . . I love you, Thomas."

He took Mildred's hands and pressed them together between his. "Well, then why? Why won't you marry me?"

"Thomas, you still love your first wife. You don't really love me. You need someone." Mildred removed her hands from his. "I'm certain you *think* that what you feel is love, but it's only friendship, the need of a woman's touch in your life. And that's not enough for me."

"You're right. I do love my wife. She was a wonderful woman, and I'll always love her. But that doesn't mean my heart can't love you as well."

"Thomas, your house is exactly the same as it was when she was alive. You haven't changed anything. You still have pictures of her throughout your home."

He stared at Mildred and didn't respond.

"I know you care for me, but you're still too much in love with Gwenn."

"The house is the same because I'm used to it that way. I didn't see any reason to change it."

"And if I were to move in? What then?"

Thomas hesitated a moment too long before he answered.

"Of course you can arrange it any way you like. It would be your home too."

"No, Thomas. It wouldn't be, not really." Mildred thought she was beyond heartbreak. It was something she was too old to feel. But she felt the crushing pain of it. She needed to get away. *I'm not breaking down in front of him*, she told herself.

"I don't know how to convince you." He reached for her hand and clasped it. "Please, I don't want to return without you."

Mildred wanted to believe him, but she couldn't. "I'll need time."

"I can't wait any longer. My business is nearly in ruins now."

"Then go ahead. And we'll correspond. I promise to give your proposal serious consideration."

Thomas gazed at her for a long moment. Then finally he said, "This is not what I wanted." He lifted Mildred's hand and gently pressed his lips against the back of it. "I won't forget you."

19

Daniel stood silently watching Jessop haul up an auger. The thickset man knelt and emptied dirt from the drill. Crumbling the soil through his fingers, he studied it and then chucked it aside. With a glance at Daniel, he sent the auger back into the earth.

Fear of what could be had held Daniel in a suffocating grip for days. Jessop had drilled thirty feet and still not located water. Studying the staid bushie, Daniel wondered if he'd made the right choice in hiring the man. *He's found water for others in the district,* he reasoned. *Supposed to know all there is to know about well drilling.*

Since going to work for Daniel, Jessop had come up with nothing more than dry holes and rock. And it didn't appear the outcome would be any different this time.

Maybe there isn't any water. Daniel blew out a dry breath. Just the thought was too fearsome to contemplate. He stepped closer, leaning on the rigging. "You have any idea when we'll hit water?"

"Ya can't know 'bout a thing like that, not for sure." Jessop picked up a bottle, uncorked it, and took a long drink.

After wiping sunburned lips with the back of his hand, he replaced the stopper and set down the jug. Pulling a filthy rag from his back pocket, he sopped sweat from his deeply lined face, then stuffed the foul cloth back into his pocket. "I've dug through some shale; that's a good sign. And we've 'ad a run of luck . . . not hittin' rock." He stared at the borehole. "If we don't hit rock, the water shouldn't be too deep. I figure a few more days."

Daniel remembered hearing similar words when the first well had been dug. But they *had* hit rock. After days of pounding their way through it, the water below had been foul and unusable. "Couple of days, eh?"

"Yep." Jessop returned to his job. Leaning against the drilling works, he seemed unaware of Daniel.

"I'll be back later, then."

Jessop didn't look up.

Daniel climbed onto his horse. He watched the drill shaft sink a few inches, and then he turned and rode across the dry grasslands. *We have to find water. We've lost too many cattle already. And too many calves.* Grazing was so poor that the cows' milk production had been down; without enough milk, calves didn't do well.

Daniel hadn't ridden far when he saw what had become a familiar sight—circling buzzards. He stared at the scavengers and then scanned the dry landscape. A cow lay on her side. He didn't want to look at the animal. Not today. He'd had enough. But with a light tap to his horse's flanks, he moved closer. There was a calf too. It was dead. The cow let out a weak bawl and blew air from her nostrils. She didn't rise.

Daniel dismounted and walked to the suffering bovine. Her nose was dry and cracked, but her eyes were focused and alert. "You may have a chance after all." He patted her neck and then stepped back a pace to get a better look at her. She was thin but not wasted. Two buzzards landed on the calf

221

and greedily tried to strip away a piece of hide. "Hah!" Daniel yelled, running at them. Their heavy wings lifted them into the sky, where they joined the circling mob.

Hating the sight of them, Daniel turned back to the cow. He looped a rope around her neck. "Come on, then. Give it a go. You can't stay 'ere." He glanced at the scavengers. "You'll end up as tucker for them." He pulled, but the cow didn't budge. "Get up! There's water in the creek." He hauled harder on the rope. "Come on, now." The cow only shifted slightly but remained prone.

Daniel walked to his horse and tied the rope to the saddle horn. "You're coming with me one way or the other," he said, climbing onto his stallion's back and kicking him in the sides. The horse moved forward, and the rope tightened. The cow didn't move. Daniel kicked the horse and urged him on. The rope grew taut, and the cow's neck stretched. Her eyes widened, and she let out a bawl. Daniel wouldn't relent. "You're not going to lie 'ere and die!" Finally the cow stumbled to her feet. For a moment she looked as if she might go down again, but she managed to maintain her footing. When Daniel moved ahead slowly, she followed.

Some of the herd was at the creek. The ailing cow trotted toward the stream and buried her nose in the water, slurping up blessed moisture. Daniel removed the rope, realizing that he'd probably only prolonged the animal's life by weeks. Feed was sparse, and each day the water level in the creek dropped. When it dried up the animals would succumb.

He moved upstream before climbing from his horse. The stallion walked into the creek and sucked up the water. Staying clear of the muddied water, Daniel stepped into the coolness and knelt. He cupped his hands and drank, then filled his hat and dumped water over his head. He repeated the indulgence twice more. Combing back wet hair, he reluctantly replaced the hat.

After that, he refilled his canteen, led his horse out of the creek, and climbed into the saddle. He rode to a nearby barn where there were hungry cattle to feed.

A mob waited for him. Rather, they waited for the hay he'd put out. Hot and weary, Daniel dragged himself off his stallion and walked into the barn. Why was he bothering? The supply of hay wasn't nearly enough to see them through. He was only putting off the inevitable—the starvation of his cattle and the end of Douloo. Nevertheless, he lugged hay out of the barn and scattered it in a crib. He couldn't give up. He'd work until there was nothing else to be done.

Daniel moved back and forth between the barn and the cribs until he'd put out just enough to diminish the hunger of the skinny mob. With the herd munching, Daniel slipped off a bag from his saddle and walked to the shade, just inside the barn doorway. He sat, knees bent, and leaned against the wall.

His stomach rumbling with hunger, he opened the canvas bag. "So, Lily, what did you make today?" He dug into the sack and lifted out a sandwich wrapped in a napkin. After uncovering it, he bit into meat and cheese pressed between slices of fresh-baked bread. Resting his head against the building, he chewed. Here in the shade the heat seemed tolerable. He studied a cluster of plump, white clouds and tried to envision them building into black billows filled with moisture. If only it would happen.

Without warning, a searing pain pierced Daniel's left hand. Jumping to his feet, he clutched the hand to his chest. It pulsed like a hot poker had been rammed into it. He looked at the ground around him. What had bitten him? A tiger snake cut a path across the dusty ground and slipped away, hiding among dry grasses.

Daniel looked at his hand. Already it was swelling. Blood seeped from the wounds where the snake had buried its fangs. "Blimey!" he uttered, grabbing the handkerchief from around his neck and wrapping it tightly about his arm just above his wrist. *That ought to slow the poison*, he thought, knowing he had little time to get home. It wouldn't take long for the venom to dispense itself throughout his body and bring him down.

Bracing his hand against his chest, he walked toward his horse. Careful to keep his left arm tucked close against his body, he reached up and grabbed the saddle horn with his right hand. Shooting pains stabbed; he sucked air and groaned. Pressing his forehead against the horse's side, Daniel waited for dizziness and nausea to diminish. "Keep moving," he said, and planted his foot in the stirrup. It felt awkward mounting from the right side, but he managed to push up and drop into the saddle.

The earth swirled about him. He leaned forward, taking slow breaths and trying to steady himself. His heart hammered. Nausea was nearly overwhelming. *I gotta get home.* Grabbing the reins and kicking the horse in the flanks, he turned toward the house.

Flat land stretched endlessly in front of him as he moved across it. Sun baked the ground, and the wind swirled dust into the air. Daniel struggled to breathe. Spikes of pain shot through his hand. He gazed at a blue sky, and despair swept over him. "Why, God? Haven't we enough trouble?"

The horse plodded toward home, and the minutes clipped by. Daniel knew each breath carried him closer to death. The world tilted at an odd angle, and it was so hot . . .

He slumped over the saddle.

☙

Woodman saw him first. He ran into the yard. "Daniel! Daniel!" He dragged his friend off his horse. "What's 'appened ta ya, lad?"

Daniel managed to whisper, "Snake."

Jim ran up to the two men, glanced at Daniel, and said, "I'm going for the doctor." He sprinted to the corral.

"Daniel!" Rebecca screamed, running down the steps. "Daniel!" Holding up her skirts, she raced across the yard. "What's happened to him? He isn't dead, is he?" she asked tentatively.

"No. He's alive but real sick." Woodman picked up Daniel as if he were a child.

"Oh, Daniel," Rebecca said, caressing his cheek. "He's burning up!" Her eyes searched his body, seeking out what could have caused this. When she saw his swollen, discolored hand and arm, she gasped. "Oh, my Lord! His hand!"

Woodman glanced at the wound. "Snakebite."

Rebecca walked alongside Daniel and Woodman. "Is he going to die?"

Woodman didn't answer but kept moving toward the house.

Willa and Mildred waited on the porch. Willa looked from her son to Woodman. "How bad is it?"

"Don't know, mum. We need ta get him ta bed."

"Of course," Willa said, sounding as if this were just another everyday difficulty that needed sorting out. She hurried up the stairs in front of Woodman. Rebecca and Mildred followed.

"What kind of snake was it?" Rebecca asked, her heart pounding beneath her ribs.

"Don't know, mum." Woodman settled Daniel on his bed. "Need Lily," he said, looking at Daniel's hand. He loosened the handkerchief.

"Lily! Lily!" Willa called, stepping into the hallway.

Lily appeared a few moments later. She shuffled into the bedroom. "What is it, mum?" Her eyes went to Daniel.

"He's been bit by a snake. Jim's gone for the doctor, but you know more about these kinds of things better than anyone else here." Willa's eyes pleaded. "Can you help him?"

"I'll 'ave a look-see." Lily sat on the bed beside Daniel. She felt his face and the skin on his arm, then examined the wound.

"Was it a king brown?" Rebecca asked Woodman.

"Don't think so, mum. If it was, he'd already be gone. More than likely it was a tiger snake."

"Is he going to die?" Rebecca stared at Daniel. She'd never seen him so sick.

Lily continued to probe. "He's roight bad, but he could live, eh?"

Lily cleaned the wound and, after making a poultice, placed the putrid-smelling mash on his hand and wrapped it. "Can't do no more than that." Her dark eyes were sad. "Try ta get 'im ta drink some water," she said before leaving the room.

🜍

Dr. Walker strode into Daniel's room. "Heard he's got a snakebite?"

"Yes, doctor," Willa said. "But Woodman doesn't think it was a king brown. He thinks it was a tiger snake."

"Let me 'ave a look." The doctor leaned over Daniel and, after removing the poultice, examined the wound. He ran his hand up Daniel's arm, lifted his eyelids, and listened to his heart. "I think Woodman's right. Tiger snakes can deliver a fierce bite and make a man real sick, but it's not always a killer."

His eyes sorrowful, he turned to Rebecca and Willa, who stood side by side, hands clasped. "The poultice was a good idea. Could draw out some of the poison. Keep him from getting chilled, and give him plenty to drink." He shrugged. "Other than that, all we can do is wait." He gazed down at Daniel. "We'll know in the next day or so." He glanced about the room at the observers. "Anyone with him when this happened?"

"No," Willa said. "He was by himself. Out working somewhere on the station."

"And he got back by himself?"

"Yes."

"Always knew the lad had spunk." He smiled. "Don't give up hope. If he came this far, could be he'll make it."

Rebecca didn't leave Daniel's bedside that first day and night except for brief intervals to nurse Joseph. She wanted to be with her husband, needed to be. Her prayers never ceased.

Callie sat with her from time to time. She never said a word, but her presence was a comfort.

Daniel's fever raged. He groaned and thrashed about. There were moments of lucidity when Rebecca would spoon water into his mouth, but those were few. Two more days passed before Daniel began to improve. Still, Rebecca remained with him, sometimes dozing in a chair.

"Rebecca dear," Willa said, "you must get some rest. And Lily's made a lovely beef pie. Go down and have a bite and then take a nap, eh?"

"I can't. Not yet. Anyway, I'm not hungry." Rebecca looked at Daniel. "I think he's getting better. He's not so hot, and he seems to be resting more comfortably."

"Yes. I agree. And his color's improved as well." Willa turned a resolute expression on Rebecca. "And what good will you be to him if you collapse?"

Rebecca compressed her lips and studied her husband. "He's still so sick. I'm afraid if I leave . . ."

"Nonsense. He's going to be fine. If he was going to die, he would have done it by now. You go. I'll stay with him."

Rebecca bent close to Daniel and whispered, "We've barely started our life together . . . I can't lose you now." She kissed his cheek.

Daniel's eyes fluttered open. He gazed at Rebecca for a moment and then returned to sleep.

ⅅ

Daniel's first thought was one of thirst. He needed a drink. His second was a question—why was his head pounding? What had happened? He struggled to open heavy eyes. His mother sat at his bedside. "Mum?"

She looked up from her sewing. "Daniel?" She smiled. "Ah, you've come back to us."

"Where've I been?"

"You've been dreadfully sick. Unconscious for days—a snakebite."

Daniel pressed his good hand to his forehead and then combed his fingers into his hair. "Right. I remember. I'd been eating lunch . . ." He searched for the memory as if trying to gaze through fog. "How many days now?"

"You rode in five days ago." Willa smiled. "I dare say, it's a good thing that stallion of yours is loyal to you. He could have taken you anywhere."

"It's not me, it's the feed." Daniel smiled. "He knows he gets a handful of grain when we get back to the barn. Good thing, eh?"

He tried to push himself upright and winced. Dropping back into the pillows, he held up his hand and looked at it. It still throbbed and was swollen and red. The bruising had diminished some.

228

"How have you managed while I've been sick? Is everything all right?"

"Yes. And we've handled everything that came our way just fine."

"We've had a run of bad luck. Can't say why." Daniel glanced at the curtains fluttering in the breeze. "Prayers seem to do little good. God doesn't seem to be listening to me."

Willa pursed her lips. Her eyes moved across the floor to the window. "I'd say we've much to be thankful for. You could very well have died. It's astonishing that you made it back to the house and even more unbelievable that you lived."

"I suppose you're right. But it would have been better if I hadn't been bitten at all. I'm needed 'round 'ere. If things don't improve, Douloo may very well be ruined."

"Daniel, we live in the world, not in paradise. Troubles abound. What matters is how we face those difficulties."

Daniel nodded slightly, wincing at the pain in his head.

Willa reached out and covered his undamaged hand. Tears washed into her eyes. She lifted his hand and pressed it against her cheek and then resettled it at his side. "Try not to worry so much about Douloo. It's only a piece of ground. There are things in this life of much greater worth."

20

Daniel handed Rebecca up into the stagecoach. She hesitated at the door and looked down at her husband. "I wish you were going with us."

"I wish I could, luv. But six weeks is too long for me to be gone. Especially now."

Rebecca knew that, but she'd had to ask. "I was just hoping, that's all." She stepped into the coach and sat beside Willa. Resting her arm on the open window, she looked out at Daniel. "Maybe I ought to stay."

Daniel laid a hand on her arm. "This holiday will be good for you. And Mum will feel more secure with you along."

"She has Mildred." Rebecca glanced at her aunt, who sat on the seat opposite her. She looked as if she'd been crying.

Daniel spoke softly. "They're both getting on . . . they may need someone to look after them."

Rebecca nodded. She'd looked forward to spending time with her aunt and her mother-in-law. Still, it didn't seem right to leave Daniel behind for so long, especially during such trying times.

"I'll write to you," she said.

"Can't promise I'll write back, but I'll try."

Rebecca glanced at Callie sitting beside Mildred. She bounced Joseph on her knee.

Callie gave Rebecca an encouraging smile. "I think Joseph will like the trip, mum. A real adventure for a young lad, eh?"

"He won't remember any of it."

"Yais, well, maybe not. Never know what stays in a mind."

Rebecca turned back to Daniel and laid a hand over his. "I'll miss you."

"Douloo needs me, and you need some quiet, cooler days. I'll be thinking of you." Daniel grinned and his cheek dimpled.

Rebecca felt the pace of her heart quicken. "I love you."

The driver climbed into his seat atop the stagecoach.

"I love you too." In one effortless movement, Daniel stepped up and inside the coach, lifted his son, and planted a kiss on his cheek. "Be a good lad." He set him back on Callie's lap and turned to Rebecca. "I'll think of you every moment you're gone." He kissed her tenderly. Holding her arms a moment longer, he studied her face. "Pray, eh?"

"I'll be praying."

He leaned over his mother and dropped a kiss on her cheek. "I'll miss you, Mum."

"We'll be back before you know it. Don't forget to take some leisure now and again."

"Right. I won't forget."

Thomas stood on the sidewalk, his eyes on Mildred. "My coach will be along day after tomorrow. I'll be thinking of you. I'll miss you."

Mildred's eyes brimmed with tears. "I'll miss you."

"Don't forget me, now."

Mildred's chin quivered, and she dabbed at her tears.

The coach jolted forward and then moved away from the sidewalk. Amidst a roiling cloud of dust, it rocked and swayed as it rolled down the street.

"Auntie, you are going to return to Boston, aren't you?"

"Yes."

"And you'll marry Thomas?"

"I don't know. I just don't know." She blew her nose delicately into her handkerchief. "I'd rather not talk about it just now."

Willa pushed back into her seat, trying to get more comfortable. Rebecca did the same. But her mind remained with Daniel. It would be three days' journey overland to Toowoomba and then several days more on the train. She'd be so far from home.

Rebecca wondered what it would be like in Melbourne. She'd heard that the weather was cooler and that the countryside was lusher than the flats. And there was the ocean shore. Images of lapping waves with diving, squalling gulls eased her misgivings about going as she imagined a stroll on the beach.

The miles passed, and Mildred became more distressed. Her mind stayed with Thomas. He'd looked so unhappy when they'd pulled away from Thornton Creek. *Maybe I should go with him to Boston,* she thought but immediately told herself the idea was ridiculous. She'd decided to vacation with Willa and Rebecca in Melbourne, and that was that. *We'll have a splendid time. And I can't go back; I haven't even decided whether I ought to marry Thomas or not. Nothing has changed. He still loves his first wife. He always will.*

"I do hope it's cooler in Melbourne," Willa said, fanning

herself. "I remember the summers as being quite nice." She smiled softly. "I met Bertram there, did I tell you?"

"Yes," Rebecca said. "You did."

"He was quite dashing in those days. I'll never forget the first time we met—I was smitten almost immediately."

Mildred was not one to pry, but she needed to know more about what Willa felt about her deceased husband. "Please forgive me if this question is too personal, but . . . how do you feel now that Bertram is gone? Do you love him like you did?"

"Yes. Perhaps more. Now I'm more aware of what an extraordinary man he was. And I've certainly forgotten some of the things he did that aggravated me."

"Do you think your love will wane in time?"

"Oh no. Never."

Mildred nodded slightly. *So it is true. Once you're deeply committed to a person and married, you'll never be able to completely love another.* Mildred felt the ache of loss. Thomas could never love her the way she needed him to.

"Willa, do you think you'll ever remarry?" Rebecca asked.

Willa studied her a moment. "I thought not, but I suppose it's possible. The idea of spending my life without a partner is a bit disheartening."

"So are you saying that if you did marry it would be for convenience only?" Mildred pressed, embarrassed but unable to restrain herself.

A surprised expression touched Willa's face. "Why, no. I would never marry simply for convenience. That wouldn't be right."

"But you just said you love Bertram."

"Yes. But that doesn't mean I can't love someone else."

"Mildred, I told you that," Rebecca said. "And now Willa

has said it as well. You must believe her. She's a widow, after all."

"What must she believe?" Willa asked.

Rebecca looked at Mildred. "Auntie."

Her embarrassment deepening, Mildred knew an explanation was necessary. She cleared her throat. "It feels awkward speaking so openly about private matters."

"You needn't if it bothers you," Willa said.

"I do need some advice." She folded her hands delicately in her lap. "It's about Thomas. He wants to marry me, as you know. However, he still loves his first wife, Gwenn. She died many years ago, but he continues to be devoted to her."

Willa nodded, but she didn't speak.

"You've heard him speak of Gwenn, always with tenderness. His affection for her is so strong that he hasn't changed a thing in the house since her death. The furnishings, photographs, and paintings remain the same. There is a coverlet still on the settee that she crocheted. It's as if he wants to keep her with him."

"I suppose that's possible," Willa said. "But more than likely, he simply feels comfortable with the familiar. And of course, she was the only woman of the house. Men know so little about decorating."

"Yes, that may be, but I'm certain he feels her presence. And a marriage to me would be one of convenience."

"Has he said that?"

"No. He insists that he loves me."

"Can you be so certain he doesn't?" Willa asked.

"I assumed that . . ."

"You can't assume, Mildred dear. You are a wonderful woman. Why is the idea of a fine man like Thomas loving you so difficult to believe?"

"I can see how much he loves Gwenn."

"And I love Bertram. I dare say, that will never change. But

God has created us with a great capacity for love. Wouldn't you agree?"

"Yes."

"In fact, Rebecca is a good example." Willa nodded toward her daughter-in-law. "She wasn't your daughter, and yet when her mother died it was you who stepped in and took over that role. I can see how much you love each other."

"I couldn't love her more if she were my own."

"And Rebecca is only one of the people you love. Does the fact that you love her make it impossible for you to love others?"

"Of course not." Mildred stopped abruptly. She'd been so foolish. Of course Thomas could love her. He'd told her so, but she hadn't really heard. Mildred smiled. "Thomas is not one to lie. I suppose he does love me."

The stage continued on, rocking and bumping as it moved across the flats. Now as the miles rolled under its wheels, Mildred couldn't help but think that she was being carried away from the man she loved. She wanted to tell him how she felt.

I must go back! I've got to tell him I understand and that I love him. She said nothing while she considered the possibility of returning. It was a ridiculous idea. She never did anything without proper forethought and planning. And yet her heart pulled her away from her commonsense thinking. She'd been practical all her life, but now practicality seemed unreasonable.

When the stage pulled in to the next little town, Mildred said, "I'm returning to Douloo. I must speak to Thomas."

Rebecca stared at her. "Right now, Auntie?"

"Yes. I must speak to him before he leaves." She stood. "I'm sure there will be a stage heading back to Thornton Creek." She opened the door and stepped down. "Driver," she called.

The tall, whiskered man who'd been driving the team climbed down from his perch. "Ya need somethin'?"

"Can you tell me if there's a stage returning to Thornton Creek today?"

A quizzical expression touched his face. "Wal, I don't know 'bout t'day. Maybe tomorrow though. Ya can ask inside the hotel." He nodded at a small, weathered building, one of the few that made up the town.

"Will you wait for me?"

"I 'ave a schedule ta keep. Ya got two minutes is all."

"Yes. Of course." With a glance at Rebecca and Willa, she strode toward the hotel. It was dark inside. A man with a drooping mustache and heavy eyebrows stood behind a counter. She hurried across the room. "Please, sir. Can you tell me when the next stage leaves for Thornton Creek?"

The man gazed at her a moment, then scratched his chin. "What's a lady like you doing traveling alone, eh?"

"Sir, that's of no consequence to you." She glanced at the stagecoach. The driver stood alongside the horses. Turning back to the man at the desk, she said, "Please, can you check your schedule?"

He turned and studied a timetable nailed to the wall. "Let me see. Ah. Right. There's one due 'ere tomorrow 'bout ten o'clock in the morning."

"And it goes directly to Thornton Creek?"

"Right. It does at that."

"Good. And do you have rooms available here at the hotel?"

"We do."

"Thank you, sir. I'll be right back." Mildred trudged back to the stagecoach. "Driver, could you please unload my bags? I'll be getting off here."

He gave her an odd look but climbed atop the stage.

"Mine are the matched set of tan bags."

236

Without a word, the driver unfastened her baggage.

Mildred moved to the coach step and stuck her head in the door. "I'm going back."

Rebecca's eyes filled with tears. "Oh, Auntie. I'm so happy and so sad. I know it's the right thing for you to do." She moved to Mildred and hugged her. "I love you. I'll miss you."

"I'll miss you too." Mildred squeezed her tightly. "I'll write often. And I'll notify you of my wedding date." She smiled. "That is, if Thomas will still have me."

"I have no doubt of that," Willa said. She grasped Mildred's hand. "I'll miss you. You're a grand woman. And any time you and Thomas want to visit, you come right along. We'll have room for you."

"Thank you. You've been very gracious to me."

Mildred scooped up Joseph and hugged him. "You be a good boy for your mommy and daddy." She kissed his cheek. Tears washed her face.

"I got ta go," the driver called. "Yer either on or off, lydie."

"Yes. Of course. I'm coming." She turned back to Rebecca and hugged her again. "I love you. Please take good care of Daniel and Joseph. And come to visit."

"We will. I love you, Auntie."

Mildred stepped off the coach and stood on the walkway. The driver climbed onto his seat and slapped the reins, and the coach pulled away.

Rebecca and Willa waved. Rebecca dabbed at tears. Mildred stood and watched the coach until it disappeared. Then she turned and walked into the hotel.

☼

The stagecoach bounced over the uneven road as it headed for Thornton Creek. A businessman who wanted only to sleep and another man who glowered at anyone who dared look at him were Mildred's traveling companions. She didn't mind their lack of communication. Her thoughts were with Thomas and their future together. However, fear stirred in the back of her mind. What if her leaving had caused Thomas to change his mind?

When the stage pulled into Thornton Creek, Mildred stepped out and onto the sidewalk. She peeked inside the hotel but saw no one she knew except the proprietor.

"G'day, Miss Williams. I thought ya were on yer way ta Melbourne."

"I was, but I changed my mind." She dropped one of her bags on the floor. "Do you know someone who might give me a ride to Douloo Station?"

"Right. I can. But I think Mr. Thornton will be into town. Mr. Murdoc is checking in. His stage leaves bright and early tomorrow."

Mildred glanced at the clock. It was four o'clock. Thomas would probably be here anytime. "Well, then I believe I'll check in."

After signing the registry and putting her bags in her room, Mildred returned to the hotel lobby. "I'm going down to the eatery for a cup of tea. If Mr. Thornton or Mr. Murdoc come by, would you tell them I'm there?"

"Right. I'll do that."

$\mathcal{D}$

Mildred sat in the café, quietly sipping tea. Her mind was occupied with thoughts of Thomas and his possible responses to her change of mind. Her hands trembled as she set her cup back on its saucer.

Thomas walked past the window. Mildred straightened her spine and waited.

The café door opened, and he stepped inside. His eyes immediately found her and didn't leave her as he walked to the table where she sat. Standing directly in front of her, he said, "The man at the hotel told me you were here. I don't understand, Mildred. I thought you were going to Melbourne?"

"I was, but then I realized I needed to be here. That I couldn't bear the idea of your returning to Boston and leaving me behind." She stood. "I know it doesn't make sense, but I suddenly realized that I love you too much to let you go sailing off. I don't want to live my life without you."

"And what about Gwenn? I haven't stopped loving her."

"Yes. I know. And you shouldn't. I was being foolish and unfair."

Thomas smiled. He took her hands in his. "Will you marry me, Mildred?"

"I'm rather set in my ways. I don't know that I'll be a good wife."

"You're more than I ever dreamed of."

Mildred smiled. "Yes, Thomas. I will marry you."

21

"Melbourne is the social capital of the country," Willa said, gazing out the window at thirsty grasslands. "It's a grand city. I remember that even as a girl I enjoyed the activities. There were cotillions to attend, and we often went to the symphony or the opera. I do hope we'll have time for the opera." She closed her eyes and smiled softly. "Such music is a delight to one's soul."

"I enjoy the opera," Rebecca said, watching Joseph gallop a wooden horse back and forth across his lap. She rested her elbow on the window ledge. "But I must admit, it has never been one of my favorite entertainments. The language is a bother. Not knowing what's being said breaks the spell of the music."

"Indeed, but they all have a story to tell. One only need know the tale, and the music conveys the emotion. There's no call to know every word." Willa smiled. She looked radiant, her blue eyes brighter than usual. "I remember my first visit to the opera. I was mesmerized—the splendor and the music absolutely carried me away. Afterward, I declared it the most wondrous thing ever created. Mum and Dad laughed. But

I knew they were pleased to discover their daughter had a taste for the arts. And I've never lost my wonderment.

"After that first introduction I convinced my parents to take me often." A furrow creased Willa's forehead. "My parents were grand people. Not grand in the sense that they were wealthy or powerful, but they were vigorous and loving. I'm certain you and Mum would have gotten along splendidly, and my father . . . well, his exterior could be rather stern, but he had a heart as soft as pudding."

"I wish I'd known them," Rebecca said, watching as a mob of kangaroos leaped and darted through a grove of acacias. Pressing her hand against her unsettled stomach, she wished the coach rode more smoothly.

Willa cooled herself with a fan. "I must say, this is the perfect time of year for a trip south. The weather will be more tolerable in Melbourne. And it may even be green there." Her eyes sparkled. "I do so look forward to that."

"It's a pleasant thought," Rebecca said.

Joseph put his toy horse aside and reached for his mother. "Mama."

She lifted the tot and stood him on her lap. He placed his hands on her cheeks and planted a wet kiss on her lips. Rebecca hugged him and he giggled.

"He's such a love," Willa said.

Rebecca smoothed Joseph's silky hair. "He's like his father. I'm thankful he's not willful like I was." She smiled, remembering the stories she'd heard from her father and from Mildred. "Aunt Mildred said I was a handful." She looked out the window. "I hope she's well. I'm still stunned at her leaving so suddenly. I can't help but worry a little."

"I'm sure she's just fine."

Rebecca clapped Joseph's pudgy hands between hers. "I'm absolutely thrilled for her."

"I was looking forward to sharing Melbourne with her, but this is better."

"She and Thomas deserve happiness."

"That they do."

"Other than the arts, what other plans do you have while we're in Melbourne?" Rebecca asked.

"I'd like to visit some of the shops. There are some fine ones. There's a lovely millinery store. Perhaps we can purchase a hat for Mildred."

"Oh yes. A new hat always gave her a lift." Rebecca smiled. "However, I doubt her spirits need lifting right now."

"Is there anything special you'd like to do while we're in Melbourne?" Willa asked.

"Actually, there's a fine stable in Melbourne. And I heard of a grand colt that might actually be for sale. I was hoping to visit."

"Oh, really?" Willa asked. "And how does Daniel feel about that?"

"He said it's fine if I have a look at him, but I'm to make no purchases. At least not until the drought is over." Joseph climbed down from her lap and stood leaning against her skirts. "I'd still like to see him though."

"I do wish Daniel had joined us," Willa said.

Joseph rested his cheek against his mother's legs. He looked sleepy.

"Ya can give 'im back ta me," Callie said. "He can sleep on me lap."

Rebecca hefted Joseph up and settled him across her lap. "That's kind of you, but I'm fine with him."

"Daniel is working too hard," Willa said. "He needs time away."

"I agree, but I couldn't convince him of that. He won't leave Douloo, not while it's in trouble." Rebecca looked at

Willa. "I'm afraid of what might happen. Will we be able to stay at the station?"

"Of course." Willa's voice sounded startled. "What would we do if we were to go?"

Rebecca shrugged. "Others have moved away."

"And where would we go?"

"What about Melbourne?"

"Oh yes. Well, I suppose Aunt Ada would help if it came to that." Using her handkerchief, she dabbed at her moist face and neck. "Daniel won't leave, not if every blade of grass dies and every stream turns into dried mud. He'll stay."

A pang of anxiety moved through Rebecca. She'd known that about Daniel, but to hear it made it more real. How would they manage if the rains didn't come? "I can't imagine what life would be like. How does one live?"

Willa thought a moment. "I don't know exactly. We've never faced such a bad drought as that."

"I wish there were something more I could do to help Daniel."

"You're doing all you can," Willa said. "You've been thoughtful and supportive. And you pray. There's nothing more that can be done." She reached over and patted Rebecca's hand. "God will not forsake us."

"I know, but I've read the Bible, Willa." Rebecca didn't mean for her tone to be derisive. She softened her next words. "God doesn't always deliver his children from trouble."

"That's true, but Daniel's faith has always been unwavering. It will serve him and us well."

"His faith *is* strong. But he worries. He's restless and barely sleeps. And there have been times when he's told me about his fears and discouragement."

"Well, now, he's human, eh?" Willa smiled. "And he carries a weighty responsibility. There were many times that I watched Bertram go through similar trials." With a nod, she added, "Daniel will do fine."

✿

Rebecca leaned her head on a pillow propped against the railcar's window and gazed at rolling countryside. The rhythmic clack of the train's wheels as they passed over the tracks soothed her. There were green fields and green shrubs. She especially liked the large, broad trees that looked like great umbrellas. They reminded her of the landscape outside Boston.

"Are those vineyards?" she asked, nodding at tilled land striped with green bushes.

"Yes. Indeed." Willa's blue eyes took in the view. "There are fine wines made here." She stretched. "Oh, I've grown quite stiff. I think I'll wander through some of the other cars. And perhaps I'll have something to drink in the dining car." She stood. "Would you like a cuppa?"

"Tea would be perfect."

"Then perhaps you'd accompany me?"

"That sounds lovely." Rebecca glanced at Joseph, who slept on her lap, then at Callie sitting across the aisle. "Would you watch him for me?"

"Roight, mum." Callie stood while Rebecca carefully slid out from under her son. Callie sat beside him and gently rested his head on her lap. He barely stirred.

"We won't be long," Rebecca said. "If you need anything ask for us in the dining car."

"Yais, mum," Callie said with hesitation. She glanced down the aisle. "Should I send someone? I don't think blacks are allowed, mum."

"I'm sure if you explain that you need to speak to me, they'll let you pass."

244

Callie shrugged. "Hope so."

"Would you like me to bring you something?" Willa asked.

"I am a bit thirsty. A cuppa would suit me fine."

"Are you hungry?"

"No, mum."

"Fine, then." Willa glanced out the window. "We'll soon be in Melbourne."

The carriage pulled up to a curb in front of a charming two-story stone house. Lush gardens reached toward a manicured lawn, and ivy climbed the walls of the home. Anticipation filled Rebecca as she thought of the adventures that lay ahead. Melbourne was a beautiful and captivating city with magnificent architecture, lush greenery, and shady lanes.

"When I visit here, I'm always reminded of England," Willa said.

Rebecca stepped out of the carriage. "It's lovely. The house reminds me of some of the cottages near my home in Boston."

A frail woman leaning on a cane stepped onto the front porch.

"Oh my. Aunt Ada," Willa whispered, allowing the coachman to give her a hand down. She moved toward the house. When she started up the steps, she extended her hands. "Aunt Ada, how wonderful to see you!"

The old woman's face broke into a smile, and as tears escaped she pulled Willa into an embrace. "My dear Willa." After a few moments Ada stepped back. "Oh, how I've missed you. Five years is too long. I ought to throttle you." Her smile assuaged the words. Holding Willa at arm's length, she continued, "Let me have a look at you. Why, I'd say you haven't aged a bit."

"I wish that were true," Willa said with a grin. She turned toward the steps. "I've brought guests. I'd like you to meet my—"

"This must be Rebecca." The elderly woman smiled. She was so thin that her skin stretched taut across high cheekbones. Blue veins trailed a map across her forehead, and deep-set eyes nearly disappeared in folds of skin.

"It's a pleasure to meet you," Rebecca said. "I've heard so much about you."

"Well, don't listen to everything you hear." Ada smiled, and her blue eyes flickered with mischief.

"I assure you, I heard only complimentary words."

Ada chuckled. "That's simply the benevolence of my Willa." She held out her hand to Joseph, who clung to his mother. Gently patting his back, she said, "And this is Joseph. How handsome he is. I dare say, those blue eyes are exactly like his father's."

"Yes, exactly," Rebecca said.

"And this is Callie, one of our servants," Willa said, smiling at Callie.

"Callie," Ada said, then looked back at Willa. "Please come in."

The tired travelers followed Ada inside.

Ada looked at Callie. "You may go into the kitchen. The cook will tell you where to put your things." She turned to Rebecca. "Now, let me see that young lad. I dare say, he has the look of his grandfather."

Rebecca watched Callie quietly move toward the back of the house. She'd accepted her place with grace. *I wouldn't do so well*, Rebecca thought.

"I'll have your bags taken to your rooms," Ada said. "And

then we can sit in the garden and have a cup of tea. You must be exhausted."

"Yes. It's been a long trip. And tea sounds lovely." Willa linked arms with Ada. "I've missed this place. I have sweet memories of my days here, especially of the garden. Mum and I used to work there together."

"I remember."

Joseph whimpered.

"Oh dear. He's probably hungry," Rebecca said. "I'll have to feed him."

"Of course. You will find privacy in the nursery. I've kept it just as it was." Ada winked at Willa, then hobbled toward a hallway. "Come along, then."

The first days in Melbourne were spent relaxing and catching up on family news. However, once rested, the three women and occasionally Joseph made the rounds of Melbourne. They attended the philharmonic, where the music carried Rebecca back to Boston. Throughout the performance, she fought tears of joy and of longing for home.

They visited museums, an art gallery, and a vineyard where they picnicked along a river. Ada belied her age and was quite spry, seeming to enjoy the gadding about. And as she showed off Melbourne, her pride at the budding city was evident.

Willa had spent her early years in England, but she'd lived much of her life in Melbourne, and at every turn she found something that reminded her of her youth.

"I wish Bertram were here to share this," she said one afternoon as they walked along a sandy beach. Her eyes glistening, she gazed out at the waters of the Tasman Sea. "He so loved the ocean."

Rebecca was reminded of *her* father. She missed him.

Sometimes life was unbearably cruel, snatching away loved ones.

Joseph chortled in delight as he toddled across the sand in front of her. *I couldn't endure it if something happened to my little boy.* Joseph stopped and bent to pick up a treasure. Rebecca's throat tightened with the joy of him and at the painful thought of losing him. *No. That will never happen*, she told herself. She couldn't even imagine such a thing. It would be an endless, excruciating agony.

☙

One afternoon while Ada and Willa sat in the garden sipping tea, Rebecca approached the women. "Would you mind if I went out?" she asked.

"No. Of course not." Willa set her cup in its saucer. "Where are you going, dear?"

"Do you remember the stables I mentioned? I contacted the owner, a Mr. Brandan Sullivan, and he's agreed to meet with me."

"Hmm," Ada said. "I believe I've heard of Mr. Sullivan—in the papers. Just recently one of his horses won a very important race, as I recall."

Willa smiled. "You go right ahead. If we're lucky, that little boy of yours will wake up, and we'll have him all to ourselves."

"Callie's agreed to care for him," Rebecca said.

"She's quite good with him. And we'll let her know if we need her help." Willa glanced at Ada and smiled.

☙

When Rebecca approached the stables, she was impressed by the imposing property. There were long rows of stone fences and green pastures where handsome horses grazed. Even before her carriage approached the house, she passed by three large, freshly painted barns, each with an arena. The property was magnificent—reminding Rebecca of a southern estate. The colonial home had broad verandas on the ground floor plus another on the second story that was supported by large white pillars.

When the carriage stopped, she could feel her nerves jump. She'd never approached a horse trader on her own. Although Daniel had said they couldn't purchase a horse right now, she wanted to make a good impression. Perhaps in the future she would be in a position to do business with Brandan Sullivan. She took a slow breath and stepped out of the carriage.

A man dressed in casual attire approached. He looked rather dashing and carried himself with self-assurance. A smile touched his lips. "G'day. You must be Rebecca Thornton."

"Yes. And you're Brandan Sullivan?"

"That I am." Brandan dropped a kiss on her hand. He held on to her hand a moment too long, and Rebecca gently pulled it free.

Blue eyes coolly assessed her.

"I've heard you have a fine stable, Mr. Sullivan."

"Then you've heard right."

He continued to study Rebecca. She felt as if she were being deliberately intimidated, purposely set off balance. She hadn't been completely honest with him about her intentions. He assumed she was here to purchase an animal, and she hadn't told him otherwise. In all likelihood, he had little respect for an unescorted woman looking to buy a horse.

"I was hoping to have a look at some of your horses," she said in her most businesslike voice, enjoying the pretense.

"Yes, indeed." Hands clasped behind his back, he walked toward a barn.

Rebecca hurried her steps to keep up. Brandan was a daunting man. She'd have to be sharp-witted to convince him she was truly looking for a horse.

"She's a fine mare, just seven years old." He stopped in front of a stall where a chestnut-colored horse stood munching oats. "Michael?"

A short, balding man appeared.

"Get the lead rope, eh?"

Michael nodded and disappeared through a doorway. A moment later he returned, carrying a lead. The mare remained still while Michael clipped on the leather strap. She followed well when he guided her out of the stall.

Rebecca stepped back and studied the horse. She stood with one foot slightly in front of the other. "Could you take her outside for me?"

The man glanced at Brandan, who gave him a nod.

Once outside, Rebecca asked, "Please, would you walk her for me?"

Michael led the horse in wide circles. Each time the mare stepped forward with her left foot, her head bobbed up. "She seems a bit lame in that right foot."

"She picked up a pebble a few days ago. It's nothing more than a bruise. Right, Michael?"

"Yais. That's right, sir."

Unconvinced, Rebecca said, "Please walk her toward me."

Michael did as he was asked. The mare's gait was uneven, and she continued to favor the right foot. Rebecca quietly approached the animal, then ran a hand down the front leg, feeling for a pulse on the fetlock. It throbbed.

Rebecca released the leg. "She has pain in that foot, sir."

"Like I said, a bruise." Brandan folded his arms over his chest.

Rebecca moved around the horse. She ran a hand down its face. The mare didn't flinch; that was good. She removed a glove and let her hand rest on its soft lips and then opened the mare's mouth. Moving the tongue to the side, she studied the teeth. "I thought you said she was only seven." Rebecca turned and looked at Brandan. "She's at least thirteen."

"And how would you know that?" Brandan challenged.

"The last incisor has two hooks on it." Rebecca faced him squarely. "What is it you're trying to do here, Mr. Sullivan? I understood you to be a reputable businessman." She held his gaze. Michael handed her a cloth to wipe her hand clean.

His mouth turned up in a grin. "Just testing you to see how much you know. Seems you're right good with horses."

"And do you test everyone who comes to your farm or just the women?"

Brandan's smile disappeared. He squared his jaw. "I don't want my horses going where they aren't properly cared for."

Feeling her anger wane, Rebecca said, "I can understand that. Now, can I have a look at your better stock?"

Brandan showed her a two-year-old chestnut colt, and Rebecca's pulse jumped. He wasn't especially tall, but he was well muscled and balanced.

"He's a beaut, isn't he?"

"Yes, a fine animal." Rebecca watched him from a distance, then approached slowly. He didn't shy away or pull on the lead when she stepped up to him. He remained calm but watched her closely. Rebecca moved to his left side. He stood quietly. *That's good*, she thought. *He's steady*. His eyes were big and round. "Good boy," she said, laying a hand on his shoulder. He didn't flinch or step away. She ran her hand up his neck. He let out a blast of air from his nostrils but seemed unruffled. "Ah yes. You're a fine lad."

Rebecca quickly checked his teeth. Brandan was telling the truth—a two-year-old. She placed her hand on his forehead

251

and gently ran it down to his nose. He seemed to enjoy her touch. "So you like attention," she said.

She walked around to the side of the colt. He had a long, sloping shoulder, short back, and long hip. His legs were straight, with a nice slope to the fetlock. As her eyes moved to his legs, she could see that he had a short cannon bone and long forearm, which would make it easy for him to stretch out and cover a lot of ground quickly if needed. Drovers would appreciate that.

She studied him from the front and the back, then had Michael gallop him around the arena. There seemed to be no faults in this animal. He was exactly what Douloo needed. If only she could purchase him. She turned to Brandan. "Can you tell me about his breeding?"

"Good bloodlines. Both parents are from champion stock. I can get the papers for you if you like."

Rebecca wanted this horse. If only there were some way to convince Daniel they ought to purchase him. "How much are you asking for him?"

"He's a fine animal." Brandan acted as if he was thinking. "I couldn't take any less than fifteen hundred pounds."

"That's a bit steep, Mr. Sullivan. He's a beauty, but he's not made of gold."

"He'll bring you gold."

"I can't pay more than eleven hundred pounds."

The horseman shook his head. "No. I can't do that. But I'll drop my price a hundred pounds. That's all I can do."

Rebecca studied the colt. "Thirteen hundred."

"Thirteen hundred and fifty pounds—not a farthing less."

"All right, then. I'll wire my husband and get back to you."

Rebecca gave the horse a pat. No matter how grand the colt, she knew what Daniel would say.

"Good day, Mr. Sullivan."

He tipped his hat.

Feeling slightly guilty, Rebecca walked back toward the carriage. *I ought to turn around and face Mr. Sullivan with the truth. Tell him outright that I've deceived him.* The idea of humiliation kept her moving.

A sharp wind cut across the pastures and caught Rebecca's skirts. The air felt cool. She climbed into the carriage and settled onto the seat, the colt foremost in her mind. *He's one of the finest horses I've ever seen.* She imagined him grazing in the pastures back home and pictured the fine foals he'd throw. Then, knowing he would never reside at Douloo, she told the driver to move on.

22

Wind drove heavy rain that hit Rebecca like hard pellets. Head down and clutching her skirts, she ran for the front steps, splashing through a rivulet flowing down the center of the pathway. By the time she reached the porch, she was drenched.

The door opened. "Thank the Lord you're safe!" Willa cried, pulling Rebecca inside. "I was afraid something had happened to you." She helped Rebecca out of her wet cloak and handed the wrap to a housemaid. "Could you hang this to dry?"

The maid took the garment and disappeared into the back of the house.

"I can't believe how quickly this gale moved in," Rebecca said, holding her hands away from her sides. In spite of her cloak, her dress had gotten wet. "I'd better go up and change."

Ada stepped into the foyer. "We're gathering in the study. It's the most secure room in the house."

"It's just a rainstorm," Rebecca said. "I'm sure it will pass."

"Oh no. It's much more than a simple storm. One of the servants told me there was a cyclone just outside of town." She glanced at a window as a gust of wind pelted it with rain. "I've seen this type of gale before. They can be very dangerous, and this one's getting worse. We must take precautions."

Ada's eyes looked over Rebecca. "Oh my, you're soaking. Callie. Callie," she called.

Almost immediately the servant appeared. Her eyes went to Rebecca. "Mum, what happened ta ya?"

"I was caught in the storm is all. I'm fine. I don't know why everyone is making such a fuss."

"Callie, see to it that she has dry clothes," Ada instructed. "And then come down to the study, Rebecca. Stay away from the windows. The wind is blowing quite hard. I'm not sure this isn't a typhoon."

"Truly?"

"Truly," she said, then added in a take-charge tone, "Go on, now. Get yourself changed."

$\mathcal{D}$

Although dressed in warm, dry clothing, Rebecca still felt chilled as she hurried down the stairs. The wind shrieked. Rain mixed with leaves and other debris battered the windows. Broken limbs were hurled at the house. Rebecca had to admit this was not an ordinary summer storm. She crossed to Willa, who sat in an overstuffed chair. Joseph rested happily on her lap, eyes closed.

"May I have him?" Rebecca asked, bending to lift her son.

"I think he's asleep," Willa whispered, handing the little boy to his mother. She picked up a sewing basket and removed her knitting needles and yarn. She held up her work, a dark blue sweater. "Do you think it will fit him?"

"It looks just right." Rebecca settled Joseph against her shoulder and walked to a sofa. She took a coverlet from the back, arranged it around her shoulders, and then sat and moved Joseph to her lap, covering him with the remainder of the throw. Cuddling him close, she marveled at his peace. In the midst of a punishing storm, he knew no fear.

She glanced at the others in the room. "Children have such trust, never a care." A powerful gust of wind brutalized the windows, shaking them so hard it seemed they would shatter. "If only I possessed the same sense of security."

"Ada, do you truly think we're in danger?" Willa asked.

"Glory be, yes. This is a fierce storm. There's no telling what might happen."

Willa's needles moved more quickly.

"Where have the servants gone to, Ada?" Rebecca asked. "I'm quite fond of Callie. I don't want any harm to come to her."

"Most likely they've gone down to the root cellar. Of course, it's possible they might be in the kitchen. They usually take these kinds of things in stride."

Just as she finished speaking, the wind pounded with fresh ferocity. The women were silent and watched the glass, certain it would splinter at any moment. When the wind quieted, Ada said, "Now then, I think tea is in order. I'll go see if I can find someone to make it."

"No," Willa said. "You stay put. I'll see to it."

🎔

With wind and rain still pummeling the outside world, the women settled in. They sipped tea and did their best to concentrate on something other than the roar of the storm. Ada's arthritic hands shook as she worked on a piece of embroidery, and Willa knitted furiously, glancing at the

256

quaking windows from time to time. Rebecca tried to focus on a book, *The Fair God*, a historical romance. Some might have called it drivel, but she rather enjoyed the romantic adventure.

Something thumped against one of the windows, and glass shattered, splintering onto the floor. Wind and rain blustered into the room. Joseph startled awake and wailed his outrage. Rebecca scooped him up and hurried to the farthest corner away from the window.

"My heavens!" Willa stood. Glancing at Ada, she asked, "What shall we do?"

Using her cane, Ada pushed to her feet and shuffled toward the door. "I'll have the handyman board up the window. Come along, then. We'll retire to the sitting room. We should be fine there." Showing no sign of fear but leaning hard on her cane, she hobbled toward the doorway.

Rebecca's pulse throbbed in her throat. Would the house hold together if it were hit by a cyclone?

The storm raged for hours, but finally just before midnight the winds quieted and soft mists replaced driving rain. Exhausted, Rebecca carried Joseph to her room and placed him in the cradle beside the bed. Her eyes heavy, she burrowed beneath her blankets and immediately fell asleep.

⑦

Early the next day reports of the storm's damage moved through the gossip chain. Servants chattered about the dozen or more cyclones spotted about the district and the damage done to several areas in and around Melbourne. When Rebecca walked to the window and gazed out, she was shocked at what she saw. The grounds barely resembled the tidy quarter she'd grown accustomed to. It looked as if the neighborhood had been ransacked. Leaves and branches and other debris littered the streets and yards. There were toppled trees, their roots upturned and limbs torn away. A house across the lane had a part of its roof missing. Splintered boards and tattered shingles were all that was left of the north side of the house.

Rebecca felt unnerved and wondered how close they might have come to disaster. She longed for home, for Douloo and the safety she felt in Daniel's arms.

When Rebecca walked into the kitchen, Willa sat at the table, staring outside. "It's devastating, isn't it?"

"Yes. Horrifying." The smell of brewing tea and baking biscuits penetrated Rebecca's senses, giving her a sense of calm. "I pray all is well at home. Will we be returning soon?"

"Possibly next week, dear. But you needn't worry. I'm sure the storm didn't touch Douloo."

"I thank the Lord for that," Rebecca said, wishing they could leave immediately.

"What is it, Rebecca? You sound let down."

"I'm just missing Daniel . . . and Douloo. Right now it seems like a safe haven." As she spoke, Rebecca realized how important Douloo had become to her. It truly felt like home. "Is it possible for us to return right away?"

"I can contact the rail station and ask about the schedule." Willa smiled. "I must admit to missing it too. But Douloo is not any safer than here. We live in a dangerous world."

"Yes, of course. It just seems safe there, is all." Rebecca studied Willa. "I wish I had your faith. You've always seemed strong, always trusting."

"Not always. I dare say, like everyone I have my fears. When I'm worrying or I'm frightened, I think over all the times God has watched over me and my family, even delivering us from calamity. Even so, we live in a world full of tragedies."

Rebecca felt her heart thump extra hard. "Do you think something bad is going to happen? Or has happened?"

"Oh no. Not at all, dear. I was just thinking about how a place or a person can make us feel safe, when it's really God we ought to rely on." She turned her gaze outside. "And no matter how much I trust God, it hurts to watch Daniel and you go through trials." Willa's eyes brimmed with tears. "I love you both so much."

"We love you."

Willa managed a smile.

Rebecca sat in the chair beside Willa and placed an arm about her. "Thank you for loving us. I don't know that I would have been able to adjust to living in Queensland without you."

Willa placed a hand over Rebecca's. "You have been such a blessing. From the first day I saw you, I knew you were special. And that God had been good to my son and to me."

Rebecca squeezed Willa's shoulders and kissed her cheek. "I'm the one who has been blessed." She stood. "Now, would you like more tea?"

"I'd love some."

Rebecca walked to the cupboard and lifted out a teacup and saucer. Closing the door, she said, "I hope there's no difficulty in changing our tickets." She carried the teakettle to Willa and refilled her cup, then poured some for herself and set the kettle back on the stove. She carried her cup and saucer across the room and sat at the kitchen table.

Ada shuffled in. "Oh my, I slept so soundly. I can hardly believe the time. I can't remember when I've slept so late."

"Aunt Ada, it's only nine. Not at all late."

"You know me, six o'clock on the dot." Leaning hard on her cane, she lowered herself into a chair. "My, that was a frightful storm. It's been many years since I've seen one quite like it."

"When I lived in Boston we had nor'easters that roared quite loudly," Rebecca said. "But I don't know that I've ever experienced a squall as fearsome as this one."

"These storms are rather unnerving. I'm grateful my home is intact, unlike my dear neighbor's." She glanced out the window. Shaking her head, she continued, "The cleanup will take weeks."

The following afternoon Rebecca traveled to the Sullivan property. She wanted to see the colt once more before leaving and make certain he hadn't been injured by the cyclone. She'd heard the storm had hit the area hard. And as distasteful as the idea was, she needed to tell Brandan Sullivan the truth. Her deception had been childish and wrong.

When the carriage moved down the lane near the farm, Rebecca's apprehension grew. She stuck her head out of the window to get a better look at the devastation. Trees were down everywhere. Some lay flat against the ground, their roots exposed, as if they'd been pushed over. Others lay on top of the earth with no root base at all, looking like they'd been cut down and tossed aside.

When the carriage turned into the lane of the Sullivan estate, Rebecca's apprehension turned into outright alarm. There were no barns. Instead, piles of sticks and debris lay where barns had once been. The drive was littered with pieces of buildings, tree branches, greenery, and mud. More than once the driver had to stop and clear the road before continuing.

Lord, no. Please no, Rebecca prayed. The horse had been in one of the barns. What had become of him?

The carriage stopped, and the driver climbed down from his seat. Opening the door, he said, "Sorry, mum, but this is as far as we can go. There's too much debris." He glanced up the drive at a heap of a barn. "I doubt there's much reason to continue anyway. I can take you back to town if you like."

Rebecca stepped out of the carriage. "No. I'll walk the rest of the way." She took a few steps, then stopped. "Please wait, would you?"

"Right." The driver closed the door and stood at the head of the team.

Rebecca picked her way through and around the farm's remains. There were horses wandering about freely. She didn't see the colt.

As she approached the house, she could see it had withstood the storm better than the barns. There were trees down in the yard, and windowpanes, shingles, and boards were strewn about, but the manor stood.

Brandan sat on the top step of the porch. When he saw her, he pushed to his feet and walked down the steps. "G'day," he said. His voice sounded empty. He picked up a panel of wood and tossed it. "Cyclone hit us straight on."

"Are you all right, Mr. Sullivan?" Rebecca asked, anxious over his ashen complexion.

"Yes. Fine." He glanced at one of the damaged barns. "Wish everything else had fared as well." His eyes rested on Rebecca. "We lost several of the horses."

"The colt?"

"He made it. Got a bit bruised up, but he'll come 'round."

"Thank the Lord." Rebecca blew out a breath. "I must admit that as I came up the drive I was afraid that . . . well, that he'd perished."

"No. He was one of the lucky ones."

Rebecca needed to tell him the truth about her ruse. "I must apologize for my dreadful behavior."

Brandan looked at her with a questioning expression.

"I wasn't completely honest with you, sir." Rebecca paused,

261

putting off the inevitable a moment longer. "I hadn't intended on buying the colt."

Brandan narrowed his eyes. "Then why did you act as if you were?"

"I wanted to purchase him. In fact, I hope you'll consider selling him to me one day in the future. That is, if you still have him at that time." She glanced about. "Just as this storm has struck you down, so has the weather at Douloo Station. A drought is draining the life from our home. Buying fine horses is presently considered an unnecessary luxury."

Brandan sat on the bottom porch step. He shook his head slightly and rested his arms on his thighs. "You were pretty good," he said with a grin. "You had me fooled." He chuckled. "You might want to consider going into horse trading one of these days. You know horses, and you can fool a bloke as good as any I've seen."

"I hope this doesn't ruin hope for further transactions," Rebecca said, taken aback at Brandan's reaction.

"No. Not at all." He pushed to his feet. "In fact, it would be an honor." He gazed at his devastated property. "I'll put the place back together again. And if the colt is still here when you're ready to do business, we'll talk."

"Thank you for being so understanding. Of course, we can't know when the drought will end, but we pray soon." She extended her hand. Brandan shook it. "I'm sorry for your losses, sir."

Brandan nodded slightly and then walked toward one of the littered pastures.

Rebecca returned to the carriage and dropped onto the seat. She needed to go home. She needed Daniel.

23

Elvina Walker headed straight for Rebecca. Wishing there were some way to avoid the busybody, Rebecca glanced about the church. There must be someone she could visit with. Before she could make a move, Elvina stood in front of her. Ready for an assault, Rebecca straightened her spine and put on a smile.

"It's good to see you, Rebecca. You've been missed these past weeks." Elvina glanced about. "I don't see Daniel."

"He had business to attend to. And as for my not being here for several weeks, I thought everyone knew I was away. Willa and I took a holiday in Melbourne."

"Right. I remember now. I did hear that. I hope ya had a fine time."

"As a matter of fact, we had a grand time. It was lovely there—green and lush. We visited the opera and the ballet and even picnicked at the seashore."

"I heard there was a bad storm."

"Yes. It was rather frightening."

"Everyone fared well though, eh?"

"Yes." Rebecca looked about to see if Cambria had arrived.

She'd missed her friend, and now would be a perfect time for her to make an appearance. She looked at the white-haired woman. "It's good to be home."

Elvina nodded. "Daniel missed church a few times while you were gone. Seems he's busy these days."

Rebecca could feel herself growing angry. "I'm sure you must understand how much Daniel loves this church and would never miss unless there was no other alternative. He has a lot to do. The drought has hit us hard, just as it has everyone."

Again Rebecca searched for someone to save her from Elvina's interrogation. Cambria stepped into the sanctuary but was engaged in conversation with her mother. It would be rude to interrupt them. Willa was already sitting. She looked back at Elvina. "I'd better get seated. I'm sure the service will begin at any moment." She edged away.

"Tell Daniel hello for me. I feel badly that he's been unable to attend."

Feeling as if she were tethered to Elvina, Rebecca said, "Of course. I'll tell him. I'm certain he'll be here next week."

"Well, let's hope so." Elvina sniffed. "G'day ta ya." She sauntered toward the front pew, her Bible clasped against her stomach and her ample hips rotating from side to side.

Exhaling her frustration, Rebecca moved toward the pew where Willa sat. She sidestepped into the row and dropped down beside her mother-in-law.

Cambria strolled down the aisle, and wearing her usual bright smile, she slid in next to Rebecca and threw her arms about her friend. "Good ta see ya. Where's Joseph? Is he all right? I heard Melbourne was hit by a terrific storm."

Rebecca laughed. "I don't know which question to answer first." She smiled. "Joseph has the sniffles and is out of sorts. I thought it best to leave him home."

"Sorry ta hear he's not feeling well."

"Willa assures me he's fine. She said little ones are often down with something or other." Rebecca tucked a stray lock of hair back in place. "And Melbourne *was* hit by a ferocious storm, but no one in the family was injured."

"That's a blessing, eh?" Cambria settled back and placed her Bible in her lap. "What do ya think about us going riding this afternoon? It's been far too long since we've been out." Her expression sincere, she added, "I've missed ya."

"I've missed you too. And I'd love to go riding, but Rev. Cobb is taking our afternoon meal with us. I dare not be absent."

Cambria pouted. "Yais, well perhaps one day during the week, then?"

"Absolutely. I'd love it." With a sigh, Rebecca added, "We'll have to ride while we can. The way things are, I'm wondering if we'll have any riding horses left for use in another month."

"Having ta sell off stock, eh?"

"Yes. It's frightening."

"Us too. Things are pretty sparse at our place. Me oldest brother is droving for another station, so there's more work than ever for me." Her cheery expression was replaced by gloom. "The drought's gotten so bad, I'm not sure we'll be able ta hang on. We've lost a lot of sheep; more are dying every day. The water holes are dried up, and the stream on our place is nearly gone. Don't know just what we're gonna do."

"Will your family move away?"

"Maybe. Me aunt Elle is already packing ta go."

"No."

"There's no one ordering dresses these days," Cambria said sadly. "She's got ta make a living."

Rebecca searched the sanctuary for Cambria's aunt. She sat near the back, and when she saw Rebecca she flashed her a smile. Rebecca waved. "I'll miss her dreadfully. She's a dear person. I've always admired her." She laid a gloved hand over Cambria's. "Is there anything I can do? I just couldn't bear to lose you and your family."

Cambria's eyes teared. "I wish there were something that could be done. Elle won't be so far away though—just Brisbane."

"What will she do there?"

"She's a grand dressmaker. I expect she'll open a shop."

"I can't believe she's going. Elle belongs here."

Cambria blinked back tears. "She said when the rains come she'll be moving back."

"And you? If your family moves will you go?"

Cambria shrugged. "What else would I do? Dad said that if things don't get better he has a mate south of the Downs he can work for."

"And what of Jim?" Rebecca whispered.

"He's not made his intentions clear. I guess I'll be saying good-bye ta him too." Cambria sounded like she was trying to keep from crying.

Grief settled over Rebecca. Life was so unfair.

The sanctuary hushed as Rev. Cobb walked to the pulpit. "G'day," he said, smiling at the parishioners. "Good to have you 'ere this morning." His eyes settled on Rebecca and Willa. "And welcome back, ladies. We thank God for bringing you home safely."

Rebecca felt protected. The reverend was a kind man who truly cared for the people in his congregation. Elvina's sharp opinions came to mind, and Rebecca marveled at the differences in Elvina and the reverend. One said she cared, but the other one truly did.

He hooked a finger inside his cleric's collar and tugged slightly. "Bit warm today." He glanced out the window. "And dry. I know there are a lot of ya who are suffering. It's in times

266

like these that we need to pray for each other and reach out to one another, bearing up together. If yer struggling, let us know so the people in the church can help."

Leaning on the lectern, he continued, "For some, this might seem a harsh land, but for those of us who know this territory, it's a place of splendor. Course, these days it's stubbornly withholding its bounty, which means we need to hang on to our faith. Especially as the Christmas season descends, we may feel disheartened, but we must keep Christ and his blessed gift before us."

"It doesn't feel like the Christmas season. I'm supposed to sing on Christmas Eve, but I don't feel much like it. I'm having trouble holding fast to my faith," Cambria whispered. "Why doesn't God bring the rain, eh?"

"I don't know," Rebecca said, wishing she did and wanting to bolster Cambria's diminished faith. However, her own faith was too feeble to give confidence to someone else.

✑

As Rebecca walked toward the surrey, Cambria fell into step beside her. "Eh, how about we go riding tomorrow?"

"I'd love to. What time?"

"Early, before it gets hot." Cambria smiled. "What ya think of inviting the gents?"

"I wish that were possible, but Daniel won't take time off. And he can't spare Jim."

"Yeah, I knew that. It's just that I never see Jim these days. I'm beginning ta think he's never gonna let me know his real intentions. I fear I'll die an old maid."

"That will never happen. He'll come around. He's smitten."

"Hope yer right," Cambria said. "Bein' an old maid was

never my plan." She grinned. "Tomorrow, then." She walked off to join her family.

Rev. Cobb and Willa approached Rebecca. The reverend smiled warmly. "It was good to see yer lovely face in church again, Rebecca."

"Thank you, Reverend." She felt a need to excuse Daniel's absence and added, "Daniel wanted to be here, but there is so much to be done . . ."

"No worries. I understand. Times like these call for leniency." He smiled, and the lines at the corners of his eyes deepened. "I know he'd be here if he could."

"I enjoyed your sermon very much, Reverend," Rebecca said. "It was heartening."

"Thank you." Rev. Cobb placed a hand on his stomach. "I'm looking forward to dining with the Thorntons. I've tasted Lily's cooking before. And there's none better."

Meghan stepped up and stood in front of the minister. "My mother asked if I could extend an invitation to you, Reverend, to join us for dinner."

"I'd be delighted, but I've already had an invitation. Perhaps another time?"

Meghan's brown eyes narrowed. "Oh. Of course." She glanced at Rebecca. "I'll tell Mum." She brushed at something on her skirt and then looked back up at Rev. Cobb and gave her head a slight bob. "G'day ta ya, then." With that, she flounced off.

"Reverend, I am so pleased you're coming to our home, but now I wish I'd chosen another day," Willa said. "I don't want any more animosity between the Thorntons and the Linnells. There's too much hostility already. And now it seems our invitation has set Meghan off."

"No worries, Mrs. Thornton. I'm sure she'll get over it. I'll speak with her mother before I leave. I'm confident I can smooth things over. So if you'll excuse me, then."

Rebecca watched as the reverend walked toward Mrs. Linnell. They exchanged a pleasant greeting and chatted amiably. "Well, it appears all is well." Rebecca shook her head. "No matter what we do, it seems to provoke the Linnells."

"The reverend's right. We shouldn't fret about such things," Willa said.

"Yes, that's true. And no amount of worrying will ever change Meghan. She's spoiled and always will be."

"She may come 'round one day."

"Perhaps, but I'm not holding my breath." Rebecca climbed into the surrey.

When Rev. Cobb returned, he was smiling and relaxed. "Two Sundays in a row I have the privilege of eating at the best tables in the district. God is good."

🜁

That afternoon the Thorntons and Rev. Cobb gathered for the midday meal. Daniel managed to make it to the table just as the food was served. "Sorry for my tardiness," he said, sliding into his seat. "I didn't know we had a guest."

"Oh, I thought I told—" Willa began.

"It must have slipped my mind." Daniel took a long drink of water.

"You look like you've taken on a bit too much sun, Daniel," Rebecca said.

"Probably have. Stubborn mob kept me out longer than I planned, and rather than wearing my hat, I was waving it much of the time, trying to keep the beasts moving."

"Where are you moving them to?" the reverend asked.

"Just upstream a bit. There's a little more water and grass there."

Daniel seemed out of sorts. Rebecca wondered if something had happened.

"You going to hold out, then?" the reverend asked.

"We'll hold on, but things aren't looking good." Daniel rested his palms on the table and settled his eyes on Rebecca. "I was thinking it might be a good time for Rebecca to make a trip to Boston." He looked at his mother. "And, Mum, you might like to see America. It's grand." He tried to smile. "I'm sure Thomas and Mildred would be pleased to see you both. And you'd be able to attend their wedding."

Silence settled over the table, except for Joseph who banged his spoon against his wooden tray.

Finally Willa said, "You can't be serious, Daniel. You know I'd never leave."

"Just for a while, Mum." Daniel leaned on the table and let his eyes slide away from his mother's.

"No, Daniel," Willa said firmly.

"And I'm not leaving you either." Rebecca laid her hand over his. "To abandon you when you need me most . . . I could never do that."

"You don't know what you're saying, Rebecca. You haven't seen it. The flats are already littered with carcasses. And it's going to get worse. Disease will come. I don't want you 'ere. I don't want to worry about you and Joseph." His eyes rested on his son. Joseph was busy pushing his green beans across his tray.

Rebecca turned to the reverend. "It's not right for me to go . . . is it?"

Rev. Cobb dipped his spoon into his bowl of soup. "A wife is to be a helpmate to her husband. I don't see that you can do that very well all the way from Boston. But if Daniel insists, then you should go. A husband is the head of his family."

"I don't *want* anyone to leave," Daniel said. "But I see no other choice. I'll not watch the people I love suffer." He pushed away from the table. "I can't be worrying about my family while I'm trying to save Douloo."

"I love that you care so deeply," Rebecca said. "But I can't leave you, not like this. And Christmas is only weeks away. Perhaps things will improve."

Daniel walked to the window and gazed outside, then turned and looked at Rebecca. "Have you thought about what you'll do when the water is gone? Today I put down a whole mob of cattle. And Noble will have to be sold—along with some of the other stock."

"Not Chavive," Rebecca gasped.

"No, she'll stay," Daniel said.

"We've a well, and it's still providing enough for our needs," Willa said. "And I thought Jessop promised we'd have water soon."

"He's still drilling. And he doesn't know. Like us, he can only hope."

"All right then, we'll stay until we must leave." Willa picked up her spoon and resumed eating.

Daniel folded his arms over his chest and looked straight at the reverend. "I don't know why God is allowing all of this. He could fix things if he wanted to."

"We cannot lean upon our own understanding, Daniel," the reverend said.

"Right now, that's all I've got."

24

Daniel put a foot on the bottom rail of the corral fence and laid an arm on the top rail. "With things the way they are, I'd say you're right smart to move on. Can't fault you."

The drover shifted his hat forward and scuffed the dry ground with the toe of his boot. "Hate ta go. Yer a roight good man ta work for. But I figgered ya'd have ta let me go soon anyways." Squinting, he looked into the early morning sun. "Might get lucky though. There's reports of gold up 'round Cloncurry."

Daniel stepped away from the fence. "Right." He extended his hand.

Grasping it, the drover shook it.

"Good luck." Daniel managed a smile.

"If the weather changes and favors ya, I'll be back. Ya can count on it."

"Right. I'll be looking for you."

The young man turned and walked away.

Daniel watched until he disappeared around the corner of the barn, then gave his attention to Chavive as she trotted across the corral. It seemed like a lifetime ago that he and

Rebecca had ridden in the forest outside Boston. He'd brought her so far from home—and to what? A dying station.

His thoughts turned to Rebecca's early rebellion, and he smiled. She'd been like a wild filly. *She was spirited, all right. Wouldn't take to a bit.* He grinned. She could still be stubborn, but Daniel was proud of her. She'd made Douloo her home, and she'd done right well with Noble and the other horses.

A pang of grief hit him. Noble was gone—sold just after Christmas. *Fine Christmas gift,* he thought with derision. He grasped the wooden fence, barely feeling a splinter that jabbed his palm. What would he do if he lost Douloo? How would he take care of his family? He tried to pray, but there were no words, only an ache inside.

Woodman joined Daniel and leaned against the fence. "He's goin', eh?"

"Yeah. Can't blame him."

"Goin' up with the other blokes in search of gold?"

"Yep. I've even given thought to having a go myself."

Woodman's eyes glinted with amusement, but his plump face remained unchanged. "Minin's dangerous work. And up that way there're crocs. If a bloke's not careful, he'll end up croc tucker." He chuckled.

"No worries. I'll be staying 'ere." Daniel's eyes scanned the cloudless sky. He turned and folded his arms over his chest, resting his back against the fence. "Things got to get better, eh?"

Woodman didn't answer. His dark eyes held only a question Daniel couldn't read. Unable to face what the man really thought, Daniel changed the subject. "Mr. Linnell invited me out to have a look at a bull of his. I'd like you to come along."

"Probably good that I do. I'll 'ave ta keep an eye out for that Miss Linnell. She 'asn't landed a husband yet, and I'd say she's still noticin' ya." Woodman grinned.

"That's long past. She and I been mates since we were kids. Figure we know better how to be friends than anything else. She'll understand that."

Daniel looked up into the branches of a scorched acacia. Squawking rose from its upper branches. In the nearly bare limbs, a well-fed maggie looked down on him. "Only animals eating good these days are the scavengers."

Woodman gazed at the bird. "With so much of the mob dyin', why ya thinkin' 'bout buyin' a bull?"

"I know I'm taking a chance, but it's now or never. If times were good Rush Linnell wouldn't sell him."

𝓓

Jim ran his horse into the yard and stopped at the foot of the front steps. Willa had been sitting on the veranda. She stood. "Ma'am," Jim said, "can you tell me where I might find Daniel?"

"I believe he's in the barn. Is there something wrong?"

"Yes, ma'am." He tipped his hat and turned his horse toward the barn.

Daniel met him outside the door. "What you in such a hurry for?"

"Trouble. You better come with me."

"What is it?"

"That bull you bought a few days ago. He's sick. Looks like redwater."

Daniel's throat constricted. "Can't be. He was fine."

"Well, he's not now."

Daniel ran to his horse, which was already saddled and tied at the railing outside the corral. He shoved his foot into the stirrup and pushed up into the saddle. "Let's have a look, then."

The two men galloped toward the pasture where the bull had been released. When they reached the field, Daniel could see right away the animal was sick. He stood with his legs locked and his head down, and he was breathing in a fast pant. Daniel looked at Jim. "Why do you think it's redwater?"

"I seen his urine—dark red and foamy."

Daniel climbed down from his horse and slowly approached the animal. The bull seemed unaware of him. Before Daniel reached him, he dropped onto his front hocks, then onto his side. Daniel moved closer, shaking his head. How could this happen? There hadn't been a case of redwater in the district all year.

The bull would be gone in a matter of hours, and the rest of the herd would follow. He pulled his hat from his head and swiped it across his pant leg. "We better get the rest of the mob moved," is all he said, but inside he was angry. What had he done to deserve this?

$\mathscr{D}$

As Daniel had predicted, the bull lived only a few hours. And in the weeks that followed, much of the herd sickened and died.

Daniel took to spending more and more time on his own, riding alone in the desiccated grasslands, searching for solace somewhere in the open country. In the past it had always been there for him. But now all he could see was a frightening future, one without Douloo. Why would God allow such hardship to come upon his family?

$\mathscr{D}$

Rebecca sat on the veranda with Willa. Joseph toddled across the wooden planking toward his mother. When he reached her, she scooped him up.

"He's such a big boy for a one-year-old," Willa said.

"He's going to be tall like his father." Rebecca cuddled him. "Hard to believe a year has passed since his birth."

Wanting his freedom more than he wanted his mother, Joseph wriggled free and scrambled off her lap. Taking lurching steps, he moved toward the staircase. He dropped to his hands and knees and backed up toward the first step.

"Oh, no you don't," Willa said, catching him before he started down. "I'm not about to chase you around the yard, not in this heat. You have more than enough to entertain yourself right here." She carried him to a box of toys sitting against the house and offered him a wooden horse. He grabbed it and banged it against the porch planks.

Rebecca sipped from a glass of water and gazed out at the dry land. "It's probably icy cold and snowy in Boston," she said, her heart longing for a true winter.

"Sounds marvelous." Willa smiled. "Never thought I'd say that."

"It does sound good." Rebecca wondered if she'd find herself back there one day. *No*, she told herself, remembering Daniel's suggestion that she return to Boston for a time. *I can't leave him while things are so bad.* So much had gone wrong, and she'd started to believe that he might actually lose Douloo. With a sigh she gazed out over the open ground. He was out there—somewhere—alone.

Willa rocked forward and laid a hand over Rebecca's. "He'll be right as rain. Don't you worry about him."

Rebecca offered her mother-in-law a faint smile. "I just wish it weren't so painful for him. Nothing I say or do seems to help."

"He's not alone. God knows his struggle."

Rebecca nodded. "I've been thinking about Mildred a lot lately. I miss her."

"Have you heard from her?"

"Yes. I meant to tell you. She sent a letter."

"I hope all is well."

"Yes. She and Thomas are doing wonderfully. Thomas's business has picked up, and Mildred said they've enjoyed the holidays. They've planned the wedding for April."

"Oh, how wonderful. A spring wedding should be lovely. It is spring in Boston in April, right?"

"Yes." Rebecca sighed. "I wish I could be there."

"Perhaps you ought to go. I know Daniel would feel much better if his family were out of harm's way."

"I know. And I've considered going. But Daniel needs me. Every time I think of how hard he works and how much he's losing every day . . . well, I just can't bring myself to leave him."

"Daniel has faced difficult times before. He won't collapse without you."

"I know that. But if I'm gone all I'll do is worry about him and Douloo. And if you stay I'll be worrying about you and wishing I were here to help."

Willa watched vultures circle, gliding on the heat drafts rising from the flats. "You must do as God directs." She looked at Rebecca. "I'll be thankful for your cooking skills. Lily is leaving us."

"Lily? I didn't know."

Willa pushed to her feet and crossed to the railing. "Her family needs her. They live west of here." She gazed at the dry land stretching out to the horizon. "The drought has touched everyone."

Dust billowed in the distance, and a few moments later a carriage appeared on the road. "Now, who can that be on such a hot day?" Willa leaned over the porch slightly to get a better look. "Why, it's the reverend," she said, moving to the stairway.

He stopped the buggy, climbed down, and secured the horse. "G'day," he said, easily taking the steps.

"Good day to you. What a lovely surprise."

"You look well, Willa." He nodded at Rebecca. "As do you."

Rebecca picked up Joseph. "How nice to see you, Reverend."

"It's a hot one, eh?" Rev. Cobb said, glancing at Rebecca and then smiling at Joseph.

"Quite," Willa said. "Can I offer you something to drink?" Her sky-blue eyes were warm and friendly.

"Yes. The drive here has given me a real thirst."

"Will water do? Or would you prefer tea?"

"Water sounds grand."

Rev. Cobb stepped into the shade of the veranda and removed his hat.

Joseph wiggled free of his mother and tottered toward the man. "He's growing like a weed, eh?"

"Yes. And he's showing me he has a mind of his own."

Jabbering, Joseph moved toward the reverend. When he stood in front of him, he looked up and smiled and then held up his arms.

"Does he want me to pick him up?" the reverend asked.

"I believe so."

"Friendly lad." Rev. Cobb bent and hefted Joseph with a slight groan. "Sturdy too." He held him at arm's length and smiled. "He must be about a year old, then?"

"Yes. He turned one on January sixth. Just two days ago," Rebecca said.

Willa returned with a glass of water and offered it to the reverend. He set Joseph back on the porch and accepted the drink. After taking a drink, he smiled and said, "Just what I needed." He took another swallow.

"Reverend, won't you have a seat?" Willa asked.

Sitting, Rev. Cobb said, "I got up this morning and thought it had been too long since I'd visited Douloo." He glanced at the yard and barn. "I was hoping I might find Daniel about."

"He's working," Willa said. "I'm sure he'll be disappointed at having missed you."

"He's probably burning dead cattle," Rebecca said, unable to disguise her angst.

"That bad, eh?"

"Yes. And he won't let me help him. He says it's too ghastly for a woman." She looked out over empty fields. "I've never seen a man so filled with sorrow."

The reverend nodded. "I've been praying. Is there anything I can do to help?"

Rebecca settled her eyes on him. "Answer one question. Why? Why would God allow this to happen to a man like my husband? He's good and faithful. It doesn't seem right."

"I wish I had a definite answer for you, Rebecca. Every time I see this kind of thing, I'm tempted to question God." He leaned forward and rested his arms on his legs. "What I know is that we live in a world of sin. And sin touches everything."

He pressed the palms of his hands together. "God doesn't always shield us from the pain of life, but he always uplifts and encourages us in the midst of our troubles. And he'll walk through this with you and Daniel. You can count on his wisdom and strength. He loves you both."

Rebecca could feel the sting of tears behind her eyes. "I'm beginning to fear what each new day will bring. My faith is waning."

"I'm praying for you and all the others in the district. Don't be afraid. God's 'ere, and when you've walked through this trouble, you'll be stronger for it. I'm confident all will be well with the Thorntons." He smiled kindly.

279

At sunset Daniel rode into the yard. He nearly staggered up the front steps. His fatigue was profound. Rebecca guessed it was more than physical exhaustion, but rather weariness of his soul.

After Daniel had washed off the day's dirt and eaten his evening meal, Rebecca convinced him to take a walk with her. Their arms linked, they strolled beneath a dark sky lit only by a wedge of moon and glittering stars. The night was quiet except for chirping cicadas and the distant yip of a dingo.

"I like the evenings here," Rebecca said, leaning against Daniel.

He gazed into the darkness and then took in a slow, even breath. "I used to. Now even the darkness can't hide the ruin from my eyes. I see it always."

He glanced back at the house. Soft lights glowed from the kitchen and parlor. A blush of light came from the upstairs room his parents had once shared. Now only his mother slept there.

"It feels like Douloo is dying. And I can't save her. I'm losing everything my father and grandfather worked for. Last night I dreamed it had all died, the trees and livestock." He looked at Rebecca. "You and Joseph, everything. And there was nothing I could do to save you."

He turned his gaze upward. "I don't know what to do . . . how do I save our home? I pray and pray and ask God to bring rain and to protect us from ill fortune . . . but he doesn't hear."

"I'm sure he does, Daniel. But God's ways are not our ways."

Daniel shook his head. "I'm struggling, Rebecca. I've done all I can, and still God refuses to rescue us." Daniel held his arms away from his body. "He's walked away. And I don't know why."

"No. God would never turn his back on his children. His Word says he shall never leave us nor forsake us. It's his promise to us. And God never breaks a promise."

Rebecca turned to face Daniel and gripped his arms. "All we can do is surrender Douloo to God. It doesn't belong to us anyway. It's his and has been from the moment he created it."

Daniel gazed at her in the near darkness. "Rebecca, I can't just give it up. I won't." He turned and walked back to the house.

Rebecca stared after him, dread growing inside of her. Something terrible waited for her and Daniel. She knew it.

25

Wind sighed and dust hung in the air. Daniel pressed his rifle against his shoulder, sited in the young bullock, and then squeezed the trigger. The blast fractured the quiet. The animal dropped.

"That's the last of 'em," he said, lowering the gun and walking toward the carcass. "If the rains come soon, some of the rest might make it." How many times had he hoped and prayed for that? He studied the wasting herd. It would be only days before he'd be forced to destroy more. He reached down, grabbed a hoof and dragged the dead animal to a mound of fly-infested remains.

Woodman stood back, his eyes mournful. He glanced at gathering crows and then picked up a can of kerosene and walked toward the pile of dried cow dung, bones, and skin. "No tucker 'ere," he said, with a nod at the birds. "They won't get fat off these, eh?" He walked around the heap of dead animals, dousing them with the kerosene.

Daniel lit a torch and followed Woodman, igniting the animals. Soon the stench of burning hides and flesh permeated the air. He moved back and watched the cremation, bile rising in his throat.

With the hard edge of bitterness cutting into him, he watched his hard work, his hopes, his future burn. Cawing crows darted in and out of drifting smoke. Finally, finding no way to feast, they broke away and disappeared, no doubt in search of other remains. They wouldn't have far to look.

Daniel moved close to the pile. Leaning away from the flames, he grabbed a hoof and draped the body of an emaciated cow deeper into the fire. Detesting every moment of this repulsive duty, he and Woodman walked around the mound, lifting and shoving animals deeper into the fiery heap.

"Wish they hadn't wandered so close ta the house," Woodman said. "I hate burnin' 'em."

Daniel leaned on a pitchfork and stared at the house. The smoke and stench would drive his family indoors. *Glad Dad's not 'ere to see this*, he thought, then using the pitchfork, he hoisted a cow into the blaze. Angry and disheartened, he plodded around the pile, pushing unburned parts into the fire.

Daniel thought he heard a baby's cry coming from the house. Shoving the pitchfork into the ground, he turned and studied his home. It seemed the same as always, sturdy and commanding, rising up in the midst of the flatlands. He'd always believed Douloo could withstand any assault. Now with the stink of burning hides in his nostrils, he was no longer sure. Would the station still be here when Joseph became a man? He turned away and continued his march around the burning heap.

The creases in his black face deeper than usual, Woodman hunkered down and stared at the horizon. "Don't take the torment, Daniel. Things mean nothin'. We come from the earth naked, and naked we return ta it. Ya 'ave yer family and they 'ave ya—that's what matters. Ya've no need of property."

283

"You can't understand. You never owned anything."

"The land and what's on it can't belong ta a man."

"The aborigine way isn't the *only* way." Daniel stabbed angrily at another carcass.

"What has yer labor gotten ya, lad?"

Daniel glowered at the smoldering mass. "My grandfather worked and sweated to build this place, and my father after him. I can't abandon it."

"Ya can if ya 'ave ta."

"No. Never." Daniel shoved the pitchfork through a bloated animal and heaved it toward the inner flames. "I have a family who depends on me. You don't."

"That's not it," Woodman said. "The land is sacred. It belongs ta no man. Ya may think ya own it, but ya don't. It does as it wills."

"I'll do as I will," Daniel nearly screamed.

Knowing he had no real power over his life, the panic he'd been holding down threatened to engulf him. What came with each passing day was not his to ordain. He'd tried to release the station to God, but it still felt like his. Hadn't God given it to the Thorntons? Wasn't it his to care for?

He glared at Woodman, shocked at the ferocity of his emotions. "Douloo is not aborigine sacred land! It is Thornton land!"

Woodman gazed sadly at Daniel. "The earth belongs ta no man." His eyes moved to something in the distance. "It has a song. If ya listen ya can 'ear it. It's the music left by the gods who walked 'ere. They speak ta us." He looked squarely at Daniel. "And they would say, think of yer family, the people ya love. They're what matter."

Daniel sagged, "I'm tired . . . tired of watching Douloo die, tired of praying to a God who doesn't hear." Sorrow cut through his middle. "What am I doing wrong?" Daniel was nearly weeping.

"Every day I walk in my father's shadow. He's always with me, watching my failure. I can hear his disappointment, his correction. But I don't know what to do." Daniel looked down at a half-burned calf; its dead eyes stared back at him. "This is what I have left, this pile of bones and hides."

"Daniel, think of yer boyhood. Life held more for ya . . . and yer father then."

Daniel stared at the flames. It was hard to breathe.

"Think of the days with yer dad—the good days. Ya fished and hunted."

His voice hard, Daniel said, "I remember hard work and failure."

"No, before that. The days when yer father and ya was close. What was it that mattered ta ya most?"

Daniel thought back. As a boy, he'd always looked forward to outings with his dad. They'd hunted roos, goannas, and dingoes. He'd learned how to track and how to find his way in the vastness of the flats. They'd herded cattle, and his father had shown him how to tell the difference between a healthy bullock and a sick one. He'd taught him how to rope and how to brand calves.

There had been family picnics and games. And sometimes on special days his father had played hide-and-seek with him and Elton. When they'd discover their father, he'd leap up, scooping them into his arms. And then he'd chuckle. His laugh had been deep and rich. Daniel smiled at the memory.

"Ya remember, then?" Woodman walked toward Daniel.

"Yeah. I remember."

Resting a hand on Daniel's shoulder, Woodman said, "That's what ya need ta hang on to—the devotion, not the land. Before yer father lost his way, he knew how ta love."

"He always loved Douloo."

"Too much. As ya do."

"No. Loving Douloo was the one good thing he held on

285

to. You can't love this place too much. It's all we have, all that will last."

Woodman squeezed Daniel's shoulder. "Careful lad, or ya'll lose sight of what's real."

Daniel pointed his pitchfork at the pile of burning cattle. "That's what's real!" He turned slowly, gazing at the land. "Look 'round you. What do you see?"

"Ya 'ave ta look farther. There's more than what yer eyes tell ya. Listen ta the earth. This day is our time, and we 'ave a song of sorrow. But there are songs from the days that came before and the days ta come. Grand songs that are always 'ere. It's calling ya, but yer not listening. Ya've forgotten how ta listen, Daniel."

"There's no music!" Daniel squatted and grabbed up a handful of soil and flung it into the air. "There's nothing here but dirt and dead bones. How can I make something from that?"

Woodman was silent a long while, and then he said soberly, "Yer grandfather came from the prisons in Moreton Bay, lad. He climbed out of that hole and made his way 'ere. He lived on this land and built it up." Woodman squared his jaw. "He was tough, that's true, but he had heart and he knew how ta live. Back then there was a drought, bad as this, but he kept lookin' for the good, never stopped believin' that the land would supply. I remember thinkin' he must be able ta see into the future. He lived as if he knew about the greatness in the days ta come."

God. He trusted God, Daniel thought. *I have no faith.*

Woodman looked squarely at Daniel. "There 'ave been many droughts. There will be more. Every one brings death. But the land doesn't die. It always comes back. Yer grandfather knew that."

Woodman's eyes brightened. "I was just a lad when I came 'ere, but I remember yer grandfather. He lived hard and

286

worked hard, but he never lost himself in this place. Yer father did, and now . . . yer doin' the same. There is more in this life ya've been given than Douloo."

Daniel tried to take in Woodman's meaning, but all he could think about was how he had failed and how the station was going to die because of him. Woodman couldn't understand. "You were just a lad. How would you know what my grandfather did?"

Before Woodman could respond, Daniel walked away. He had no idea where he was going, only that he had to walk. He needed to escape the carnage. After a while he stopped and sat beneath a giant ghost gum. Then he sobbed.

🎵

"Come on, mum, come with us," Callie said. "It will be good for ya."

"I don't know. I'm worried about Daniel. When Woodman came back he said he and Daniel had an argument and that Daniel had walked off."

"Woodman wasn't afraid for 'im was he?"

"He didn't say so. But I could see he felt restless. I think he's concerned."

"Ya don't 'ave ta worry 'bout Daniel. We can go ta the billabong. I 'eard it's still a bit green there. That will be nice for a picnic."

"I've seen it. It's muddy, mostly dried mud."

"Maybe. But what if Daniel is there, eh?"

"I doubt he is. I think seeing it just makes him more unhappy."

Callie stared at Rebecca, waiting for her to make up her mind.

"I suppose it's possible. He could be there. All right. I'll go, but I have to change. I want to ride."

Willa chose to remain home. She stayed indoors, away from the acrid smoke that drifted about the house. Rebecca left Joseph in her care.

Rebecca hurried as she saddled Chavive. The stench of the burning carcasses was almost more than she could tolerate. Callie had been right. It would be good to get away from the house.

Callie stood and watched until Rebecca had finished with Chavive. "Would you like to ride?" Rebecca asked. "I'll help you saddle a horse."

"No. T'day I want ta walk."

"I thought you liked riding."

"Yais. I do. But I feel like walkin'. It will be good ta feel the earth beneath me feet."

Rebecca and Callie set off with Callie walking alongside Rebecca and Chavive. She carried a dilly bag slung over her shoulder with picnic fare inside.

"It doesn't seem like a picnic without Joseph and Daniel," Rebecca said.

"I can go back and get the bybie, mum."

Rebecca thought a moment. "No. It's hot, and I'd hate to wake him from his nap. He'll just be fussy. Besides, Willa enjoys caring for him."

"Too roight. She does."

Callie walked slightly ahead of Rebecca, moving with an effortless stride. It looked as if her feet barely touched the ground. She'd once explained that because of her reverence for the earth, she tried to pass through life without disturbing the places where gods had once walked. Although the notion was pagan, Rebecca found it romantic.

As they approached the billabong, she spotted Daniel sitting beneath a gum tree. "He *is* here," she said, urging her horse to a faster pace.

Daniel sat with his back against the tree. He rested his arms on bent legs and stared at what had once been a deep, cool pool. A puddle surrounded by hard, dry mud was all that was left. He glanced at her, then returned to studying the mud hole.

Rebecca brought Chavive to a stop and dismounted. "Daniel?" she said, approaching him. He kept staring. "Daniel, is everything all right?"

Finally he looked at her. His eyes were red rimmed. "No. Nothing's all right." He turned his gaze back to the mud hole. "First the animals and then Douloo. That's how it will be." He glanced at his hands. "I wish my father were here. He'd know what to do."

Rebecca knelt beside him. "Tell me how I can help." She rested a hand on his arm. "None of this is your fault. No one in the district is doing well. Many have moved away, but we're still here."

Daniel acted as if he hadn't heard. He shook his head. "How could I have known—the dry boreholes, the bull . . . ?"

"You couldn't have," Rebecca said gently.

"My father would have. He'd have known what to do. Now he watches my failure."

"No. That's not what he sees. He's proud of you. Proud of how hard you've worked and how much you love Douloo."

"And what would he say about the way I've let my family down?"

"You haven't let us down. You've loved us and cared for us." Rebecca sat close to him and rested her head against his arm. "This is the most difficult time we've faced. We need to lean on each other and on God."

"God? I haven't heard from him lately, nor have I seen him. I don't believe he lives 'ere anymore."

Rebecca felt as if she'd been hit across the chest. "You can't mean that."

"I don't know what I mean. I don't know anything anymore."

Rebecca had never seen Daniel so discouraged. It frightened her. She searched her mind for something she could say that would help. Knowing she was treading on unstable ground, she took in a breath and gently said, "Daniel, you thought it might be good for me and Joseph to go to Boston. Perhaps we could all go . . . just for a while, until the rains come."

Daniel stared at her as if he were seeing an apparition. "I can't leave." His eyes went to the mud hole. "But I do think you and Joseph ought to go. And Mum, if I can convince her."

"I won't go without you."

Daniel stared moodily at the ground in front of him, then turned tender eyes on Rebecca. He rested his hand on her cheek. "I love you, Rebecca."

Her heart aching, Rebecca clasped Daniel's hand. "We'll face whatever is to come . . . together."

Daniel managed a small smile. "Maybe it will rain, eh? And when it does, I'll build up Douloo again."

"Douloo doesn't matter."

"It does. I'll make this place work . . . somehow."

Woodman approached. "I was 'bout ta go, but figured I should tell ya."

"Tell me what?" Daniel pushed to his feet and helped Rebecca up.

"I got ta go."

"You're going on walkabout? Now? In the middle of the worst drought to hit the district?"

Woodman nodded.

"You'll die. You'll go out there and die."

"No. I won't." Woodman was silent for a long moment, then added, "And if I do, then that's how it's supposed ta be."

"I need you here. What am I going to do without you?"

"Heard of some men in town lookin' for a job. Said they'd work cheap."

"And you think some bloke who doesn't care about Douloo, who knows nothing about us, can replace you?"

"I gotta go." Woodman tipped his hat to Rebecca and then turned and walked away.

Daniel threw his hat to the ground. "Woodman!" The aborigine didn't look back. "Stop! I'm telling you! Stop!" Woodman kept walking. "If you go now . . . well, don't come back!"

"He's got ta go," Callie said quietly.

Woodman moved on, walking steadily until he disappeared into the haze of the afternoon heat.

26

Daniel drained the last of his tea and handed Rebecca the empty cup. "Time I got to it, then."

"Can you wait a bit?" Rebecca asked. "I was hoping for a few minutes together on the veranda before you go."

"Wish I could, luv. But I've got a couple of new roustabouts showing up this morning. They're going to stack some of that hay we've got left." He kissed her. "How would it look if the boss was late?" Settling his hat on his head, Daniel strode through the kitchen and out the back door.

Rebecca stood at the kitchen window and watched him walk toward the barn. "When will this drought end? I don't know that I can stand any more of it."

Willa set a pan of burned eggs on the counter and moved to Rebecca. Standing directly in front of her, she grasped her arms. "Life will be set right again. Give it time." She turned and watched her son. "He's carrying a great weight, more than he has reason to." Folding her arms over her chest, she added, "I dare say, when we're most weighed down, we forget God wants to carry our burdens."

"Daniel feels God's deserted him," Rebecca said barely loud

enough for Willa to hear. Looking at her mother-in-law, she added, "Nothing I say helps."

"We have to let him find his own way."

"It . . ." Rebecca choked back tears. "It just hurts so much to watch him. I know he feels alone." Despite her efforts to hold back the tears, they came anyway. Brushing them aside, she said, "Sometimes I wish he would walk away from this place, leave everything, and start over. And at the same time I'm so proud of him because he won't."

Returning to the scorched pan, Willa said, "I've seen my share of hardship, and the Lord has never let me down. Not once." She smiled at Rebecca, her eyes warm.

Rebecca nodded, but she was still afraid. She felt as if a stone lay in her gut, heavy and fearsome. "Willa, I'm scared. What if something terrible happens?"

"And why would you think something is going to happen?"

"It's just that there's already been so much suffering."

Willa moved to Rebecca and pulled her into a motherly embrace. "There now, everything will be fine, dear. I'm sure of it. We'll stick together."

Rebecca rested her head against Willa's shoulder. "I know I shouldn't be afraid, but I am. I've never experienced anything like this."

Joseph's cries carried down from upstairs. Rebecca stepped away. "I better get him."

Willa held Rebecca at arm's length. "Now, don't fret. Everything will turn out just as it should."

Rebecca nodded. "I believe you."

"Don't believe me. Believe God."

Joseph rattled off a string of "Mama, mama, mama, mama."

"I better go up. He's probably hungry."

"You go, and I'll do my best to get the goo out of this pan. I do so miss Lily." Wearing a bewildered expression, she added, "You're a much better cook than I am. Perhaps you ought to have a go at it?"

"I'd like that. But I'm not nearly the cook Lily is." Rebecca shrugged. "We'll manage. Does Callie know anything about cooking?"

"I rather doubt it."

Joseph let out a loud howl, and Rebecca hurried upstairs.

By the time she reached Joseph, Callie was already lifting him out of his bed. He tucked his chubby arms in close and rested his head against the servant's chest.

"Oh, thank you, Callie," Rebecca said. "I'll take him." She reached for Joseph and carried him to the rocker. She sat and put Joseph to her breast.

Callie turned her attention to straightening the room. "I'll wash the beddin' t'day," she said, stripping off the crib's sheets and blankets.

Rebecca rested her head against the back of the rocker. She felt tired. The morning had barely begun, but already the heat drained her. "Sometimes when I sit on the veranda, I believe I can hear the crackling of brittle grasses."

"Yais, maybe ya do, eh? When it's dry like this, strange things happen."

Rebecca looked out the window. "There are clouds in the east. Is it possible they'll give us a bit of rain?"

"Maybe, mum." Callie dropped the bedding into a clothes basket.

Rebecca continued to stare at the plump gray clouds. "I know we've had clouds before, but these look heavier and darker."

Callie walked to the window and looked out. "Ya could be roight."

Rebecca felt a surge of hope. Feeling a bit more light-hearted, she asked, "Callie, do you know how to cook?"

"Just damper, mum, not much else."

"Oh. I was wondering if you knew how to make decent eggs."

Callie smiled. "Is that what I smell?"

𝒟

By late morning, a brisk breeze cooled the flats. The distant clouds now scuttled across the sky, shutting out the sun.

"Glory be!" Willa said, stepping onto the veranda. She breathed deeply. "I believe I smell rain." She looked at Rebecca. "You don't suppose we might get a bit of wetness?"

Rebecca moved down the steps and into the yard. "I felt a drop!" she said, holding out her arms and turning her face skyward. More drops fell. "It's raining!"

The clouds opened up and dumped their moisture. Daniel stood at the barn and looked up at the sky and laughed, then ran across the yard. He caught Rebecca around the waist and lifted her, twirling her about. "Rain! At last—rain!" He set her on her feet and kissed her.

"Isn't it wonderful!"

"Yes." He brushed damp hair off of Rebecca's face and kissed her again. "Wish I could stay."

Rebecca thrilled at the devotion she saw in Daniel's eyes. "Can't you?"

"Sorry, luv, but I've got to check on a mob at the eastern boundary."

"Do be careful," Willa said. "If it comes down very hard, there could be flooding."

"I'll be careful," Daniel said, glancing at the gray sky. With a quick kiss for Rebecca, he hurried off.

The rain fell but only for a short time. Then, behaving like one of the few showers that had moved through over the past year, the squall was swept away, and the sun returned to bake the plains. In less than two days, the small puddles had dried out and mud congealed into hard ground.

🍃

Rebecca stood at the porch railing fanning herself. "Perhaps there will be more storms now that we've had one." She looked at the garden. "At least the flowers had a good drink."

"Yes," Willa said. "My flowers are happier."

Rebecca closed her eyes and breathed deeply through her nose. "Sometimes when the ground is damp I think I can smell home." With a smile, she said, "But today this seems like home."

Gazing out over the yard and beyond to the endless grasslands, she smiled. "If I were to leave, I'd miss this place. I've grown to love it here." Rebecca laid her hand over Willa's, which rested on the top of the balustrade. "For so long I felt like a stray. It's good to have a home again." Her gaze moved to the two new men Daniel had recently hired. "However, I do wish there were more I could do to help Daniel. In fact, he was in such a hurry today he couldn't take the time to instruct the new help."

Willa watched as one of the workers walked across the yard. "They'll do just fine. And I'm sure that if Daniel feels the need, he'll speak with them tonight."

"Perhaps." Rebecca felt uneasy. She stared at the barn door. "Just after the storm I caught them stacking wet hay. They had no idea it could mildew and make the animals sick." She shook her head. "I hate to think of what might have happened if I hadn't discovered the error." Taking a handkerchief from her pocket, she patted her damp face. "I do pray for more rain and cool weather."

"Oh yes. That would be lovely." Willa sat in a wicker chair. "Will you be traveling home for Thomas and Mildred's wedding?"

"I long to go, but not while Daniel is struggling so." Rebecca smiled. "I'm thrilled for my aunt though. Thomas is a fine man. I knew the day Auntie left that she was truly in love. She would never set off on a journey like that without making proper arrangements. It's very out of character for her, unless of course, she's in love."

"I would say you're exactly right."

Rebecca leaned against the railing. "Do you think Woodman will return soon?"

Willa looked out past the yard to the flatlands beyond. "He's left us before and always came home. But I don't know how long he'll be gone. Sometimes it's taken months for him to return."

"I don't understand why he left, especially now."

"All I know is that the aborigines say they hear from the land and that they must go."

Rebecca was confused. "How does he know it's calling him?"

Willa wore a crooked smile. "I really don't know, dear."

Rebecca nodded, still perplexed. "It's all very confusing to me." Rebecca glanced about the veranda. She searched the yard. Joseph wasn't anywhere about. "Have you seen Joseph?"

"Callie took him for a walk. They left a short while ago. He does so love to be strolled about in his carriage."

Rebecca's taut nerves relaxed. "He seems happiest outdoors. He's growing so quickly; soon he'll be charging about on his own." Rebecca let her gaze move to an area of pasture just west of the barn. She saw what looked like smoke. "What's that?"

"What, dear?"

"There." Rebecca pointed at a hay pile with smoke billowing from beneath the heap. "It's smoke!" Lifting her skirts, she hurried down the porch steps and out into the yard. "There must be a fire!"

"Heavens no," Willa said.

"The hay is burning!"

"Come with me, Rebecca!" Willa said urgently as she ran for the barn.

She and Rebecca grabbed buckets. "We need help." Willa looked around. "Where did the new roustabouts go? Help! There's a fire! We need help!"

The men stepped out from the back of the barn. The larger of the two asked, "What is it? What's wrong?"

"There's a fire in the haystack! Fill these buckets with water and douse the flames before they go any farther. I'll get blankets."

Rebecca thought her heart would stop. "What about Callie and Joseph?" She looked toward the road. "Where did they go?" Fear swelled. *Dear Lord! Please don't let anything happen to them.*

Willa took Rebecca by the shoulders. "Rebecca, Callie will know what to do if the fire spreads. But we must stop it here."

She nodded but didn't feel assurance. Everything in her screamed to search for her son.

A woman with an infant strapped across her front stepped out of a cabin. Clutching the baby against her, she sprinted to Willa. "I'll get water, mum," she called and ran for a bucket.

"We must put out the flames—now!" Rebecca shouted.

"You help with the buckets. The blankets are in the tack room." Willa disappeared inside the barn.

"Callie!" Rebecca screamed as she grabbed a bucket and ran to the watering trough. "Callie!" The servant didn't appear. "Callie!"

Rebecca dipped her bucket into slimy water. When it was nearly full, she ran for the hay pile. Already the fire had more than doubled, and flames had leaped to the field. The blaze burned toward the barn.

"Oh, my Lord!" Rebecca stared at the sight. What good would one bucket of water do? Even though it seemed a worthless effort, Rebecca ran, stopping just out of reach of the fire and emptied her bucket. Voracious flames consumed the moisture.

Willa met her with sopping wet blankets.

"We can't stop it!" Rebecca shrieked.

"Beat it with these," Willa said, handing a blanket to Rebecca and then running toward the fire. The men tossed water on the barn walls, but the flames were already licking at the back of the building.

A handful of men and women worked to douse the fire or beat it back, but their efforts were met by what seemed an impenetrable, gluttonous blaze. While slapping the flames with a wet blanket, Rebecca continued to look for Callie and Joseph. They were nowhere. A servant carrying a wet canvas bag ran toward the fire. Rebecca grabbed his arm and stopped him. "Have you seen Callie? Or my son?"

"No. I 'aven't seen 'em." The man pushed past.

Each bite of land consumed by the fire added to Rebecca's fright. What had happened to Joseph? Eyes tearing, she peered through heavy smoke. *Where is he? Lord, please protect him.*

Fire ate up dry grass and wood, burning across fields and through buildings. The barn blazed. "Chavive!" Rebecca cried.

She'd planned to ride her later that day, and after brushing the mare, she'd left her in a stall. She raced toward the barn and charged inside. Horses screamed their fright, and panicked cows mooed.

"Chavive!" Rebecca called, running to her stall. Throwing open the gate, she grabbed the horse's halter. Barely able to see through dense smoke, Rebecca choked and coughed as she guided her cherished mare outdoors. She slapped her rump. "Go! Run! Go on!" she hollered and then turned back to the barn. Flames and smoke billowed throughout the structure. Rebecca ran from stall to stall, freeing captive animals.

Gasping and struggling to breathe through the acrid smoke, she stepped out of the burning building and watched a portion of the roof collapse. Her eyes and throat burned. She longed to sit and cry, but there was no time. The insatiable blaze moved toward the house. It was ruthless.

Woodman stepped out of the smoky haze. His eyes red and watering, his skin sooty, he looked down at Rebecca.

"Oh, praise the Lord! Woodman!" Rebecca was so glad to see him, she nearly leaped into his arms. "Is Daniel with you?"

"No, mum." He coughed. Gripping her arms, he looked intently into her face. "Ya all roight, mum?"

"Yes. No. I can't find Joseph and Callie."

He glanced about. "Can't worry 'bout them now, mum." Woodman picked up two blankets and wet them, then swinging them both, he fought down hungry flames.

Willa flogged the blaze, trying to protect her flower garden. "You won't have these!" she shouted.

Daniel galloped into the smoke-choked yard. He jumped from his horse and ran for Rebecca. "How did this happen?"

"There was a fire in one of the hay piles." Rebecca wiped

stinging tears from her eyes. "I don't know where Callie and Joseph are."

"Where were they last?"

"I don't know. They went for a walk."

A burning tree cracked and fell toward them. Rebecca screamed and Daniel grabbed her, dragging her clear of the torched eucalyptus.

Willa and the others continued their fight. The fire grew fiercer.

"Daniel, it's no use," Rebecca said. "Everything is burning."

An ember landed on Willa's dress, and her gown flared. Flames climbed up her skirt. Using her damp blanket, Willa slapped at the burning cloth. The blanket, however, was little more than a singed rag and of little use.

Daniel snatched Rebecca's soaked blanket and sprinted for his mother. He wrapped the moist cover about her skirts, smothering the fire. Picking her up, he carried her to an area already burned out and gently set her on the blackened ground. Squatting beside her, he said, "That's all, Mum. There's nothing more to do."

Willa nodded and pulled her burned legs close to her chest.

"Daniel, the house is burning!" Rebecca yelled.

"Could Callie and Joseph be inside?"

"I don't think so. I'm sure she wouldn't hide there."

Daniel looked about frantically. Everything was already burned or burning. "The house would be the only refuge. Stay 'ere with Mum. I'll go in and have a look."

"I'm coming with you."

Daniel didn't seem to hear. He ran to the house, calling, "Joseph! Joseph! Callie!"

Paint curled and exposed wood torched as Daniel pushed

through the front door. "You check downstairs. I'll go upstairs."

Rebecca grabbed Daniel's arm. "What if they're not here?"

Daniel looked at her, but he had no answer.

"Be careful. Please, be careful," Rebecca called, then watched as he charged up the staircase. She hurried toward the back of the house. "Callie! Joseph!" she screamed. "Please answer me! Where are you?" She ran from room to room, checking every nook, every closet. She even looked inside cupboards. They were nowhere.

Choking smoke seared Rebecca's lungs as she ran toward the front of the house. Daniel ducked into the parlor and then reappeared a moment later. "Did you find anything?" Rebecca asked in a husky whisper, then choked.

"Nothing." His face was black with soot, his eyes red and tearing. He coughed and wheezed, struggling to breathe. A curtain hanging at a front window flamed to life. "We have to get out." He placed a protective arm around Rebecca and steered her toward the door.

Once outside, they scanned the blackened yard. The barn was ablaze and the cottages were flaming. Trees looked like torches, and burning leaves and small limbs rained down on the yard. Daniel guided Rebecca to an open area where the rest of the household had gathered. Willa tended to the injuries of others.

"Mum, what about Callie and Joseph? Have you seen them?"

Willa shook her head no.

Woodman strode up to Daniel and placed a hand on the younger man's shoulder. "Ya find Joseph?"

"No. He's nowhere." Daniel peered through the smoke-filled yard and then scanned the flaming fields beyond. "Joseph! Callie!" he yelled.

"Oh, God! Where are they?" Rebecca sobbed.

Daniel pulled her into his arms and smoothed her hair as he would a child's. They clung to each other and watched as the house blazed. Glass splintered and wood popped and crackled. The family and the few workers still left at Douloo huddled together on the dirt yard, their soot-covered faces imprinted with shock and revulsion. The fire burned through the house and outbuildings and then raced across the prairie. A black ruin was all that remained of the Thornton estate.

Daniel and Rebecca huddled together on the ground. Rebecca felt as if the fire had consumed her like it had everything else. Aching and empty, she pressed in close to Daniel.

ᘓ

Daniel pushed to his feet and pulled Rebecca up with him. He gazed over the wreckage of what had been his home. "We have to find Joseph," he said.

Rebecca looked at the seared earth. As far as she could see, nothing had lived. Trees stood like giant, blackened cornstalks. Singed brush huddled, shriveled and indistinguishable.

"Daniel, nothing could have survived. Joseph and Callie are dead. Our son is dead," Rebecca sobbed and slid to the ground. Drawing up her legs, she pressed her face against her knees. "He's dead, he's dead, he's dead . . ."

"No!" Daniel yelled. "He's alive! We'll find him!" He kneeled beside Rebecca and gripped her forearms. "We'll find him."

Rebecca pressed her forehead against his chest. Daniel held her so tightly she could barely breathe. And yet it was not tight enough.

Woodman rested a hand on Daniel's shoulder. "Callie and that lad of yers may still be in this world. They could be needin' help."

"Do you think they're still alive?" Rebecca asked, feeling a spark of hope.

Woodman didn't answer.

Rebecca tried to quiet her trembling. She gazed all around her. Everything was decimated. Her eyes moved across charred earth, taking in blackened trees that stood like the bones of dead loved ones. "Where could they be?" She looked at one burned building and then another and another. "Where?"

Daniel cupped the back of her head in his hand and then smoothed her hair. He stood and squared his chin, blinking back tears. "Woodman said they might be alive."

Rebecca continued to gaze at the devastation. "No one could have survived out there." Using her sleeve, she wiped dirt and moisture from her face with her sleeve.

Willa moved close to Rebecca and settled an arm gently about her shoulders. "Whether here or in heaven, that little boy is all right. God's looking after him."

Rebecca choked back a sob. "I can't bear it. Oh, God, please . . . I can't bear it. Please . . . not Joseph." Sobs shook her body.

"We've got to look for him," Daniel said.

Willa held Rebecca close to her. "If anyone could survive, it would be Callie."

Rebecca nodded and stepped away from her mother-in-law. Her gaze fell upon the house. Brick chimneys stood like charred towers amidst black ruins.

"Yer roight, Mrs. Thornton. That Callie's a clever one," Woodman said.

For the first time, Daniel seemed to actually see Woodman. He stared at him and then said, "I thought you'd gone on walkabout. Why did you come back?"

"Don't know. Just had a feelin'."

"I'm glad you did."

Woodman gripped Daniel's shoulder and gave it a brotherly squeeze. "Me and the boys will round up the horses."

He called for Jim, and the two of them, along with a couple other blokes, walked away, disappearing into the ghostly, smoke-filled world.

Willa let out a slow breath. "We must have faith. God has not forgotten us." Her chin quivered and her eyes filled with tears. She turned to Daniel and rested a hand on his chest. "Don't give up hope."

He pulled his mother into his arms. In little more than a whisper, he said, "Keep praying, Mum."

She nodded. "I won't stop."

Daniel stepped away. "Fire started in a hay pile?"

"Yes," Rebecca managed to say. "I saw the smoke and we tried to put it out." Fresh tears gathered in her eyes. She couldn't continue.

"It was my fault," Daniel said. "I didn't watch over the new roustabouts. Heard they'd stacked wet hay and figured on getting to it, but . . ." He shook his head slowly back and forth. "Should have made sure it was scattered and dried."

305

"What does that have to do with anything?" Rebecca asked.

Daniel turned tortured eyes on his wife. "When you stack hay it's got to be dry."

"Yes, so it won't mildew."

"Right. But damp hay can heat up in the sun. Get so hot underneath that it bursts into flames." His eyes roamed over the smoldering station. He tightened his jaw. "If Dad had been 'ere this wouldn't have happened. It's my fault."

"It's no one's fault," Willa said. "It was a mistake."

Rebecca returned to Daniel's arms.

Daniel crushed her to him, and pressing his cheek against her hair, he cried. Finally he held Rebecca away from him. He looked at the burned-out house and said, "I was so wrong. None of this matters. I thought it was so important. Curious how things change." His voice was laced with bitterness. "All that matters now is Joseph and Callie. We have to find them." He looked down at Rebecca and gently wiped away dirt and tears from her face. "We *will* find them."

"I pray you're right."

Daniel took a deep breath. "I better help find the horses."

🍃

Willa put her arm around Rebecca's waist. "Come along, then. We've got work to do." She guided Rebecca toward the well. "We'll need water for drinking and cleaning. I'll get some buckets."

Hearing the authority and calm in Willa's voice helped Rebecca feel quieter inside. With more resolve, she asked, "What about Joseph? We have to find him."

"And we will. But I doubt you want to walk, not out there." She nodded at the burned-out flatlands. "Wait for the horses, dear."

306

"Right. I left a bucket beside Callie's cottage," Rebecca said. "I'll get it." Feeling as if her insides had been seared, she walked slowly toward a pile of smoldering rubble. It had been a home. "Callie," she whispered, staring at the ruin. A pain cut into her chest, as if a knife had been buried there. *Please, God, keep her and Joseph safe. Please bring them back to us.*

Daniel appeared, leading Chavive and one of the Morgans. "Have a look 'ere," he said.

"Chavive!" Rebecca shouted and ran to the horse. She wrapped her arms about the animal's neck. "You made it. You made it." She pressed her cheek against the mare's neck.

"Don't know how she managed to find her way through the flames."

Rebecca took a closer look at the horse. "Is she all right?"

"Yes. Right as rain." He offered a dismal smile.

"Where did you find her?"

"She found me, actually. Came trotting up the road toward home."

"If she's alive, maybe . . ."

"Maybe. Don't hope for too much, Rebecca."

A pulse of fear surged through her. "I thought you believed they were still alive?"

"I do, but we've got to be . . . prepared. I found a lot of dead animals. And most of the stock is dead."

Woodman joined them with the other Morgan and Daniel's stallion. He handed the stallion over to Daniel along with two pieces of rope. "No bridles, but these ought ta work, eh?" He tied the cords to the horses' harnesses. Resting his hand on Chavive's withers, he settled bloodshot eyes on Rebecca. "We'll find 'em."

Her grief felt like a raw wound, and it choked off any reply. All she could manage was a nod. Resting her hands on the horse's back, she realized that with no saddle she'd need a hand up. "Can you help me?" she asked Daniel.

"I want you to stay," he said.

"No. The more people looking, the better." With her eyes fixed on her husband's, she said, "I'm going."

"All right, then."

Rebecca turned back to Chavive and pressed her left foot into Daniel's cupped hands. Throwing her right leg over the horse, she settled onto the mare's back and waited for the men to mount their horses. It was decided Woodman and Jim would ride east and Daniel and Rebecca north.

Riders came up the road. It was Cambria, her father, and two of her brothers, Ran and Tanner.

"Saw the smoke," Mr. Taylor said. "Figured you could use some help." He glanced about. "Looks like we're too late."

"No. We need you," Daniel said. "Callie and Joseph are missing."

"Oh, Lord," Cambria said, her eyes filling with tears. "Rebecca, I'm so sorry."

Fresh tears pooled in Rebecca's eyes. "We'll find them," she said with more conviction than she felt.

"All right, then, we better get to it," Daniel said. "Jim, is it all right if you and Cambria ride together?"

"Yeah." Jim looked at Cambria, and the love in his eyes startled Rebecca. Strange how tragedy puts things into perspective.

"Woodman, you take Ran," Daniel continued. "And Tanner can ride with his father. The more of us looking, the better, eh?"

Fearing the worst, Rebecca searched the charred land. Was it possible Callie and Joseph were still alive? The grass was ugly black stubble. Trees were scorched, their leaves shriveled and seared. There were animals too—charred. They'd fled yet still died. Rebecca's hopes dwindled. But she continued on.

They moved past dead cattle and horses. A lizard had tried to flee but had been roasted and left in the middle of the road. Cooked corpses of roos unable to outrun the blaze lay along the roadside and among groves of scorched trees. How could a woman and a small boy have escaped?

"What will we do?" Rebecca asked Daniel.

"What do you mean?"

"We have no home. No son." She choked back a sob.

Daniel let out a long breath, his eyes continuing to search. "I don't know." He rode slumped forward. "This is my fault. My father was right to despise me. He knew I was too weak to manage the station."

"No. He didn't feel that way, Daniel. He knew you had a good mind and courage. But he also understood that he'd kept such a stranglehold on you that you would need time to build confidence and discover your abilities."

"How can you know that?"

"The day I planned to leave Thornton Creek, your father's attorney gave me a letter. It was from your father. In it he told me how he was to blame for your pain—that he'd been too heavy-handed with you. He wrote about what a fine lad you'd been and how his harshness had hurt you so.

"He was proud of the man you'd become, and he said that in spite of him you had a strong spirit and he knew in time your strength would be renewed along with your compassion." Rebecca hesitated. She hadn't wanted Daniel to know that she'd stayed because of his father's urging. "He thought I was the one God had chosen for you—to stand at your side."

"I thought you stayed because you wanted to."

"I did want to. But it was your father who helped me see how deeply I love you." She reached across to Daniel and grasped his hand. "I loved you long before I knew I did." Meeting his eyes, she continued, "You're a good man, and I'm proud of you. You've done a fine job of running Douloo. No one could have done better."

"My father would have."

"Your father was not perfect . . . remember?"

Daniel was quiet.

"No man can do more than his best. And you have done that."

Rebecca's eyes fell upon something lying in the burned grass. She let out a gasp. She knew what it was and moved Chavive ahead slowly.

Daniel joined her.

They stopped, and the horses stood side by side. Daniel and Rebecca stared at the charred remains of Joseph's buggy. Shards of burned cloth clung to its metal frame, and like miniature flags they flapped in the breeze. Four melted wheels looked like black, blistered feet.

Daniel jumped from his stallion's back and dropped to the blackened earth. Kneeling beside the buggy, he lifted out a piece of Joseph's blanket. "Where is he? Dear God, where is our son?" he demanded, then pressed the blanket to his face and wept. He looked at Rebecca, who knelt beside him. "I wouldn't do this to someone I loved. Why is God allowing this?"

Rebecca took the fragment of blanket. "I don't know. But I know we can trust him," she said, feeling a renewed faith. "He won't forsake us." Looking up and over the blackened grasslands, she could envision Callie grabbing Joseph and sprinting across the dry prairie. But where would she have run to? She took Daniel's hand. "We'll find them."

Hands clasped, Rebecca and Daniel returned to the horses.

Daniel helped Rebecca onto Chavive's back. "I know God's 'ere," Daniel said. "He hasn't abandoned us." With a shuddering breath, he continued. "And he can have Douloo. I'll do whatever he wants with it. I'll walk away forever if that's what he wants. If only he'll return my son."

Tears spilled onto Rebecca's cheeks as she looked down on her bereft husband. Rather than feeling weak and hopeless, she felt strength and trust. "God will do as God will do," she said. "We have to trust him."

Daniel nodded. He climbed onto his horse and led the way forward.

Rebecca's thoughts returned to the question of where Callie would have gone. She felt as if she should know. Probing memories, she tried to grab hold of the scrap of information she knew lay hidden somewhere in her mind. She couldn't grasp it.

"Maybe the others have already found them and are searching for us, eh?" Daniel said, trying to sound cheery.

Still struggling to listen to her inner self, Rebecca kicked Chavive's sides and moved on, clutching the piece of tattered fabric that had been her son's blanket.

Daniel and Rebecca continued their wretched search. Praying and hoping to find Joseph yet afraid of finding him. The fire had spared nothing. Rebecca felt as if she had awakened amidst a nightmare of charred plants and trees and dead animals. She gazed out across the station at billowing smoke that told of the fire's continued life. It would eat its way across the district. She feared for her neighbors.

Daniel pressed his feet hard into the stirrups and straightened his legs, lifting himself out of the saddle. He stared at something in the distance. "What's that?"

Rebecca squinted, trying to see what was moving toward

them. "It looks like someone's walking!" *Lord, let it be Callie. Let it be Joseph.* Rebecca kicked Chavive's sides and galloped across the sooty ground. Daniel's horse ran alongside.

"Callie?" she called. "Callie, is that you?" And then her eyes told her what she'd been hoping to see. It was her friend carrying Joseph in her arms. The little boy didn't move. He lay limp in Callie's embrace. *Please let him be alive. Please. Lord, be merciful.*

Callie's dark skin was dusky with soot. Her feet and ankles were burned, and she was limping. Joseph lay still across her arms.

Rebecca pulled up Chavive and leaped from her back before the horse had completely stopped. "Callie! I'd nearly lost hope!" Rebecca cried, stumbling toward her friend and never taking her eyes from the child in her arms.

Daniel threw one leg over the side of his horse and jumped to the ground. He strode toward Callie.

"Glad ta see ya. And I'm thankful."

Rebecca's eyes remained on her son. "What happened?" She braced herself to hear the worst.

"When I seen the fire, I run."

Rebecca closed the final steps between herself and Callie. Joseph was nearly as black as the servant.

"I run for the cave, mum."

"The cave?"

"Yais. With the paintings."

"Oh. The cave." Rebecca felt as if she were sleepwalking. "Yes. The cave. I remember."

"Roight. Wal, the fire was going so fast I picked up Joseph and we run." She hugged him more closely. "I was truly scared. Didn't know if we would make it. But I went fast as I could."

"I knew you would do all that was possible." Rebecca reached for her son. "Can I have him?"

"Yais, mum." Callie held out the little boy.

Her heart breaking, Rebecca clutched her son. And then he stirred.

"Mummy," said a tiny, raspy voice.

Astonished, Rebecca looked down at the soot-covered child. "Joseph?"

"Mum." He opened his eyes and circled Rebecca's neck with his chubby arms.

Rebecca pressed him against her chest. "You're alive!" She smiled broadly at Daniel. "He's alive!" Closing her eyes, she said, "Thank you, Lord!"

Daniel's smile was broad, and his blue eyes brimmed with tears. He rested a hand on Joseph's head.

"Yais, mum. Course he's alive. We hid in the cave, and the fire went 'round us. It was roight smoky, but we stayed close ta the ground and it was all roight." She smiled at Joseph. "He was a brave lad. Didn't even cry."

Daniel swept Rebecca and Joseph into his arms. Husband and wife clung to each other, their son between them. Still holding on to one another, they dropped to their knees. Finally Daniel scooped Joseph into his arms. He hugged him and said, "Thank you, God, for my son."

He looked at Callie. "Thank you."

Callie smiled and bobbed her head. "I love 'im too, Mr. Thornton."

With Joseph tucked safely away in his arms, Daniel looked at Rebecca. "You asked what we should do. We'll begin again. There will be a new Douloo." He looked up at the blue sky and closed his eyes. "I praise God for his mercy. I had no faith, but he remained faithful."

He looked at Rebecca and smiled. Draping his free arm about her shoulders, he pulled her close. "The Thorntons are not done in, not yet . . . not ever."

Bonnie Leon dabbled in writing for many years but never set it in a place of priority until an accident in 1991 left her unable to work. She is now the author of more than a dozen historical fiction novels, including *The Heart of Thornton Creek* and *Journey of Eleven Moons*. She also stays busy teaching women's Bible studies, speaking, and teaching at writing seminars and conventions. Bonnie and her husband, Greg, live in Glide, Oregon. They have three grown children and four grandchildren. You can contact Bonnie at www.bonnie leon.com.

New beginnings
spark Rebecca's search for freedom

book one of
The Queensland Chronicles

Available at your local bookstore